Praise for Donis Casey

FORTY DEAD MEN
The Tenth Alafair Tucker Mystery

Barnes & Noble Nook First Look pick for 2018
Barnes & Noble Press Presents pick for 2018
Barnes & Noble "20 Favorite Indie Books of 2018" pick
Finalist for the 2019 Oklahoma Book Award for Fiction

"A poignant novel of heartache, pain, love, and grace. Brilliant and memorable."
> —Carolyn Hart, award-winning author

"Casey expertly nails the extended Tucker family—some 20 people—and combines these convincing characters, a superb sense of time and place, and a solid plot in this marvelously atmospheric historical."
> —*Publishers Weekly*, Starred Review

"A compassionate look at PTSD, this tenth series entry again showcases the savvy mother hen Alafair, who has a lot in common with Mette Ivie Harrison's Linda Wallheim, another loving western mother whose curiosity and common sense always come in handy."
> —*Booklist*

THE RETURN OF THE RAVEN MOCKER
The Ninth Alafair Tucker Mystery

Finalist for the 2018 Oklahoma Book Award for Fiction

"Readers may find Alafair's huge extended family hard to keep straight, but the homespun mood remains winning, while the impact of world history on the Ozarks is skillfully evoked."
> —*Publishers Weekly*

"Vividly rendered and psychologically astute, this somewhat transparent puzzler provides an unusually immersive perspective on familiar historical territory."

—*Booklist*

"The mystery comes in second (or maybe third) to history lessons and paeans to traditional American values in this folksy tale of small towns and big hearts."

—*Kirkus Reviews*

ALL MEN FEAR ME
The Eighth Alafair Tucker Mystery

"Casey's skill at making you care about the injustices of a time and place not often covered in history books is second to none. The admirable mystery is the cherry on top."

—*Kirkus Reviews*

HELL WITH THE LID BLOWN OFF
The Seventh Alafair Tucker Mystery

2015 Oklahoma Book Award Finalist, Fiction

"Casey provides an engaging portrait of the close-knit society that was commonly found in the rural Midwest at the time. Alafair Tucker, her large family, and their friends are a pleasure to spend time with."

—*Publishers Weekly*, Starred Review

"The tornado's destruction is a perfect metaphor for the man-made destruction done by Jubal Beldon. Both forces, unthinking, impersonal, unstoppable, feared when contrasted to the sympathetic, loving Tucker family creates the best mystery novel of the year. It is suspenseful and gripping, with superb writing and unforgettable characters. If you can only read one book this year, *Hell with the Lid Blown Off* should be that one."

—*New York Journal of Books*

"A good mystery with an odd final twist is eclipsed by frighteningly detailed descriptions of the terrors of tornadoes."

—*Kirkus Reviews*

"This edgy historical mystery works as a powerful picture of the times."

—*Booklist*

THE WRONG HILL TO DIE ON
The Sixth Alafair Tucker Mystery

2013 Oklahoma Book Award Finalist, Fiction

"Alafair Tucker deserves to stand beside Ma Joad in literature's gallery of heroic ladies."

—Tony Hillerman, *New York Times* bestselling author

"Casey's warm and wise heroine handles her multiple roles gracefully."

—*Publishers Weekly*

CRYING BLOOD
The Fifth Alafair Tucker Mystery

2012 Oklahoma Book Award Finalist, Fiction

"Will appeal to history buffs and Hillerman aficionados. The book includes sections on hog butchering, favorite old-time recipes, the history of the Indian Territory and land allotment, as well as a guide to Creek pronunciation."

—*Kirkus Reviews*

"Casey's nuanced portrayal of settler and native lives in early 20th-century Oklahoma lends soul and depth to her atmospheric fifth Alafair Tucker mystery."

—*Publishers Weekly*

THE SKY TOOK HIM
The Fourth Alafair Tucker Mystery

2010 WILLA Literary Award Finalist, Historical Fiction
2010 Oklahoma Book Award Finalist, Fiction

"Those who like their puzzles cloaked in local color from a different time will be amply rewarded."

—*Publishers Weekly*, Starred Review

THE DROP EDGE OF YONDER
The Third Alafair Tucker Mystery

Winner of the 2008 ABPA Arizona Book Award, Best Mystery/
   Thriller

"Casey gives convincing voice to the early Midwest much as Sharyn McCrumb does for her Appalachians, including period recipes that help to convey the literal flavor of the era."

—*Publishers Weekly*

HORNSWOGGLED
The Second Alafair Tucker Mystery

"Hornswoggled is a tremendous novel from a gifted writer. Donis Casey's voice flows like tea syrup, transporting you effortlessly to the Oklahoma frontier. If you fondly recall The Walton's clan, you'll adore Hornswoggled's richly drawn characters. A welcome invite to your great-grandmother's front porch swing."

—Julia Spencer-Fleming, *New York Times* bestselling author

"Dialog rich with Midwestern speech patterns and a consistent, unobtrusive narrative voice lift this small-town historical, which should particularly appeal to Margaret Maron fans. An appendix of down-home recipes is a bonus."

—*Publishers Weekly*

THE OLD BUZZARD HAD IT COMING
The First Alafair Tucker Mystery

Named an Oklahoma Centennial Book
Winner of the 2007 ABPA Arizona Book Award
2006 Benjamin Franklin Award Finalist, Mystery/Suspense
2006 Oklahoma Book Award Finalist, Fiction
2004 Best Unpublished Mystery by the Oklahoma Writers' Federation

"As an Okie farm boy of the dust bowl Depression days, I can testify that Donis Casey sounds like she's been there and done that. She gives us a tale full of wit, humor, sorrow and, more important, the truth. Her Alafair Tucker deserves to stand beside Ma Joad in Literature's gallery of heroic ladies."

—Tony Hillerman, *New York Times* bestselling author

"Donis Casey's debut mystery is as vivid and unforgettable as a crimson Oklahoma sunset. The Old Buzzard Had It Coming is a book to savor, lyrical, authentic, and heartwarming."

—Carolyn Hart, award-winning author

"This debut novel is a remarkably tactile historical mystery ... A lot of writers of historical mysteries tell us about the places their stories are set in; Casey actually takes us there."

—*Booklist*

Also by Donis Casey

The Alafair Tucker Mysteries
The Old Buzzard Had It Coming
Hornswoggled
The Drop Edge of Yonder
The Sky Took Him
Crying Blood
The Wrong Hill to Die On
Hell With the Lid Blown Off
All Men Fear Me
The Return of the Raven Mocker
Forty Dead Men

THE WRONG GIRL

The Adventures of
BIANCA DANGEREUSE

DONIS CASEY

Poisoned Pen
PRESS

Published by Poisoned Pen Press, an imprint of Sourcebooks
P.O. Box 4410, Naperville, Illinois 60567-4410
(630) 961-3900
sourcebooks.com

Library of Congress Cataloging-in-Publication data
Names: Casey, Donis, author.
Title: Wrong girl / by Donis Casey.
Identifiers: LCCN 2019027168 | (hardcover)
Subjects: GSAFD: Mystery fiction.
Classification: LCC PS3603.A863 W75 2019 | DDC 813/.6--dc23
LC record available at https://lccn.loc.gov/2019027168

Printed and bound in the United States of America.
SB 10 9 8 7 6 5 4 3 2 1

*With love for the great Carolyn Hart, who has helped
and encouraged me and a whole generation of authors;
and for the great Barbara Peters, who has stuck with me
through thick and thin;
and for my great-grandmother, Alafair Wilson Morgan,
for raising such a bunch of tough cookies.*

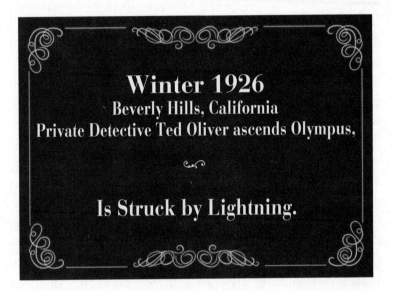

Winter 1926
Beverly Hills, California
Private Detective Ted Oliver ascends Olympus,

Is Struck by Lightning.

Ted Oliver drove up Santa Monica Boulevard to Beverly Drive, then turned onto Summit and wound up the steep side of San Ysidro Canyon until he reached the ten-acre estate of beloved motion picture celebrity Bianca LaBelle, star and living embodiment of the *Bianca Dangereuse* serials, the biggest money-making movie franchise in the entire Western world. He showed his identification at the wrought-iron gate to the guard who, having already been apprised of his arrival, gave him directions to the main house. He drove down a winding dirt road for nearly a quarter mile before he turned onto the palm-lined drive leading to a California Mission-style mansion. LaBelle's estate was not situated at the top of the hill, but the property still boasted a commanding view of the ocean on one side and mountains on the other.

Oliver had only seen one Bianca Dangereuse flick in his life. There wasn't much of a plot to it, but there was a lot of action. Bianca Dangereuse had been kidnapped by pirates off the Tripoli coast and had saved herself by leaping overboard and swimming to shore, where she escaped by donning a burqa and hiding among the sympathetic wives in the harem of the local sheik. Oliver had enjoyed it, but he didn't have time to go to movies very often and so had never seen another.

The actress who played Dangereuse, Bianca LaBelle, was an enigma. In a world of insecure people with giant egos who lived to see their names in print, Bianca had managed to keep her private life as private as possible ever since she had burst into the public consciousness only four years earlier with the release of her first movie, *The Adventures of Bianca Dangereuse*. Bianca Dangereuse was a Nellie Bly–type journalist and adventurer who would go to the ends of the earth for a story. She also had a talent for getting herself into impossible situations and making uncanny escapes. In the years since the first Dangereuse adventure came out, Bianca LaBelle had been in great demand. She worked continually, making half a dozen feature films a year. Historical adventures, oaters and romances, and three more Bianca Dangereuse thrillers. It was widely advertised by United Features Studios that Bianca LaBelle wrote her own scripts and did all her own stunts, but after seeing the character swing herself off a yardarm on a rope, dive headfirst into the ocean, and swim a hundred yards to what he suspected was one of the Channel Islands standing in for Tripoli, Oliver had his doubts.

Bianca's relative invisibility on the social scene didn't mean that the press never wrote about her. There was not one issue of a fan magazine or industry newspaper that didn't have at least a filler, and more likely an entire feature, speculating about the mysterious beauty from who-knows-where, who suddenly appeared out of nowhere in 1922 and instantly became a star. Bianca had done a couple of interviews with the fan magazines and cooperated on one feature in the *Examiner*. The only thing she had ever publicly said about her background was that her first appearance in the moving pictures was in a Tom Mix feature in 1921, when she had ridden stunt double for the female lead, the luscious Alma Bolding. In the Dangereuse features, Bianca was absolutely fearless, whether the role called for her to go over waterfalls in a canoe, swing on a rope over a canyon, leap onto a galloping horse, or climb a cliff face. That much was known. Where Tom Mix had found her, why Alma Bolding had decided to take the total unknown under her wing, or why Pickford and Fairbanks had decided to produce her first Bianca Dangereuse film, was not. The Tom Mix flick had been shot near Prescott, and there was some speculation that Bianca may have grown up on a ranch in Arizona.

But her name was definitely French, and she did have a dark, exotic, Mediterranean look about her, so the most popular scuttlebutt about her background was that she was the scion of a noble French family, who had escaped to America in order to avoid an arranged marriage with a sybaritic Italian count. It didn't matter that Del Burke, publicity director for United Features, had fabricated that story out of thin air. It was romantic and appealing, so it was widely believed by the movie-going public and Bianca's adoring fans. Was her real name Bianca LaBelle, Oliver wondered? Probably not. Yet no reporter had ever gone to the trouble of digging into her background. Or else the studios had quashed the truth in favor of the fairy tale.

Bianca was not often seen at parties with the rich and famous. She did not frequent the dance halls and country clubs where her contemporaries whiled away their time with bootleg booze, illicit drugs, and other unsavory activities that usually involved sex with whoever was handy.

Not that she was a virginal goddess. The studios presented

Bianca as independent and totally self-sufficient. She was wealthy, gorgeous, a fashion icon, the perfect modern twentieth-century woman, only seen with the most eligible bachelors, usually a costar, at one official studio function or another. No serious romance had ever been hinted at. That fact had lent itself to some innuendo, especially since Bianca and Alma Bolding frequently traveled together and stayed at one another's homes. Of course, Alma was twenty years older and had been married five times. Which still didn't do much to quell the prurient rumors about her relationship with Bianca.

Bianca's inaccessibility merely increased the public's appetite for any tidbit of news about her. She was one of the most popular actresses in the industry, a friend of the elite; besides Mix and Bolding, she hobnobbed with Chaplin, Marion Davies, Mary Pickford, and Doug Fairbanks. None of whom had any gossip to share about her, either. A studio conspiracy, Oliver thought, to add to her mystery.

Oliver parked his auto at the head of the drive and made the long trek up the steps to pound on the massive Mission-style doors. He figured that a polite tap wouldn't do to alert whoever was inside this monstrosity that someone was outside and wanted in.

He was beginning to wonder if he'd pounded hard enough, but it must have taken a few minutes to traverse the foyer's acreage to reach the door, for just as he raised his fist for another try, the door swung open and a creature of remarkable size and aspect blocked his view of the interior.

Oliver had seen all kinds since he had come to California, but this being took the cake. He was well over six feet tall and well over three hundred pounds, dressed in a tuxedo, white gloves, and spats. Or was he a she? One red chili pepper-shaped earring dangled from a pierced lobe and a surprisingly delicate face sported a tasteful hint of blush and a bit of lip rouge. No hint to gender could be gained from the hair, it being covered by a black turban.

In fact, judging by his or her dusky complexion, the person could very well be an Indian or a Parsee, or from somewhere else in the Mysterious Orient.

"May I see your identification?" he/she asked, in a hoarse, mid-timbre voice that gave nothing away. A careful once-over of both man and calling card, then, "Come in, Mr. Oliver. Miss LaBelle is expecting you. She is in the garden, but if you will wait here in the foyer, I will inform her that you have arrived."

Oliver stood with his hat in his hand, taking in the details of the grand entryway—gleaming marble floors, a sweeping oak staircase, ceiling two soaring stories high—before the unfathomable personage reappeared and said, "Please follow me." The individual turned and strode away, leaving Oliver to follow or not, whichever suited him.

It suited him to follow.

Oliver had had his share of dealings with some of the motion picture elite, directors and producers and such, so when he was ushered into Bianca's airy sunroom by her butler, or whatever its title was, he was prepared to be treated like something Her Highness had just stepped in.

The solarium consisted of more windows than walls, and was alive with potted plants: bamboo, palms, other tropical varieties, including a small orange tree in a turquoise ceramic planter that graced one corner. A radio encased in a cherrywood cabinet shaped like a gothic window sat on a sideboard next to the wall. Velvet rugs and streamlined furniture completed the decor.

Bianca LaBelle was draped across a chaise-lounge situated between two feathery fan palms, holding a small, hairy, brown dog in her lap.

Oliver paused between steps. He had never before been face-to-face with a real movie star. He had known she was beautiful. Her image was everywhere—trade papers, magazines, posters, and billboards. But in living color, she was stunning. It was impossible to tell on film how remarkably green her eyes were—spring grass flecked with gold, and almond-shaped over her famously high cheekbones. Her short, wavy bob was a rich, deep brown, glinting with mahogany highlights where the sun shone on it through the windows. She was younger than Oliver expected. On the motion picture screen, in black and white, she looked like a mature woman, but in the flesh, it was obvious that she was not long out of her teens. Her expression was wary as she sized him up. Oliver approved of her caution. Hollywood was not kind to young women.

"Mr. Oliver," the usher announced.

"Thank you, Fee," Bianca said.

Oliver couldn't help but cast a glance at the person as he (Oliver decided to call it "he") withdrew.

Bianca smiled at his poorly masked curiosity. "Fee is my majordomo."

"Quite an interesting individual."

"Fee likes to keep people guessing and is generally quite successful at it." She put the dog on the floor, and it immediately trotted over to inspect Oliver's shoes. The beast gave an accusatory "whuff," which indicated that he was withholding his approval until presented further evidence. He stalked back to his mistress and flopped down under her chaise. Bianca leaned back and stretched out one long, brown leg, then picked up a glass of something icy from the side table before sliding a languid glance at Oliver. She was barefoot. The man/woman had told Oliver that Bianca had been in the garden when he arrived. She was dressed casually in a plain white cotton shirt with a sailor collar, and a dark skirt. She had tied a wide, bright-green scarf around her brunette waves, its long ends trailing down her back. She had on no makeup, which surprised Oliver. These days no actress would let herself be seen without her cheeks rouged, her eyes kohled, and her lips a crimson slash.

Instead of the peaches-and-cream complexion that was all the rage at the moment, Bianca was unfashionably bronze, which made

Oliver think there might be some truth to the Mediterranean noblewoman story. Her slender body was long, half legs. A tall woman, yet she had an elfin look about her. Or some sort of not-quite-human-like-the-rest-of-us look, anyway. Oliver braced himself sternly, determined not to be swayed by her otherworldly beauty.

"Thank you for agreeing to see me, Miss LaBelle."

She graced him with a nod. "I understand that you are a private detective from Santa Monica."

"That is so."

"Now tell me why you made an appointment to trek all the way up here to Beverly Hills to speak with me. How can I help you?" Her voice was low-pitched, and she spoke slowly, deliberately. Oliver detected a slight accent but couldn't put his finger on what variety of accent it was.

"Last week, a couple of citizens found human remains on the beach near Santa Monica."

"Remains?"

"Bones. Sticking out of a hillside at the foot of the Palisades, just north of the park. Been there a long time. The storm last week finally eroded the hill enough to expose part of the body."

Bianca seemed unaffected by this revelation, but Oliver noticed that her eyes had darkened. He reminded himself that she was an actress.

"And why did you make a special trip to tell me about these old bones, Mr. Oliver? I'm as interested as anyone in Mr. Carter's recent discoveries in Egypt, but that doesn't mean that I know anything about archeology."

"These bones are nowhere near as old as King Tut's, Miss LaBelle. I was able to examine the remains before the police removed them. They were still clad in parts of a man's suit. A nice one, too, from what I could tell. Still had his wallet on him. It was much the worse for wear, but his driving license was still readable. Have you ever heard of Graham Peyton?"

Bianca's expression didn't alter, but the atmosphere in the room changed utterly, as though time had paused. "Should I have?"

"Miss LaBelle, screen stars usually can't keep their pasts a secret or their lives private for long, considering the press's appetite for every detail about the lives of the rich and famous. But you've been pretty successful at keeping yourself to yourself. In fact, you're famous for your air of mystery. The enigmatic Bianca LaBelle, star of the many adventures of the intrepid Bianca Dangereuse, daring journalist."

"Do you have a point, Oliver?"

"Graham Peyton, if that's indeed who our body was, was a bag man for whoever needed money physically carried from the East Coast to the West. I've discovered that he was also well known around Southern California for recruiting high-class prostitutes for the studios. I've been told that he specialized in young girls who wanted to get into the pictures. He disappeared off the face of the earth back in the fall of '21, and from what I hear, nobody much cared except for the people whose money he was transporting. At the time of his disappearance, a Pierce-Arrow like the one he drove was found at the top of the bluffs, but no one connected it to Peyton until now. It was generally believed that he either stole a lot of money and left the country, or that he finally ran afoul of one of his business associates and whatever was left of him was feeding the fish in the Pacific Ocean."

"This is a fascinating story, but—"

"It's not that I much care about justice for the late Graham Peyton," Oliver said over her. "In fact, I wouldn't care if all the low-life mugs around here ended up bumping each other off. But my client does care very much and has paid me well to try and discover what happened to the unfortunate Mr. Peyton."

Bianca replaced her glass on the side table and sat up on the edge of the chaise. "Who is your client?" Her sharp tone caused the dog to lift its head and glare at him. Oliver figured that if he made a wrong move the little mutt would try to gnaw his ankle off.

"He prefers to remain anonymous."

"This does not encourage me to be helpful. What do the police have to say about your investigation?"

"Not much. I get the feeling that they'd just as soon not trouble themselves."

"Well then, neither would I. What on earth could possibly have made you connect me to an old skeleton, anyway? I can promise you that I never worked as a prostitute, unless you consider motion picture work prostitution."

"A slim but intriguing connection, Miss LaBelle…"

"Bianca!"

Alma Bolding, star of stage and screen, was standing in the door behind them. She had not appeared in a movie in years, but she was not one to hide herself from any adoring fans she might have left. It was not unusual to catch sight of her around Hollywood or Beverly Hills in her sporty convertible Bugatti, roaring down Hollywood Boulevard.

Oliver hardly recognized her. She looked terrible, wrapped in a yellow silk Chinoise dressing gown, a few strands of too-black hair coming loose from the twist on top of her head. She was pale and blousy, puffy dark circles under her eyes. He knew that she wasn't that old in normal human terms—perhaps around forty—but in movie star years, she had reached the age when most actresses resorted to desperate measures to retain their youthful looks, started taking supporting roles as the heroine's mother, became businesswomen, or killed themselves. Her shocking appearance made Oliver wonder how long it would be before she chose one or the other. Still, she was the great Alma Bolding in the flesh, motion picture queen for nearly twenty years, and Oliver couldn't help but be awed. He stood up.

"Miss Bolding," he said.

Alma straightened, lifting her chin to look down her aristocratic nose at him. "Who the crap are you, young man?"

Oliver had grown used to such language from women in

Hollywood. "The name is Ted Oliver, Miss Bolding. I'm a private consultant who has been hired to find some information about a man named Graham Peyton."

Alma's eyes narrowed. "Peyton? Did that son of a bitch turn up again? I thought he skipped to Buenos Aires years ago. Why are you bothering Bianca about him?"

"You knew Graham Peyton?" Oliver had not expected this.

Alma swept into the room and flung herself into a chair next to a table sporting a gilt and ivory telephone. "Keep your lip zipped, Bianca," she said, reaching for the receiver. "I'll have Del over here in a jiffy."

Bianca cast a glance at Oliver. "Don't be so dramatic, Alma. I've already told Mr. Oliver that I've never heard of the man."

"Well, I have. He was before your time, honey. Everybody in Hollywood knew about Peyton, and believe me, he wasn't the kind of guy you'd hang around with." Alma pointed an accusing finger at Oliver. "He'll make up a story anyway, Bianca. They all make up stories. No matter what we say."

"Now, Miss LaBelle—" Oliver attempted, but Bianca stopped him with a gesture.

"Perhaps she's right, Mr. Oliver. It won't matter that I can't help you. I don't know you, but I do know what this town is like."

"I'm not going to sell some half-fabricated story to the *Hollywood Examiner,* Miss LaBelle."

Alma snorted. "So you say, Mr. Detective. You can't be in the motion picture business for as long as I have without learning that most people are scumbuckets who are only out for themselves. I doubt if your word is worth the paper it's written on."

"Perhaps you'd better go, Mr. Oliver," Bianca said. "Fee, please show our guest out." Oliver turned to see that the majordomo was already standing in the doorway, glowering at him in a most alarming fashion. He didn't argue.

Oliver couldn't blame the women for their attitude. The studios owned the newspapers and the police, and if an actor didn't toe the line his studio set for him, he could find himself destroyed overnight. It was ten times worse for women. And here was Oliver, sniffing around Bianca LaBelle, Bianca Dangereuse herself, trying to find out if she knew anything about the death of a dealer in whatever shady enterprise was going; drugs, booze, money laundering, whores, and who knew what else.

"How long have you worked for Miss LaBelle?" Oliver asked as he followed Fee's bulk down the marble hallway to the front door. Fee's icy silence chilled the air.

——

Oliver returned to his apartment in Santa Monica. He hung his fedora on the hat rack beside the door and sat down at his desk. From everything he had discovered over the previous week, he surmised that Graham Peyton had been a royal son of a bitch. Perhaps there were mysteries best left unsolved.

People get forgotten in a hurry. Graham Peyton was a bootlegger, a bag man, and a frequent violator of the Mann Act, which forbade the transportation of underage girls across state borders for immoral purposes. The man who hired Oliver had indicated that when Peyton had disappeared without a trace, so had fifty thousand dollars and a leather-bound ledger. Oliver could understand why his shadowy client was looking for that much money and a missing ledger full of incriminating information. But why would anyone care if somebody murdered a character like Graham Peyton? There were plenty of other guys with no conscience who would be happy to do his job.

Oliver had just decided to think about supper instead of murder when his party line telephone jingled, two short rings and a long. It was for him.

It took him a moment to recognize Fee's low rasp on the other end. "Mr. Oliver, Miss LaBelle would like to see you. Would you come to the estate for luncheon tomorrow?"

But there is more to this story than first meets the eye.

The walk from Bianca's house to her stables had been long and twisty, down bridle paths encircling the estate and through a small citrus orchard. Fee conducted Oliver down a gravel path that led around the swimming pool, through a neat vegetable garden, more scattered fruit trees, mostly apple this time, to the small paddock at the back of the property, backing up to the rocky side of the mountain. It was dark inside the stable after the sun-drenched hike, and it took a moment for Oliver's eyes to adjust.

Bianca was standing at a stall halfway down the central aisle. She was dressed for riding, in high lace-up boots and jodhpurs, an embroidered white shirt, her hair once again covered with a scarf, yellow flowered silk. This was the first time he had seen her standing up, and he was surprised to note that she was easily as tall as he was. She was communing with a blaze-faced roan whose massive head was hanging over the door of his stall. Bianca had pressed her forehead to the horse's and was murmuring to him, so softly that Oliver couldn't hear what she was saying. He suspected it wasn't anything that he would understand, anyway. She didn't move when they came in, though her green eyes shifted in his direction. Oliver nearly collided with Fee when she/he stopped walking. He couldn't get around the majordomo's bulk, so had no choice but to stand and wait until Bianca deigned to acknowledge them.

Finally she sighed into the horse's nostrils, and the horse sighed back. She turned to face Oliver. "Hello, Oliver. Thank you for interrupting your investigation long enough to come out on such a lovely day. Have you turned up any more skeletons in the rocks since yesterday?"

A pang of annoyance hit him. "You wanted to see me, Miss LaBelle."

Her amused expression did not dim. She straightened, suddenly businesslike. "Fee, would you please ask Norah to set out our luncheon in the library? We will be inside shortly."

Oliver had to squash himself up next to the slats of one of the stalls in order to let Fee pass. He was just about to say that he was not here for damn tea and cakes, but Bianca forestalled him.

"Do you ride, Detective?"

"What? No. I…"

"That's too bad. I grew up around horses, you know. When I was a kid I thought I didn't want anything more than to get away from the smell of horse sweat, but nowadays nothing soothes my soul like a leisurely ride. Horses ask very little of you. Oh, well. There's nothing for it, I suppose. Let's go inside to talk."

She led him briskly up the path to the house (a much shorter route than Fee had led him, Oliver noticed), and they entered through the sunroom where he had first spoken to her. He followed her down a hall with a black tiled floor so shiny that he briefly wondered if the modesty of women in skirts was compromised when they walked over them. The decor of the house was surprisingly plain, the walls painted white and mostly bare except for black, white, and gold fan-shaped sconces covering the wall lighting. They passed through a cavernous, white-carpeted living room with sleek, metallic furnishings and into a sizable library. There was some interesting art on the walls in the living room, rather exotic, Oliver thought, but Bianca was moving fast and he didn't have time to examine the objects and still keep up with his hostess.

The library was different from the rest of the house, at least what he had seen of it. This room was full of wood and had a simple, almost Japanese look to it. Three walls were lined with bookshelves and the fourth with floor-to-ceiling windows. A semicircular bench in the center of the room curled around a round mahogany table. A small secretary's desk was tucked into one corner. Bianca settled herself into a comfortable-looking white leather chair, and gestured for Oliver to take a seat in its twin, next to her. The funny little dog that Oliver had met on his first trip trotted into the room, following a maid who was holding a tray of sandwiches. The pooch did his usual sniff and warning "whuff" before taking up his vigil at Bianca's feet.

"That's some dog. What kind of dog is that?"

"Thanks. I think he's some kind of dog, too. We've decided he's part rat and part drain hair. But I love him. I call him Jack Dempsey." Jack Dempsey looked up at the sound of his name and Bianca scratched his chin. "We adopted each other a few years ago." She gestured toward the tray the maid had put on the side table. "Have a sandwich."

Oliver picked one out, had a bite, then got to the point. "Do you have some information for me, Miss LaBelle?"

"Have you learned anything more about what happened to Peyton?"

Oliver shifted in his chair. He was used to hearing people dance around his questions. He didn't like it. "Since we spoke yesterday? I'm in the early stages of my investigation. The police are still maintaining that his death was an accident, that he must have fallen from the cliff. And maybe he did."

She sat in silence for a long minute before her eyes wandered to the bookshelf behind his chair. "Do you like to read, Mr. Oliver?"

"Miss LaBelle, I…"

"I love this room. If heaven is really a place where I would want to go, it'll look like this. If I get a choice, I'll spend eternity riding horses and reading books." Her gaze shifted back to his face, her eyes green ice that made him catch his breath. "Tell me about yourself, Oliver."

"Well, Miss LaBelle, there's not much to tell. Besides, if I'm going to give you my autobiography, I think it's only fair that you return the favor."

She favored him with the enigmatic smile for which she was famous—small, quirky, knowing.

"My past is hardly classified information, Mr. Detective. Anyone who really wanted to know the truth about me only had to look. Most people don't want to know."

"I disagree. Everyone wants to know the truth about the beautiful French princess with the broken heart."

Her voice was tinged with irony. "I can assure you that no one in Southern California is still the person she was born as. The publicity director at United Features was the one who created the heartbroken French aristocrat."

"So you're not an aristocrat."

"Hardly. Not from France, either."

"Are you heartbroken?"

"Not at all. In fact, thus far my life has turned out remarkably well. I'm still young, of course, so who knows what the future holds? But that's true for all of us, so I don't worry about it. Now, I've told you about my life. It's your turn to tell me about yours."

Oliver almost pointed out that aside from admitting that she was not really a French aristocrat, Bianca had not told him anything. He changed his tactic. Perhaps if he gave her reason to trust him, she could be coaxed. "I haven't been in California very long. I moved down here from Oregon, thinking I was going to be the next John Gilbert. I wasn't as lucky as you, movie star-wise."

"How do you like California?"

I don't, he thought. "Miss LaBelle, why did you want to speak to me? Surely not just to exchange life stories."

"I wanted to ask you if you will keep me informed about the progress of your investigation. I will of course pay you for your time."

"I can't do that. I owe my client my discretion."

One sculpted eyebrow inched upward. "Well, that's unusual. Could it be that you are the only ethical man in Hollywood?"

"I wouldn't go that far. But I do maintain certain standards for myself, if no one else. Why do you want to know?"

"Is your client K.D. Dix?"

Oliver's eyes widened, but he said nothing. How did she know about K.D. Dix?

Bianca laughed. "I'll take that as a 'yes'. But it doesn't matter, Mr. Oliver. I don't need to know who your client is. If you do decide to keep me in the loop, I'd appreciate it if you wouldn't tell your client of my interest. I guarantee that it has nothing to do with Dix's operation."

"I understand your concern, Miss LaBelle. But why have you suddenly developed an interest in the investigation? I thought you were afraid that I would make up some celebrity gossip about you to sell to *Photoplay* for a bundle. Or blackmail you into paying for my silence."

"I've done a little investigation of my own since you were here yesterday, Oliver. Some of my friends have told me what you've done for them, and discreetly, too. And Mr. Laemmle vouches for you, which goes a long way in my book."

Oliver didn't say it, but it did strike him as ironic that it was Laemmle who had recommended his services to K.D. Dix in the first place. His skepticism must have shown on his face, because Bianca said, "Don't say anything bad about Carl Laemmle, not in my presence, Mr. Oliver."

"I was just thinking that it must be Laemmle who told you about Dix. No, never mind. Let's just agree to trust each other on this one." The Laemmle connection didn't surprise Oliver that much. Carl Laemmle had founded Universal Studios in a deserted area of the San Fernando Valley more than a decade earlier, and was the man who had first signed Mary Pickford. "Uncle Carl" liked betting on the ponies and playing high-stakes poker, but unlike many studio moguls, he was not a lecher. In fact, he was known for hiring women to write and direct his pictures. He had a reputation for liking smart women. It was no wonder he liked Bianca.

"All right, Miss LaBelle. I'll try to keep you informed."

"I appreciate it." She stood, and Oliver stood too. He was aware that Fee had entered the room and was standing behind him. His sandwich was half-finished, but the audience was over.

Santa Monica, California
One week earlier...

Ted Oliver was a good-looking man. He knew it, but he didn't put much stock in the fact. Southern California was chockablock with good-looking men. Most of them with the character of a weasel, and in certain cases that comparison was insulting to weasels everywhere. He had originally come to California to get into the moving pictures, but it didn't take long for him to realize that he could make a much better living as a private agent. Oliver had carved out a nice business for himself by doing favors for the studios, mostly by tracking down and paying off blackmailers who threatened to release incriminating evidence about the indiscretions of high-earning movie stars. On the side, he located runaways and deadbeat husbands, spent a lot of time sitting outside of hotels with a Brownie camera, waiting for his client's spouse to walk out the front door, arm in arm with his or her latest dalliance.

He met most of his clients at their homes, or in Santa Monica at his usual table in Bay Cities Italian Deli on the corner of Broadway and Lincoln. On the rare occasion that a potential client preferred a neutral location, or more privacy than a public dining room could afford, Tony DiTomasi let Oliver use his office at the back of the restaurant. Oliver was a good customer, so as long as it didn't discommode anyone, Tony didn't charge him for the privilege. If the client objected to the aroma of garlic and oregano, then Oliver didn't particularly want to do business with him, anyway.

He had been at the private agent business long enough to have formed a less than favorable opinion of his fellow man. His fellow woman didn't win any prizes in his estimation, either.

On this day, a man by the name of Ruhl had arranged a meeting with him at Bay Cities. When Ruhl showed up at two o'clock on the dot, Oliver was already ensconced behind Tony's desk, which was big enough to be intimidating even if it was located in a closet-sized room lined with shelves of tomato sauce and olive oil.

Oliver was surprised when Tony ushered the man in. Usually Tony couldn't be bothered to do more for Oliver's clients than wave his hand in the general direction of the office.

But when Oliver got a gander at the guy, his eyebrows inched upward.

The man was seventy if he was a day. He was dressed in a homburg hat, a cutaway coat, and a pair of skimpy trousers of a style that hadn't been popular for thirty years. His outfit was expensive, though, and new. The man had money enough to have his clothes tailored and prestige enough not to give a rat's ass about fashion. Oliver and Tony exchanged a pregnant glance over the man's head before Tony shut the door and left them alone.

Oliver stood up long enough to shake the man's hand and invite him to make himself comfortable in the upholstered chair in front of the desk. Once back in place, Oliver looked the man over while the man pointedly did the same to him. Eventually Oliver decided that somebody ought to start the ball rolling.

"What can I do for you, Mr. Ruhl?"

The man's eyes were the color and, it seemed, the consistency of steel. "I understand from my friend, Mr. Laemmle, that you are good at what you do, and discreet."

The mention of motion picture producer Carl Laemmle gave Oliver confidence in Mr. Ruhl's bona fides. "I've done some investigative work for Mr. Laemmle on previous occasions," he said. He explained his terms and conditions to Ruhl, and when he padded his usual fee plus per diem by twenty percent, Ruhl didn't blink, which told Oliver something about his prospective client.

Often very rich people would try to bargain him down or ask for a discount, which is why they were rich, Oliver figured. But Mr. Ruhl didn't argue, so he was both rich and extremely motivated. He said to Oliver, "A couple of lovers walking on the beach found a skeleton this morning, buried under rocks below the cliffs of Palisades Park."

Oliver had heard worse. "You want me to find out who it is?"

"I know who it is. I want you to try to find something that he stole from me."

Oliver considered this for a moment. "You said they found this guy's skeleton. And you know who he was?"

"Yes. They found his wallet on him. I know who it is."

Oliver noted that the man's aggressive attitude was covering a bad case of nerves. "And he stole something from you. How long ago did this happen? Long enough for him to thin out, apparently."

Mr. Ruhl did not appreciate Oliver's humor. "You don't need to look so skeptical, young man. His name was Graham Peyton. He used to work for my company. He disappeared five years ago, along with a great deal of money and a book that belonged to me. The money is of little interest, but I would like to retrieve the book."

"A book."

"You're very talented at repeating everything I say, if at nothing else. Yes, a book. A ledger, actually."

"How much money did he get away with?"

"I told you, I don't care about the money."

"Peyton may have cared, and a lot of other people too."

"All right. About fifty thousand."

Oliver gave low whistle. "Somebody may have taken a notion to conk your boy over the noggin and buy himself a ticket to Santiago. Or for fifty big ones, Peyton could have decided to hand his wallet to some schmuck, push him over the cliff, and take a steamer to South America himself. Besides, if this ledger has been missing for five years, you have obviously been able to get along all right without it. Why is it so important to get it back after all this time?"

"The ledger contains some very valuable information. When Peyton disappeared, it was generally supposed that he skipped and took the book with him, perhaps with blackmail on his mind. After a few months with no contact, I began to suspect that Mr. Peyton had come to a bad end. He did not keep the best company. Still, I've had people looking for him all this time. When I learned this morning what had become of him, I wasn't surprised. Peyton was a shady character."

"Mr. Ruhl, if Peyton took the ledger from you five years ago, he probably sold it to someone or someone found it and kept it after he disappeared. The likelihood that it can be found is slim at best."

"Mr. Oliver, if he sold it or the wrong person found it after he died, I'd know."

"How could you possibly know that?"

"I'd be dead."

"Well, now you've got my attention, Mister. What is in this book that is important enough to kill for?" The moment he asked the question, he knew the answer. He took a breath. "Mr. Ruhl, you say that the police discovered the remains at the foot of the palisades this morning, yet you already know who it is. Could it be that you know how he got there because you put him there?"

Ruhl looked shocked. "Certainly not. I have friends in the Santa Monica Police Department who were kind enough to inform me of the deceased's identity. It is generally known among my circles that I have been looking for him for a long time."

"Before I take on the job, I'm going to need a little more information, then."

Ruhl sat back and perched his forearms on the arms of the chair. "I was given to understand that you are…let us say, nonjudgmental about a person's line of work. If that is not so, tell me now."

"Mr. Ruhl, if it weren't for people's vices, I wouldn't be in business for long. As long as it doesn't involve killing people, I'm not interested in how a man makes his living."

His answer seemed to satisfy Ruhl. "You have not been in the Los Angeles area for long. Have you ever heard of K.D. Dix?"

Oliver got a sour feeling in his stomach. Perhaps he wasn't as blasé about a person's profession as he had thought. "K.D. Dix runs whores, mostly for studio bigwigs and money men, and has a profitable side business turning dirty money into clean money for rich people who got rich the wrong way. I've never had the pleasure, if you can call it that, and as far as I know, neither has anyone else. Of course I've heard of him. Big operation, but no one seems to know Dix himself. What does he have to do with this?"

"K.D. is my employer, and your client, if you decide to take the job."

"The ledger belongs to Dix?"

"It does. It contains potentially damaging information about some very powerful men."

"If we are going to work together then let us not get off on the wrong foot by not being perfectly honest. If you are K.D. Dix, then say so."

"That is an amusing notion, Mr. Oliver. No, I am not K.D. Dix. I have been with K.D. for many years, however, and am in my employer's complete confidence."

"Why didn't your boss come himself?"

"My employer prefers to shun the limelight. I handle most of K.D.'s business, public and private. I have men at my disposal who can take care of some of my less savory chores, but I want an outsider for this particular task. I also wanted to meet you in person, and judge for myself if you are up to the job. I want to find out what happened to that ledger, if it still exists, who has it, and if it can be got back. I'm willing to pay well to find out. K.D. particularly wants to find out if Peyton's death was an accident or if someone killed him. And if so, who. If he was murdered and you can find out who did it, that greatly increases the chances of finding the book."

"Mr. Ruhl, don't you think that if someone was going to use the information in that ledger, they'd have done it by now?"

"Maybe. Maybe they don't know what they have. Maybe it's hidden somewhere, a safe deposit box, under a bed."

Oliver sat back in his chair. Knowing the type of clientele who utilized K.D. Dix's services, Peyton had most likely collected plenty of incriminating information over the years. Yet why wasn't a ledger full of five-year-old dirt too old to be useful? It must hold proof of something shockingly illegal or shockingly filthy against someone shockingly rich or famous or powerful. If it came to light that a man frequented brothels, his reputation would suffer. But tax evasion and money laundering, now that was a thing that could ruin a man's life, whether he was a mobster, movie mogul, businessman, or President of the United States. K.D. wanted that power back.

"What more can you tell me about the last days of Peyton's life? When was the last time you saw him? Do you remember?"

"I don't remember the exact day, but it was sometime in the last week of September 1921. I had given him the cash and an assignment to travel to Chicago to pick up a shipment of merchandise…"

Oliver interrupted. "What kind of merchandise? Hooch?"

Ruhl's put-out expression scared Oliver a bit. "Does it matter?" Ruhl said.

"I don't know. Maybe. I have to have all the pieces before I can put together a puzzle. You wanted someone discreet and I can guarantee you that I am."

Ruhl still didn't look happy, but he said, "Not liquor. We have a Canadian connection for that. Cocaine and heroin, mostly. The government controls on dope were getting stricter by the minute, so in '21 we decided to open up our own supply lines. Just in the nick of time, too. By the next year it was almost impossible to get the stuff legally, so our market exploded. Anyway, Peyton took the dough and was supposed to catch the train to Chicago the next morning, but our contact telephoned a couple of days later and said he never arrived. He didn't catch the train. He never made it to the station, as far as we were able to tell. He was gone and so was the money."

"And the ledger?"

"I know he had it in his house the day before. I saw it myself. I searched his house as soon as we knew he had disappeared, maybe a week later. But there was no trace of the ledger then. We removed everything from his duplex that could lead back to Dix. K.D. thought from the beginning that Peyton was dead. My boss had a soft spot for the guy and never did believe that he took the money and scarpered."

"But you believe it."

Ruhl didn't opt for subtlety. "Peyton was an idiot. It's a wonder somebody didn't knock him off years earlier. He liked to seduce young girls with stories of love or fame or riches and then sell them to pleasure establishments. If some outraged father was after him with a shotgun I have no doubt he'd have purloined that money and sailed for Hawaii on the next steamer out of

Long Beach. That's why we've had our agents hunting for him overseas. Until now. Maybe the outraged father got him after all."

"Did Peyton gamble?"

"Was he in hock to the Chicago outfit? Dix says no. I don't know, but I wouldn't be surprised."

"So...he died before he got on the train to Chicago, and the ledger disappeared, sometime during the last week of September in 1921. I assume that once you knew Peyton was missing, you talked to all his known associates in the L.A. area."

"Of course. No one knew anything."

"Someone could have been lying."

"No one would be stupid enough to lie to K.D. Dix."

If Oliver agreed to take the job, he'd have to be careful. If Peyton had been murdered for the ledger, the killer would go to bloody lengths to keep hold of it. His hesitance must have shown on his face, because before he could refuse, Mr. Ruhl said, "I'll give you five thousand to get started, on top of your usual fee. If you get the book back for me, I'll give you a twenty-thousand-dollar bonus. More if you can find out what happened to Peyton."

Oliver uncapped his pen. "Tell me everything you know about Graham Peyton."

Boynton, Oklahoma
1920

It Had All Started Five Years Earlier, in the Fall, when a Starstruck Girl Went to the Movies.

Blanche Tucker and her sister Alice Kelley had gone to the flickers at the O&B Theater in Boynton, Oklahoma, to see *Stella Maris*, with Mary Pickford and the ever-so-dreamy Conrad Terle. Their parents didn't approve of their offspring going to the movies. Who knew what sort of unsavory ideas impressionable young people might pick up? But Blanche was staying at Alice's house for a few days to help her with her three-year-old daughter, Linda. Alice was expecting again and hadn't been feeling well. Blanche saw in the *Boynton Index* that the Mary Pickford flick had arrived in town at last. Boynton, Oklahoma, was the back-est of the back of beyond, and it took forEVER for anything cultural to finally show at the O&B. Blanche concocted an elaborate plan to sneak out of Alice's house and see that motion picture come hell or high water before she had to go back out to the farm. She would not miss her one and only chance to see her very favorite actress in action.

But she never had to execute her plan. After three days of lying around, Alice was bored to tears and she made the suggestion that they go to the pictures herself. If there was one thing about Alice that Blanche had always admired, it was that Alice usually did whatever she felt like doing and managed to not just get away with it, but charm her way out of trouble, to boot. So Alice and Blanche made a pact one warm, hazy September afternoon. Blanche would not tell Alice's husband or the doctor that Alice had been out of bed, and Alice would not tell their parents that she had corrupted her little sister by taking her to the purveyor of shocking ideas that was the O&B Theater. Blanche worried that Linda, little magpie that she was, would spill the beans. But Alice knew her baby well. A cautionary word and a box of Good & Plenty was enough to seal her lips. Linda was used to keeping her mother's secrets, anyway. She had learned early that her collusion would always be rewarded.

After the picture ended, when the lights came up in the theater, Blanche was sure that her life had been changed forever. The divine Mary Pickford had played two entirely different characters—the sheltered, crippled Stella Maris, and Unity, the poor servant girl. Unity had fallen for her benefactor, the kindly, married John Risca, but John only had eyes for Stella. In the end, the selfless Unity shot John's evil wife and then killed herself so that John would be free to marry his one true love, Stella Maris.

What a story. What sacrifice. What unbridled, unselfish love. What a gift Mary Pickford had, to be able to move and inspire one the way she had inspired Blanche. Blanche would do anything…

> *~Anything, Blanche?~*
> "Yes, anything at all."

...to be able to evoke such emotion.

"Let's get some ice cream before we have to go back to prison," Alice said, jolting Blanche out of her dream.

Alice took Blanche and Linda to the soda fountain at the Owl Drug Store. They didn't stop at Williams Drug Store across the street from the theater, where the entire Tucker clan usually shopped, lest they be recognized, in which case word of their outing would certainly get around. Not that Alice or her husband, Walter, would care, but it was just too much trouble to put up with the family's disapproval. When the ice cream was finished, Alice took a tired Linda home, but she didn't bat an eye when Blanche asked to stay behind for a while and peruse the magazines in the long rack by the front window. Owl Drug Store was smaller than Williams', with a small soda fountain and two little round tables at the front. All around the back and side walls of the store, a U-shaped counter displayed an assortment of patent medicines and a few sundries.

Mr. Williams never seemed to mind when Blanche thumbed through the magazines, but five minutes after Alice left, the sour-faced woman who was working the register at the Owl Drug informed Blanche in no uncertain terms that if she was going to read all of the motion picture periodicals from front to back and get her finger marks all over then, she at least had to buy one.

Blanche felt her cheeks flush, but before she could respond, a voice behind her said, "I would be most pleased to buy any magazine the lady wants." Blanche turned to find herself facing the handsomest, most sophisticated man that she had ever seen. His gaze lowered to her face and he tipped his white boater. Unimaginably dapper, dressed in his black suit and bow tie, he spoke with an exotic clipped accent. His blue eyes shone with good humor. "Kindly allow me to be of assistance, Mademoiselle."

She had been told that she shouldn't accept gifts from a stranger. She had been told a lot of things. But her parents were desperately old-fashioned, and Blanche could tell at a glance that this stranger was a gentleman. The only reason he could possibly have for offering to buy a magazine for her was his own natural gallantry.

After allowing him to spend a quarter on the October 1920 issue of *Photoplay* with the picture of Mary Pickford right on the cover, Blanche and the gallant gentleman sat down at the corner table and talked for half an hour, until Blanche feared that Alice would come looking for her. Graham Peyton was his name. He had seen her at the movie house, sitting two rows ahead of him with Alice and the little girl. He had noticed the tears in her eyes when her little party left the theater. It was a happy coincidence that he had run into her here at the drug store.

Graham was only passing through on his way to Los Angeles from New York City. He was a Broadway impresario, he told her, as well as a Hollywood motion picture producer. She didn't know what an impresario was, but when he explained it to her, she was impressed. His latest Broadway revue had recently closed after a two-year run, and he was returning to California to take up the reins of his motion picture production company. He had tired of New York and wanted to spend more time concentrating on the movie industry. Besides, his mother lived in Los Angeles and she wasn't getting any younger.

It occurred to Blanche that Boynton, Oklahoma, was not exactly situated on the direct route from New York to Los Angeles, but when Peyton told her that he had decided to take his time getting out to the West Coast and see a bit of the country, she didn't wonder about it again. Especially once he told her that he intended to hang around Boynton for a few days because he particularly liked the scenery. Since the scenery around Boynton consisted of fields, a bunch of cows, trees, and endless barbed-wire fences, Blanche got his drift immediately.

Though Alice was feeling better by the end of the week, their mother let Blanche stay on a few more days. As long as she had returned in time to fix supper, Alice and Walter didn't seem to mind that Blanche was a little late coming back to their house after school. Blanche didn't feel guilty about meeting Peyton on the sly to talk about Hollywood. After all, he was only going to be in town for a couple more days.

But then he told her that he thought he would spend some extra time in Boynton before he made his way out west. He looked deep into her eyes and said he had found a compelling reason to delay. He had the most poetic way of putting things.

"Your eyes are emerald pools. Your hair is living waves of sable."

The first time she and Peyton had met at the Owl Drug, he spun tales of all the Broadway stars he had worked with. The second time, he had told her how many of those stage actresses were now Hollywood stars, acting in motion pictures that he had produced. The third time, Peyton told Blanche that she was too beautiful to bury herself in Boynton, Oklahoma, only to find herself hitched someday to a hayseed husband and raising a bunch of snot-nosed kids. The very next day he brought her flowers. By the end of the week, he told her he loved her.

After that, Blanche contrived ways to meet Peyton in whatever out-of-the-way place she could, as often as she could manage. Alice would have been happy to have Blanche take up residence at her house and become a permanent cook and nanny, but their mother knew both her daughters' scheming ways too well. Finally, she insisted that Blanche vacate Alice's neat little house in town and come home. To the farm. Located two endless miles outside of town. Far from the Owl Drug Store and the fascinating Graham Peyton.

Blanche had to think fast. She volunteered to spend a month helping the first grade teacher, Mrs. Trompler, ready her classroom and prepare lessons in the mornings before school started. After all, she told her mother, it was so much easier to get to school from Alice's house in town, rather than have to make that two-mile hike so early in the morning.

She didn't know how long she would be able to get away with her ruse before her mother smelled a rat. Her parents had reared ten children and Blanche was the eighth, which put her at quite a disadvantage. Her mother had already heard every lie and figured out every sneaky trick an adolescent could devise.

Blanche had never known she was capable of feeling such desperate, wild longing. Was it love? What else could it be? Surely not simple lust for adventure. No, she had never met anyone as sophisticated as Graham Peyton, and she was never likely to again. It was love for sure.

They made their plan. Another of Blanche's married sisters, Ruth, lived with her husband and their elderly benefactor in an enormous confection of a house on the northern outskirts of town. Blanche knew it wouldn't be much longer before her mother saw through her, so she and Graham had to put their plan into action quickly. She told her mother that Alice didn't need her anymore and she didn't care to outstay her welcome, so could she please spend a few nights at Ruth's place, at least until she finished off her job as Mrs. Trompler's aide? Just till the end of the week. Ruth was fine with it since her husband had pulled a month's night duty as a policeman in the neighboring town of Muskogee.

Her mother agreed. It would have been the perfect plan but for one snag. Blanche's younger sister Sophronia wanted to join her at Ruth's, and Blanche could not come up with one convincing argument as to why she should not. Their mother thought it was a great idea.

Blanche managed to get away long enough to tell Graham the bad news. She was practically in tears, but Graham thought it was funny. "That just makes your getaway more exciting, toots. Now, listen. Here's what we're going to do."

~Determined to embark on a life of excitement
and adventure, Blanche does a midnight flit.~

Fourteen-year-old Sophronia Tucker was as straightforward
and open as Blanche was secretive. But Sophronia knew her older
sister better than anyone in the world. There was only a year's
difference in their ages, after all. As soon as the two girls settled
into the ground floor bedroom in Ruth's big house, Sophronia
knew something was up. In the first place, they were only going
to be at Ruth's house on the edge of town for a few nights, but
Blanche had brought enough clothes for a month. Sophronia
asked Blanche about it, but Blanche snorted and icily informed
her that you never knew when an occasion might arise, and it
was best to be prepared.

Sophronia grudgingly bought it. Blanche had always been
something of a clotheshorse. Still…she couldn't put her finger
on it. There was something furtive about Blanche at supper that
evening, and after they went to bed, Sophronia could have sworn
that Blanche was just pretending to have fallen asleep a mere ten
minutes after lights out.

But sleep overtook Sophronia before she could wonder about
it for long.

~As Mark Twain said, "Everyone is a moon, and has
a dark side which he never shows to anybody."~

Sophronia woke with a start. The moon was shining through
the open window, two hands above the horizon. Sophronia figured she had been asleep for about an hour.

It was cold. She flopped over onto her back and realized that
she was alone in the double bed. Where was Blanche? The window was open and her bedmate was gone. No wonder she was
cold. Sophronia forced a disgusted breath and sat up. She was
not going to be able to go back to sleep until she located Blanche.

She climbed out of bed, slid her feet into her knitted booties, and threw a shawl over her shoulders before slipping out of the room and down the hall to the bathroom. She could tell before she had traversed ten feet that Blanche was not there. The door was standing open and the light bulb hanging from the ceiling was unlit. Sophronia went back to her room to ponder her next move. She stood beside the bedroom door for a moment, thinking, until it slowly dawned on her that she was not seeing Blanche's carpetbag in its accustomed place on top of the bureau.

Sophronia's heart leaped into her mouth. She pulled open the bureau drawer where Blanche had stored the magazines she had brought with her. Empty.

Sophronia rushed to the window and looked out onto the night. Not that she expected to see anything, but her feet seemed to move of their own accord. Far across the long front yard, Blanche's thin, dark-haired figure stood with the carpetbag in her hand and her back to the house, facing the road that led out of town. Before it quite registered on Sophronia what was happening, a convertible roadster pulled up beside Blanche. It was too dark to see the driver clearly, just that he was a man in a white straw hat staring determinedly at the road before him. Blanche tossed her bag into the back.

"Blanche," Sophronia cried, and Blanche started and looked behind her. She lifted a finger to her lips, then climbed into the roadster. The driver pushed the car into gear and took off down the road. He never turned his head.

> ~*The devil comes disguised*
> *as everything you ever wanted.*~

"She saw us, she saw us, Graham! My sister Ruth will call the sheriff! They'll be after us!"

"Don't worry, angel. We'll be long gone before they can figure out what happened." He stepped on the gas. The roadster roared forward into the night, and Blanche squealed with delight.

Graham's giant seven-passenger Pierce-Arrow roadster was unstoppable, even over the rutted dirt roads that Oklahomans euphemistically called "highways." It took them a mere seven hours to traverse the 140 miles between Boynton and Oklahoma City, and they never had to stop once for a flat tire. Graham had roused the proprietor of a Pure Oil station in Shawnee from his bed in the middle of the night in order to fill the gasoline tank, but they didn't stop for long. They wanted to put as much distance between themselves and Boynton as they could. Dawn was just breaking over the prairie when Graham finally stopped in Oklahoma City long enough for them to refill the tank and get a bite to eat at a little diner on Twenty-third Street, across from the state capitol building.

The waitress asked Graham what she could get for his daughter. Blanche was mortally offended, but Graham laughed and ordered bacon and eggs and a big stack of pancakes for both of them. When they had made their escape from Boynton, Blanche had been so excited that she thought she would never need to sleep again, but after they left Oklahoma City she slept for a few hours in the Pierce-Arrow's spacious back seat.

West of Oklahoma City, the aspect of the country changed. There were few rolling hills and little forest land here, mostly flat, featureless grassland as far as the eye could see, broken only by an occasional farm outlined by a windbreak of scrubby trees. The road was dusty and difficult and the only easy going came when they drove through one small backwater town or another. Paved streets were rare, but at least most towns could afford to grade their roads every once in a while.

Blanche slept through much of the endless trip through western Oklahoma, but perked up considerably when they reached New Mexico and the country changed again, turning into a strange, arid landscape without grass, but covered with small, spiky plants and miles of barbed-wire fence that stretched endlessly until it disappeared over the horizon. Sometimes she caught a glimpse of a herd of beautiful deerlike animals that Graham called "pronghorns," but before she had time to admire their graceful forms, they would bound away from the road and the roar of the automobile.

In order to put distance between Blanche's old life and her new, Graham stopped only for meals and to let Blanche out of the auto long enough to relieve herself behind a scrubby mesquite or yucca. They would drive into the night, either stopping in some forlorn little New Mexico town with a boardinghouse, or if no town presented itself, pull off the road and camp in the car. Blanche never minded sleeping under the stars, talking with Graham for hours, making plans for their life together.

Albuquerque was as foreign to her as China. The pueblo-style buildings around the town square were flat-roofed, with long *portales* stretching along the facades, and adobe benches called *bancos* built into the walls. Graham drove directly through the central square and pulled up at the grand entrance to the Alvarado Hotel, a sprawling red-and-white Fred Harvey hotel located next the railroad station. He helped her out of the auto and she followed him into the lobby, trying not to stare like a rube. She had never seen such a fancy hotel, even the time she had gone with her parents to a Grange convention in Tulsa. The large lobby was beautifully decorated in a Spanish and Indian style, with a beamed ceiling, carved wooden furniture, huge potted desert plants. Colorful Indian rugs lay on the saltillo tile floors and hung from the walls.

Graham led her to the carved cedar registration desk, where a tall, black-haired clerk in a red vest and black bow tie looked up and broke into a grin.

"Hello, Mr. Peyton. Welcome back. Your regular room is made up and ready for you." The clerk didn't spare a glance for Blanche. Graham didn't introduce her, or ask for a second room, either. She had been traveling with Graham for more than a week. When they weren't camping out, Graham had paid for separate rooms in the various inns and boardinghouses where they had stayed. Until now. Blanche felt her heart quicken. She said nothing.

Graham accepted a key from the clerk. "Our luggage is in the trunk, Bernardo."

"Allow me to escort you." Bernardo snapped his fingers at a liveried bellhop, who scurried out the front door.

Blanche was impressed.

Graham took her arm as Bernardo led them through the lobby and down a long, carpeted hallway to a door at the end. Blanche whispered as they walked, "You have a regular room? You must come here a lot."

"This is my regular stop when I make the drive between New York and Los Angeles. I spend a lot of cabbage here and send a lot of business their way, so it's in their interest to treat me right."

Bernardo stopped in front of a door at the end of the hall. He stood aside as Graham gestured for her to enter first.

She half expected a suite, but it was just one large room with a door that led to a private patio in the back. One large room, one large bed.

Once Bernardo had made his exit, his palm well-greased, Blanche turned and raised an eyebrow at Graham.

Question unasked, but question answered. "Darling," Graham said, "this week that I have spent traveling with you has been the happiest of my life. By this time next week we'll be married, but I don't want to wait another day to begin the rest of my life with you. I think of us as married already. But I won't force you to do anything you don't want."

"Oh, Graham, I feel exactly the same way. I love you so much. I know we're already married in the eyes of God."

He chuckled. "You know it, honey. I'd take you to the court-house right this minute, but California is going to be our home. I think it would be better to do the deed there, among all our friends. Well, my friends. But believe me, they'll be your friends too."

> *~It is the dawn of the morning after…*
> *and the point of no return.~*

Blanche had spent her entire life on a farm, so the ways of males and females were not a mystery to her. Her older sisters had seemed so pleased with their husbands that Blanche had been looking forward to the glories of the bedroom for a long time. But all in all, it was a disappointment. To begin with, it hurt. Still, it was all over very quickly, and it was entirely wonderful to stay in fancy hotels and be waited on hand and foot. Graham only went first class. She was going to be the wife of a very wealthy and important man.

The next morning Graham ordered room service and she lay in bed and ate fresh peaches with clotted cream and flaky little biscuits called "scones" off of china plates. Then he took her to the square and bought her a turquoise-and-silver necklace before they took off down the road, toward California.

When they reached Flagstaff, Graham turned south and they wound through steep mountain roads to Prescott, where he rented another fancy room in the Hotel Vendome on Cortez Street, just off the tree-shaded town square. The hotel was smaller than the Alvarado but just as classy, a two-story red brick building with wraparound porches on both stories.

The man at the desk didn't know Graham, but that didn't matter after Graham asked for the best room they had and paid cash in advance. Then he took Blanche shopping at J. Goldwater and Bros. General Merchandise.

He showered her with gifts. She had never in her life owned such luscious clothing and jewelry. When she looked at herself in the full-length mirror, rouged and painted, dressed in a gray serge tunic embroidered with intricate Russian designs, and saw a wildly beautiful, grown-up woman looking back at her, it wasn't hard for her to decide that in order to spend her life with this man she could put up with a few minutes of discomfort every night.

When they got back to the room late in the afternoon, Graham left her while he conducted some business, giving her time to unwrap her gifts and take a nap before supper. When he returned, it was heading toward evening. She had just gotten back to the room after a long, luxurious bath in the big tiled bathroom down the hall.

She was combing out her freshly washed hair in front of the mirror. He came up behind her and studied her reflection with approval.

"Now, honey, I want you to don your ritziest duds tonight. I just met up with a friend of mine from Hollywood who's here to scout out a location for a William S. Hart oater. I told him I'm traveling with a future star and he wants to meet you. This one-horse town ain't exactly the Big Apple but there's an eatery downtown that won't put us to shame. We're going to meet him there at eight o'clock."

Blanche wasn't completely sure what he just said, but she got the gist. Dress up, go out to eat at a nice restaurant, meet someone important in the motion picture industry who just happened to be in Arizona at the same time they were.

She picked out a simple black silk jersey dress that had been stenciled with Cubist designs around the bodice and scalloped hem.

"You look swell, honey. Really hotsy-totsy! You'll have old Schilling eating out of your hand." He ran his hands down her back and gave her a lingering kiss. He was breathing heavily when he pushed away. "No time for that right now. But we'll have us a time tonight."

Blanche was not as happy about that pronouncement as she was about a fancy dinner with a movie mogul.

> ~*Prey to his avaricious nature,*
> *Graham seeks out an old crony.*~

Darkness had fallen by the time they left the hotel on foot. They walked around the square to South Montezuma Street, which was bustling with noisy life. Unfortunately, it was not the kind of high-class activity Blanche was expecting. In spite of the fact that the entire street was lined with restaurants and ice cream parlors, the sidewalk was bristling with disreputable-looking cowboys and miners for whom the newly enacted Eighteenth Amendment to the Constitution, prohibiting the production, transport, and sale of intoxicating liquors, seemed to be no more than a suggestion.

"Are all these people drunk?" Blanche was incredulous. "Where did so many people get moonshine and why ain't they all arrested?"

"Honey, Arizona has had Prohibition for the last five years, long before the whole country decided to go dry. These folks have had plenty of time to get over the idea." He made a sweeping gesture that encompassed the entire street. "Most of these 'soda fountains' sell liquor out of the back room, and most of the time the sheriff pretty much looks the other way. For a regular monetary consideration, that is."

She didn't comment. Over the past weeks on the road, she had seen too many things that were unheard of in her previous life to be much shocked by a little lawless behavior.

Graham took her into an establishment in the middle of the block called the Palace Restaurant, located on the bottom floor of a two-story gray granite building decorated with ironwork and ornamental bricks. A round medallion bearing the image of a man leaning against a shovel, posed between a bear and a lion, had been impressed into the pediment beside the front door. The dining room was dark, long, and narrow, graced on one side by an ornate mahogany bar which was a remnant, Blanche supposed, of Prescott's bawdier, pre-Prohibition past. Round tables covered with white tablecloths took up most of the floor. Graham seated her at a table toward the back of the room and Blanche relaxed. The diners were quite respectable-looking. Waiters in long linen aprons bustled back and forth between the tables and the kitchen.

"We're waiting for a friend," Graham told the hawk-nosed waiter who appeared with pad in hand to take their order. "We'll start with some of your special lemonade."

The lemonade tasted funny, Blanche thought, but Graham assured her that the more she drank, the more she'd like it. She had to admit that was oddly true, even though the taste didn't improve with longer acquaintance. By the time they were joined by a fat man in a three-piece suit with a gold watch chain stretched across his stomach, Blanche had finished her first glass and started on another and was feeling inexplicably mellow.

Graham introduced the man as Mr. Schilling. Blanche took an instant dislike to him. He had piggy little eyes that narrowed hungrily when he looked at her, as well as a swollen red nose and jowls that jiggled when he talked. When he wasn't smacking disgustingly over his bloody rare steak, he was paying her far too much attention of a kind she didn't appreciate. He reached across the corner of the table to touch her when he spoke to her, even though she didn't try to hide her distaste. She moved her chair closer to Graham.

Graham and Schilling ignored her during their conversation, and a boring conversation it was, too. They didn't talk about the flickers, only mundane things like the weather and the state of the roads and business ventures. Graham asked Schilling if he was pleased with the deal. Schilling said that he was very pleased indeed. Blanche was beginning to wonder what the point of her being at this meeting was, when Schilling laid his utensils across his plate and excused himself to go out back and use the facilities. As soon as he was out of the room, Graham grabbed her arm roughly enough that she winced. A look of irritation flitted over his face, quickly replaced with a pleasant smile.

"Honey, I want you to be nice to Mr. Schilling. Act like you're interested in everything he says. Schilling is one of my best customers. He's rich as Midas, too, and he could be a big help to you in getting your career started."

"I'm sorry, Graham. He's just so... And nobody has said anything about the moving pictures yet. I was beginning to wonder..."

"There's no need for you to wonder about anything. You just let me handle it, baby. I know how these things are negotiated. Now, put on your prettiest smile."

Schilling returned, rubbing his hands together in a way that reminded Blanche of a fly who had just landed on a pile of manure, and plopped down in his seat. "That was good grub. But now let's get down to business. Peyton, your asking price is certainly reasonable. I'll come to your hotel and we'll settle up." He turned to Blanche. "Now, little lady, tell me all about yourself."

Blanche had not realized that Graham was an actor's agent as well as a moving picture executive. But now that the conversation had turned to Blanche's favorite topic, herself, she forgot to wonder what offer Graham had proposed on her behalf. She relaxed back into her chair and regaled the loathsome yet rich and important Mr. Schilling with all the considerable charm at her disposal.

Schilling walked back to the Vendome with them, Blanche between the two men, arm in arm with both of them. Graham sent her to their room while he and Schilling repaired to the bar for a nightcap. Blanche was annoyed at being dismissed like a child while the grown-ups talked, but she didn't argue. This was probably how business was conducted in the moving picture industry.

She removed her face paint with globs of cold cream, brushed out her hair, and changed into the pale pink silk peignoir that accentuated the roses in her cheeks. She was sitting in an upholstered chair, tapping the arm impatiently and wondering if she should go to bed, when Graham returned with a bounce in his step.

He threw his hat on the bed. "Good news, honey. Schilling thinks you've got a lot of potential. Tell you what, tomorrow you get dressed up real nice and we'll meet him for breakfast.

Then after he's agreed to put you in one of his productions, and you've signed the contract, we'll head on over to the courthouse and get married."

Blanche blinked at him as though he had grown a new head, but only for an instant. Her heart leaped. "But I thought you said…"

> ~ *"Marry me, Blanche,*
> *and satisfy my every desire."*~

He knelt down before her and took both her hands in his. "What the hell, honey, we might as well get it done. I figure it'll be just as legal in Arizona as it would be in California. We can have a big reception and invite everybody after we get to Los Angeles."

She threw her arms around his neck, happier than any human being had a right to be.

After the usual ten minutes of discomfort with Graham, she went to sleep that night in a state of bliss. All her dreams were coming true. In a few months, after she was married to a rich man and had starred in a couple of motion pictures, she'd pay to have her parents come out to California, first class all the way, and stay with her in her Hollywood mansion. They'd be proud of her, then.

> ~*Blanche learns the hard way that*
> *"all that glisters is not gold."*~

She woke up with the sun streaming in through the window. She was alone in the bed. She sat up and stretched, still muzzy and euphoric. Until she noticed that the closet door was standing open and all the clothes were gone. His suits. Her new dresses.

Her forehead wrinkled. She swung her legs out of the bed, stood up, and walked over to peer into the closet as though the clothing had just decided to become invisible and would reappear any second. Still confused, she opened the bureau drawers. No silk underwear, no jewelry, no lovely beaded purse. No money. The outfit she had worn to scarper out the window of her sister Ruth's house was draped across the armchair, along with the little carpetbag she had brought with her.

Before she could decide that the situation called for panic, she found the note he had left for her on top of the dresser.

> I've gone to make arrangements for the wedding. I've had the luggage taken to the auto. Go downstairs. Schilling will give you a ride to the courthouse.

Relief flooded through her. She dressed quickly, and since all her toiletries had disappeared, she did her best to arrange her long wavy hair by running her fingers through it and tucking it back behind her ears. She caught sight of herself in the full-length mirror as she turned toward the door. No makeup, a long-sleeved white sailor-collared blouse and dark calf-length skirt, dark stockings, and clunky oxfords. She was a fifteen-year-old girl again.

Her lips thinned as she averted her eyes and walked out the door. She had seen her stunning future self and she was determined to put the farm girl in the mirror behind her forever and become that glamorous creature again.

Blanche trod down the hall and into the lobby. She walked around and checked all the lounge chairs but no Schilling was to be found. She went up to the counter, which was manned by a black-haired man in a bow tie who was not the same man they had met the night before.

"Excuse me," she said. "I'm supposed to meet a Mr. Schilling here, but I don't see him."

A look she couldn't identify crossed the clerk's features. "Yes, darling, Mr. Schilling is waiting for you in the dining room. Go on in."

Really, this was all too annoying. What was Graham thinking?

He knew perfectly well that Blanche didn't like Mr. Schilling and certainly would not want to be escorted to her own wedding by such a man. And speaking of her wedding, how inconsiderate of Graham to pack all her nice clothes and leave her to get married in something a child would wear to school. She paused at the dining room entrance. Perhaps he intended to surprise her with a beautiful new outfit. She felt her mood lighten. Yes, that was just the kind of thing that he would do.

She caught sight of Schilling—sitting at a table next to an iron stove in the corner of the small, wood-paneled room, shoveling eggs into his mouth—and her mood sank again.

The waitress gave her the once-over. "Can I help you, dear?"

"I'm meeting that man there," she said, just as Schilling gave her an oily smile and waved her over.

She squared her shoulders and made her way to the table. He pushed out a chair for her with his foot and she sat down.

"Good morning, honey," Schilling said. "I like the schoolgirl look. Fresh as a daisy."

Blanche didn't care to banter. "Graham said you'll give me a ride to the courthouse."

"That's right, sweetheart. Graham has a big surprise waiting for you. But there's plenty of time. Have some breakfast."

A wave of relief washed over her. Her emotions had taken such violent swings this morning that she didn't know how much longer her heart could take it. "Oh, no, sir, I couldn't eat a thing."

Schilling laughed, setting his jowls aquiver. "Why, it's your wedding day. No wonder you're excited. Now, come on and have some eggs."

"Well, maybe just some tea."

"Tea. That's a good idea!" Schilling gestured to the waitress. "Bring the little lady a big cup of hot tea."

"But can we hurry?"

"Don't worry, baby. We'll get you sorted out in a jiff."

The waitress brought the tea in a china cup, but before she

could taste it, Schilling took a silver flask out of his breast pocket and poured a healthy slug of something amber into it. "This'll calm you down, honey. Better than any nerve tonic."

Whatever his 'nerve tonic' was, it tasted horrible. Sort of like last night's lemonade but with a bitter, herby aftertaste. She pretended to sip on it, but poured most of it into a potted plant that was handily positioned within arm's length. Blanche could hardly stay in her seat, fidgeting with her empty cup, her silverware, her hair, her collar, ready to scream before Schilling finally, finally mopped up the last of his gravy with a biscuit and called for the tab.

He led her out the front entrance to the hotel, where two matched roans were hitched to a fancy brougham parked on the street. Schilling put his hands on her waist and lifted her bodily onto the leather-padded bench before climbing in next to her. He flicked the reins and the high-stepping pair took off at a trot.

Blanche felt much better now that they were moving. "This here is a nice carriage."

"I ought to get an auto, but I have a particular fondness for this brougham. Makes me feel like the king of England." The thought struck Schilling funny and he guffawed. "King Otto. I like the sound of that."

It took them only minutes to reach the square. Blanche straightened as they sailed past the courthouse and turned onto the main street leading out of town.

"Mr. Schilling, you passed the courthouse."

Schilling didn't look at her. He flipped the reins and the horses picked up their pace. A cool breeze ruffled her hair. "I know, honey. I told you Graham has a surprise for you."

She should have been reassured, but something didn't feel right. "What surprise? Where are we going?" She had to raise her voice over the clatter of hooves and wheels on the road.

"I want to introduce you to my business partner, Mrs.

Fredrickson. She runs a nice establishment just west of town, and she's agreed to give you a really good job."

Oh, my Lord, I'm being kidnapped. The thought formed in her mind as clearly as if she had spoken it aloud. "Where is Graham? We're getting married today." She meant to sound forceful but the words came out more like a high-pitched squeak.

Without taking his eyes off the road, Schilling patted her knee with one hand, all avuncular good humor. "Oh, you sweet little idiot. Peyton never had any intention of marrying the likes of you. He's not tying himself to a half-breed whore."

Blanche had always thought that it was stupid when some frail flower of an actress in the movies pressed the back of her hand to her forehead and swooned. She didn't think real people did something like that, not until this minute, anyway. Her vision dimmed and she swayed on the seat.

Schilling put out a hand and seized her arm to prevent her from falling to the floorboard. She leaned over and put her head down so she wouldn't faint. "I will not cry," she said to her lap. She had made her bed. Now she had to lie in it. She sat up with an effort and took a shaky breath. "Do you know where he went?"

"Off to find some other tasty merchandise, I expect. If I was you, I'd forget him. I paid a lot of money to take you off his hands. But don't worry. Him and me fixed it so that you can work off your debt."

It took her a moment to understand what he was talking about. "He sold me?"

"Well, I wouldn't put it exactly like that. But, yes, I paid Peyton a pretty penny for your services. I reckon you owe me big-time. So don't give me any trouble."

~*Finding herself in an impossible situation, Blanche takes a desperate leap to freedom.*~

For a long moment she said nothing, frantically trying to figure out her next move. There was no way in hell that she was going to cooperate. She was quite sure that the job with the aforementioned Mrs. Fredrickson had nothing to do with teaching Sunday School. It hadn't taken long to leave town. They were driving at a fast clip over open roads now. No one around to hear her scream for help. Schilling was driving too fast for her to jump out without injury, though that was a last resort. She cast a glance around the interior of the carriage, looking for a weapon, something to smack him with. No weapon within reach. She balled her fist. He was twice her size but a punch in the face would at least slow him down enough for her to attempt escape. An alternative presented itself when a wave of nausea overcame her.

She clutched her middle and leaned over. "I'm going to be sick."

Schilling's lip curled with disgust. "Not all over my new brougham, you aren't."

"Stop the carriage, stop the carriage."

Schilling regaled her with an imaginative collection of words that she had never heard before, but he did pull over to the side of the road. The girl was deathly white. "Go on, get out! If you're going to upchuck, do it over there away from the carriage."

Blanche staggered toward the bushes and bent over with her hands on her knees. She heaved a couple of times, expecting that she might actually be sick. She steadied her breathing and willed her stomach to settle. She realized full well what kind of situation she was in, and this was no time to indulge her very real terror.

No one was going to save her. She was going to have to save herself. She made a few retching noises to keep Schilling away from her while she took the lay of the land as best she could without straightening. The road meandered through woodland, alive with early fall greenery. She was surrounded by huge cottonwood trees, just beginning to color at this high altitude, and she recognized oaks and willows, and tall pines. The forest floor was fairly open, with the occasional box elder or wild rose bush growing in the shade, but strewn with boulders, some large enough to hide behind if it became necessary.

She realized that she had stopped making sick noises when Schilling barked at her to get back in the carriage.

Blanche stood up and cast a look back over her shoulder. Schilling was still in the driver's seat, but his buggy whip was in his hand as he prepared to dismount. His face was thunderous. When there is nothing else you can do, you take the only action you can.

She took off into the scrub. She could hear him scramble down from the brougham and bellow a few salty words at her, but fear gave her wings. She was a healthy, long-legged fifteen-year-old, and he was fat and fifty if he was a day. She outdistanced him easily, but she could still hear him screaming after her as he crashed through the woods in pursuit. She was surprised. He hadn't seemed like a man who would take the trouble to retrieve something (or someone) he could easily pay to replace. He must have given Graham a bundle for her.

She doubted he was much of a tracker, but his resounding curses were getting louder. She cast about for a likely hiding place. The ground under the pines was bare and carpeted with needles. The trees did not grow that close together, so her field of vision was pretty wide. That gave her a certain amount of comfort. She would be able to see Schilling coming before he could see her. She climbed up on a boulder that was big enough for her to reach the bottom branch of an ancient ponderosa pine and hoisted herself up. She had managed to climb fairly high into the canopy when she caught sight of Schilling, huffing and red-faced, coming through the scrub in search of his troublesome investment. His buggy whip was in his hand and he was muttering to himself—words not fit for civilized ears.

She drew her knees up and pressed back against the rough red bark. He stopped walking right under her hiding place, and she held her breath.

"If I find you, you little bitch, I'm going to beat you within an inch of your life," he said in a normal voice, and her heart skipped. Did he know she was directly above him?

She was surprised to see that she had lost one of her shoes. Her stocking was ripped to shreds and her foot was bruised and full of stickers. She hadn't felt a thing until this minute. Slowly, slowly, she untied her remaining shoe and slipped it off. If she had to brain him with an oxford, she'd be only too happy to do it. Below her, Schilling put one hand on the tree and leaned forward to catch his breath. He straightened and cocked his head, listening. Nothing but the shushing of the wind in the pines. He took a few steps this way, then turned around and took a few more steps that way. Blanche could only see the top of his felt fedora. She seriously regretted that she didn't have a rock the size of a pumpkin to drop on him.

She started and had to catch herself when Schilling suddenly burst forth with a voluminous barrage of filth and stomped all around waving his arms like a two-year-old in the full throes of a tantrum.

Don't let him look up, she prayed. Her prayer was answered as Schilling stalked off in the direction of the road, still turning the air blue with his epithets. His curses faded out, and she allowed herself to breathe again.

She had no idea how long she perched on her branch after Schilling disappeared, but it seemed like hours. She could no longer see the road, so she couldn't be sure he wasn't sitting in his carriage, waiting for her to reappear. Eventually, she began to hear birdsong again and a squirrel chittering. The raging intruder who had frightened them off was gone.

Blanche slipped her shoe back on and clambered down to the ground. She made herself as small as she could next to the tree trunk and looked around carefully. To her supreme relief, Schilling was nowhere to be seen. She took some time to hunt for her lost shoe, but had no luck. She was afraid to go back very far in the direction she had come, in case he was waiting for her to retrace her path.

The forest had changed in just the half mile or so she had run from the road. She was at a higher elevation now. She walked for a while through a steep-walled ravine that had been cut through the mountain by a burbling stream lined with reeds. People had been here. A narrow footpath followed the creek up the mountain, eventually leading her to a clearing, a high grassy meadow dotted with yellow wildflowers. She hesitated before walking out into the open, fearful of being seen. Her unshod foot hurt, and she had been limping for a while. But since she had no option but to try and find help, she continued on the path across the meadow and back into the woods, now dominated by tall, straight pines and scrubby oak.

When she felt she had put an adequate distance between herself and Schilling, she squatted down on the path, trying to catch her breath and calm down enough to take stock. The air was thin and cold. She had gained a lot of elevation. She looked at the sky to get her bearings. The sun was climbing toward its zenith. She could tell that she was facing north, but otherwise she had no idea where she was.

If she had been in her native country she would have known where to go, and even if she had decided to hide for several days, she would have known how to survive. She had been to Arizona before, a few years earlier when she was ill with bronchitis and her mother had taken her to her aunt's house in Tempe, south of Phoenix, to recover. But this was northern Arizona. Not the rolling, cactus-bestrewn desert of the south, but high forested mountains covered with trees and shrubbery she had never seen before.

She found a likely tree to lean against and sat down to ponder her situation and formulate a plan. She took a deep breath and felt the tension in her body lessen. It was very quiet, this forest, and fragrant, like pine and vanilla.

She knew enough about outdoor survival to know that birds would fly toward water come sundown, and that she could keep herself warm enough not to freeze to death tonight by making a leaf burrow. Surely by morning Schilling would be long gone and she could walk back out to the road and hitch a ride south to the nearest town. That is if anybody would stop for a dirty-faced girl with one shoe and pine needles in her rat's nest of hair. Maybe she would look so pathetic that some kind passerby would take pity on her.

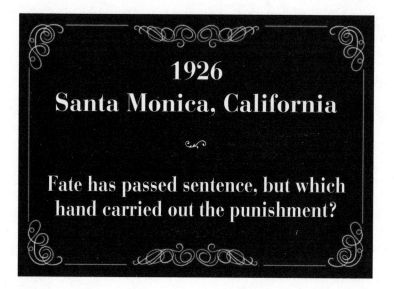

1926
Santa Monica, California

Fate has passed sentence, but which hand carried out the punishment?

Ted Oliver wondered who the "friend with the police" was who had tipped off Ruhl about the body at the foot of the cliff. It didn't matter. He had friends of his own. He only thought that if there was some overlap in their list of snitches, it would be more efficient for his investigation. Oliver parked his Ford at the side of the coastal highway and crossed the road and railroad tracks to where his friend Officer Hal Poole was standing guard over the remains of Graham Peyton.

"How come you haven't removed him yet?"

"We're waiting for the coroner to get down here and have a look. Once he says it's okay, somebody will haul the drunk wagon out of the toolshed and bring it down here."

Oliver snorted. The Santa Monica Police Department's "drunk wagon" was nothing more than a garden wheelbarrow. "Did the coroner say when he might drop by?"

Poole shrugged. "Don't know when he'll make it over. Truth is this guy has been lying here for a long time, so I don't guess there's any big hurry."

"Any idea yet how he got here?"

"There's nothing left of him," Officer Poole said. "No telling when he ended up here, or how."

Oliver lifted his gaze from the skeleton and looked out to sea. The sun was hovering over the horizon, a fuzzy disc of light behind the afternoon haze. He didn't bother to speculate. You could come up with a hundred reasons a person might end up dead under a pile of rocks at the foot of a cliff, and in the end they would all turn out to be wrong.

"My client tells me that you found the guy's wallet on him and it still had his driving license in it."

"Who's this client of yours who knows about a body on the beach practically before the police do?"

Oliver briefly considered telling him. He expected that the name K.D. Dix might open a lot of doors in certain circles. But he liked the policeman, and there was no reason to drag him into something seedy. Poole was reasonably honest, and Oliver didn't think that he was a member of said certain circles. "You don't need to know," he told Poole. "Just tell me about the wallet."

Poole didn't argue. "Yeah, we found one. It's still there, too. The chief said to leave everything as we found it until the coroner releases the body."

"Suppose I could have a closer look?"

"I don't know, Ted. If the chief finds out I let you dig around in there he'll have my hide."

"Well, how about if you take a break and I'll stand guard over the body for you?" Oliver dug a five-dollar bill out of his wallet. "Maybe take a walk on the beach for fifteen, twenty minutes."

Poole didn't even make an attempt to demur. He pocketed the fiver and walked away. Oliver waited until the cop was across the highway and strolling across the sand before he scrambled up the rock pile and squatted down next to the partially exposed skeleton.

Oliver simply looked for a while, trying to imagine the last moments of the man's life. The little cove at the bottom of the steep sandstone bluffs on the northern end of Palisades Park, past Adelaide Drive, was isolated and hard to get to. There was a footpath winding below the clifftop, but it was dangerously narrow, covered with loose slag, easy to lose one's footing. That's probably what happened to the guy, Oliver thought. One slip high up and you could lie all broken up on the rocks for weeks before some unlucky passerby found what was left of you.

Still, the secluded little beach was popular with lovers. Most couples walked in beside the Southern Pacific railroad tracks running along Beach Road, or came in by boat. They mostly stayed on the beach for their hanky-panky. There wasn't anything romantic about the railroad tracks under the cliff. The poor bastard had probably loosed a minor avalanche when he fell and was immediately buried on the cliff side of the tracks. The unlucky dope had been lying there during countless illicit trysts. But just a week earlier, a violent storm had practically destroyed the Santa Monica Pier, and had driven the Pacific Ocean to erode the beach and beat on the rocks long enough to finally expose the bones. The two latest hormone-driven visitors to the cove may have been looking for privacy but had found more than they bargained for. Nothing will shrink your willie like a skeletal hand sticking up out of the rock pile in a gruesome gesture for help.

The skeleton was wearing a suit. The material was much the worse for having lain under a rockfall for who knew how many years, but it was unmistakably a man's suit. Oliver found the one intact jacket pocket with the top of a leather wallet sticking out of it. He knew that the responding cop had already rifled through it, but Oliver hoped that if he were very lucky indeed, the wallet would provide a clue about who might want to kill the wretch and dump his body over the cliff.

He didn't hold out much hope. Since the guy still had his wallet on him, this looked to Oliver more like an accident than a premeditated killing. Or maybe the death had been an act of passion. Spontaneous killers were usually so shocked at what they had done that all they could think was to get the hell out of there. The other kind of killer planned his task so that he had enough time to get rid of as much evidence as possible before dumping the body.

Oliver slid the wallet out of the pocket and sat back on his heels to examine its contents. There was a lot of money, maybe a hundred dollars. The weather had had time to do its work on most of the paper, but the California driving license had been wedged between the bills and a couple of receipts. The typewriting was beginning to smear around the edges but otherwise was perfectly readable.

"Graham Peyton," Oliver said aloud. He looked back over his shoulder to see that Poole was still contemplating the ocean before he slipped the wallet back into the corpse's pocket, careful not to rip what was left of the disintegrating material. He stood up and leaned close over the bones to see what else he could see.

Oliver repositioned one good-sized rock, exposing more of an arm bone. The arm was lying at an unnatural angle, broken between the wrist and elbow. He took a deep breath and removed a few more rocks and detritus from the side to expose more of the skeleton. The entire body slowly came into view as he shifted the rocks, exposing feet still in shoes, legs, pelvis, arms, and finally all of the grinning skull with a few strings of light brown hair still attached to a bit of mummified scalp. A fall from the cliff could have easily caused the fist-sized hole in the top of the skull.

From the area he had recently cleared, a glint of metal caught his eye. A skeletal finger on the left hand still sported a ring. Not a wedding ring, more like a signet. Black onyx with a gold insignia. No, not an insignia, not a lion or helmet or some other family crest. Initials, wound around one another in such a fancy script it was hard to tell what the letters were. One was a P, maybe, tangled up with a little G and a little E.

A gold ring, a lot of money. Ruhl's late business associate had not been poor. Graham Peyton had not been whacked on the head by a robber, not unless the thief had knocked him right off the cliff with a cosh and then was too lazy to climb down to retrieve his hard-won loot. No, this sucker took a wrong step and bashed his head on the rocks below. How he got covered with these big rocks was a question, but a Pacific storm as violent the one that had occurred the week before could have deposited a battleship on top of him without any trouble.

"Seen enough?"

Oliver started when Poole spoke to him. He had been so engrossed that he hadn't been aware of the policeman's return. He sat back on the rocks. "Did you see the driving license? You know what the guy's name was?"

"Yeah, I know."

Oliver was interested to see that Poole's nostrils had narrowed, as though he smelled something bad. "You've heard of him?"

"Oh, yeah. He was quite a presence around town. That was before you came to California," Poole said. "He was the slipperiest snake who ever slithered. I don't know that there was anything he wasn't willing to do. He sold drugs, ran whores, smuggled booze, mostly for the motion picture studios. Murder, for all I know. He always liked young girls. He supplied fresh young things to the studio pimps and madams. He was good looking, a real sheik. He'd tempt the girls with tales of stardom and they'd end up working in a whorehouse. We were never able to pin anything on him. He liked to throw money around, so he was usually able to bribe his way out of trouble. He disappeared about five, six years ago. No one knew what had happened to him, not until now. He was such a son of a bitch that when he disappeared without a trace, not even his best clients shed a tear. There was some talk that he helped himself to a wad of his boss's loot and legged it off to South America. I always figured he finally ran afoul of the scumbags he did business with. Looks like I was right."

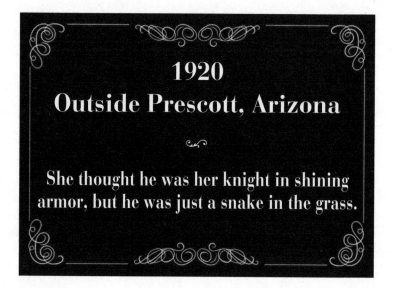

1920
Outside Prescott, Arizona

She thought he was her knight in shining armor, but he was just a snake in the grass.

She pulled her knees up to her chest and settled in to wait for evening. Fatigue allowed her mind to wander and she found herself wondering what was happening at home. Were her parents hot on her trail? How long had it taken for Sophronia to rouse the household and for Ruth to call out the cavalry? Minutes, at most. What had Alice admitted to their mother? Had they traced out her meetings with Graham at the Owl Drug Store? The sour-faced woman behind the counter would be able to describe Graham, but she wouldn't know his name. No one in Boynton knew his name. As they had flown through the night in his roadster, he had bragged that he had been staying at the American Hotel under a false name and had listed his hometown as Chicago, Illinois.

At the time, she had thought him so clever. Too clever. He had devised a perfectly conceived misdirection. The kind of perfection only gained by long practice. Now, as she sat bedraggled under a pine tree in the Arizona wilderness, she wondered how many times he had used this very ruse to lure ambitious or love-struck girls away from home. She tried not to think of her parents and sisters and brothers. If she were at home in her family's warm kitchen, her mother would lave her wounded foot and wrap it in soft cotton bandages.

No, she told herself sternly. No mother, no sisters, not anymore. She'd find that mountain creek again and wash her own wounds as best she could. She had burned her bridges forever. She was on her own.

Graham didn't love her. He had taken advantage of her naivete and used her not just for his own pleasure, but to sell her for profit. And she had believed every word he said to her.

Or had she? If she told herself the truth, hadn't she always had an inkling that the whole thing was a lie? Too good to be true? And, if she told herself the truth, hadn't she been more enamored of the adventure than she ever had been with Graham Peyton? Because what she was feeling right this minute was not heartbreak over his betrayal but burning, all-consuming anger.

Besides. Besides. Besides, if all she had wanted was to be Mrs. Somebody, there were plenty of Somebodies to choose from around Boynton, Oklahoma. No, she grew up among good, gentle, religious people whom she loved and who loved her, and in their way of thinking she had done the worst thing ever: thrown away her virtue, shamed her parents, and broken their hearts. But if she admitted to herself the raw, ugly truth, she didn't care. She was free, and she knew that she would do whatever she had to in order to remain free.

Jays began to chatter in the trees as the light turned golden. She watched as attentively as if her life were on the line, which it was. There was a sudden flurry in the treetops and a swirl of small birds of an unfamiliar species rose into the air and flew west.

Blanche pulled herself up and limped deeper into the woods, in the direction of the flock.

It took a while to find the creek. She could hear it before she could see it. It was beautiful and cold, and she nearly wept with relief as she sipped the pure clear water from her cupped hands. Her stockings were ruined anyway, so she took one off and wrapped it around her wounded foot to make a kind of moccasin. She stood and took a tentative step. Better. Better than nothing, at least. She had walked farther into the woods, in the direction the birds had flown, in order to find the creek.

A storm came up suddenly, black and roiling, not there one minute and pounding rain the next. *Damn*. It's not supposed to rain in the desert. Her misery was complete. The storm lasted long enough to dump its load on her, almost as though it had been saving it up until it was right over her head. Then, task completed, the clouds scudded out of sight over the hilltop. Blanche didn't know if that was the natural way of the mountains. She came from flat country, where it was easy to see from horizon to horizon, where you had time to prepare for whatever was coming.

She was chilled to the bone and couldn't be any wetter than she was at that moment. The wind that had pushed the cloudburst over the hilltop was still gusting, a puff, a swirl, a gust, then dead quiet just long enough to draw a breath before blowing again. The clouds were lighter now, and only shedding a light drizzle. She heard a crack, and a slash of lightning cut across the sky over her head.

Blanche pushed a wet hank of hair out of her eyes. She was going to have to find some shelter. Walking out among the forest of tall, straight trees—natural lightning rods—was not wise. She swallowed down a lump of panic. She was in a dangerous situation, and she knew it. She might have escaped her captor, but she was alone in the wilderness, in country that she did not know.

She needed shelter—that was order number one. Food and assistance would have to wait.

No matter which way she looked, she could only see trees. She was not totally disoriented. The road from Prescott was in that direction, but what lay in the other three was a mystery to her. She could either go back the way she had come and risk recapture, or take her chances. As much as she wanted to take her chances, she knew which was the wisest course to take.

She expected that the storm had driven Schilling back to town, and it was unlikely that he was still searching for her. Still, better to wait as long as possible before returning to the road. If it hadn't been for the rain, she would have tried camping out by the creek for a day or two. She didn't know if there were dangerous animals, or dangerous people, in the woods, but she had water and she knew how to stay warm. But wet was dangerous.

She was having trouble thinking, cold and unable to maintain her concentration. The woods were busy with jays and ravens, all about their own business in the treetops and unconcerned with her plight. Blanche considered trying to knock a bird off a branch with a rock. She had seen her brother do it, though she had never tried it herself. It didn't take her long to dismiss the notion. She had no way to light a fire, and hungry as she was, the idea of eating raw bird didn't appeal to her. She squatted down under a young lodgepole pine and wrapped her arms around her knees. Quiet. Except for the wind in the pines, there was no sound—no skittering animals about. She closed her eyes and listened with all her might. It was not her ears that gave her a clue, but her nose.

A faint smell of smoke on the wind. Smoke, a wood fire, and just a hint…maybe her desperation was misleading her, but she was sure she could catch a whiff of something cooking.

She stood up and headed into the gusty, moisture-laden wind, toward the smell of hope.

> ~*A witch or an angel? Is salvation at hand,*
> *or is Blanche in for more shades and terrors?*~

The wet leaves and pine needles muffled the sound of her steps, making a slurping noise around her feet as she slopped through the muck. She followed her nose while keeping an eye on her surroundings. She didn't want to find herself face-to-face with a bear or lion or whatever other dangerous beast lurked in this unfamiliar country. She began to see signs of the humans who had been here before her. Another narrow footpath covered with piles of windblown pine needles from the squall. A tree that had had its bottom limbs trimmed. She came upon a section of wooden fence just before she topped a small rise and saw a house in a clearing. There was no movement or light in the windows, but a thin line of gray smoke rose from the chimney toward the treetops, dancing like a live thing in the gusty wind.

She would have called it a cabin, since it was made of peeled logs and stone with a shake shingle roof, but it was bigger than the house she and her nine siblings had grown up in. It consisted of two stories, with an outside staircase leading to a balcony that completely encircled the upper floor. She could see white lace curtains through the windows on either side of the front door. A circular gravel drive disappeared into the woods from the back of the house. The front of the house sported a long wooden porch, a hitching post, and batch of copper-colored chrysanthemums planted in a barrel beside the porch steps.

She squatted down again and gazed at the homey place for some time, afraid, yet desperate for help. A month earlier she would have marched right up and knocked on the front door, sure that a young girl in difficulties would be welcomed and aided. She had always taken so many things for granted—such as the idea that most people were good. She had not had personal experience with evil and had not understood the depth to which mankind can sink. Until Graham. All she could think of at that moment was the story of Hansel and Gretel. What if a witch lived in that cabin and wanted to cook her and eat her?

A shadow passed across one of the windows and Blanche straightened, her senses sharp. The figure reappeared and paused in front of the window. A Negro woman, slender and middle-aged. She busied herself with something below the sill for a moment, then moved out of sight again. It was enough.

Blanche took a deep breath and stood. "Hello-o-o…" she called, her voice rising. She sounded to herself like a scared child, which was embarrassing. But her situation did not permit her to indulge in false dignity. "Hello," she called again. "Is anybody to home? I could use some help, please."

There was no response and Blanche spent a moment considering whether to call again or fade into the woods before the woman decided to grab a rifle and take a shot at her. She was drawing a breath to call again when the front door opened and the woman appeared.

She gave Blanche a good once-over before she said, "Well, don't just stand there, girl. Come on in out of the wet."

Blanche didn't give herself time to think about it. She squished across the soggy open ground between the woods and the cabin and stopped on the wooden porch. "Take off those muddy shoes first," the woman said, and disappeared into the darkness, leaving the door open.

Blanche looked down at her feet, surprised because she only had on one shoe. But her makeshift ex-stocking moccasin was so black with mud that it was hard to tell. She sat down on the porch to take off her remaining shoe and unwind the muddy cloth before stepping into the house in her bare feet.

The ground floor was mostly one giant room, with a closed door at one end and an open door that led to a modern kitchen on the other. The walls were painted light green and the floor was wood, scattered about with rugs woven in patterns that Blanche recognized as Indian, though she didn't recognize the tribe. The white curtains at the windows were lace. Pots of herbs and flowers sat on nearly every flat surface. The woman had created a sitting area on the back wall of the cabin by grouping two quilt-covered leather chairs beside an upholstered couch that sat before a large stone fireplace.

She was pretty, this woman who was watching her quietly, small, thin, and delicate. It was hard to tell how old she was. Her face was unlined, but her hair, which had been braided and wound around her head, was graying.

The woman waited for Blanche to have a good look around before she said, "Come into the kitchen," and Blanche followed her. A Franklin stove under the front window served both as a cooktop and provided heat. One round knotty pine dining table dominated the center of the room. A second small window over a long sideboard looked out into the woods.

The woman threw a tattered blanket over one of the chairs at the dining table and gestured toward it. "Sit down."

Blanche did as she was told. She sat slumped in the chair, her bedraggled locks hanging in damp hanks over the tabletop, as the woman busied herself at the stove.

The woman returned in short order with a crockery bowl full of something that smelled like heaven. Of course, Blanche thought, after what she had been through, she would be happy to eat boiled leather.

The woman said nothing as Blanche wolfed down the stew, which was meaty, full of vegetables and herbs, and even more delicious than it smelled. When Blanche had finally scraped the last morsels from the bowl and looked up, the woman was sitting across the table from her, chin in hand and a look of vague amusement on her face.

Blanche felt her cheeks heat up with embarrassment. She had sucked up the stew like she had never seen food before. "Thank you," she said, barely loud enough to be heard.

The woman dropped her hand onto the table. "You're welcome. Looks like you haven't eaten in a while."

Blanche blinked at her, taken aback by the woman's cultured

accent. Few people in eastern Oklahoma, black or white, sounded like that. "No, ma'am. Not since yesterday."

The woman waited for Blanche to say something else, but when nothing was forthcoming, she took the initiative. "What's your story, hon? What are you doing way out here in the woods, standing in the rain like a forlorn dog?"

What to say? Would the woman toss her out when she heard what kind of a person Blanche was? Yet Blanche owed her some sort of explanation.

"A man was giving me a ride to Phoenix but he...made some suggestions that I didn't like. I got scared and jumped out of the buggy and ran."

A weary look passed over the woman's face and was gone. "That explains the condition of your feet, then. I'm Mrs. Gilbert. What's your name, baby?"

"Blanche Tucker."

"Well, now, Blanche Tucker, I think you had better get yourself out of those wet clothes before you catch pneumonia, or drip all over any more of these expensive rugs." Mrs. Gilbert stood. "I think I could find clothes that would fit you. Come with me. We'll look through the armoire upstairs and pick out something for you to wear, find some soft socks for those feet. I'll rinse out the soggy clothes you have on, and then we'll figure out what to do with you while they're drying by the fire."

Blanche followed Mrs. Gilbert up the pine log staircase to a loft bedroom—a large, airy space, filled with light from a west-facing casement window situated across from a quilt-covered featherbed.

Who was this woman, Blanche wondered? She knew many colored folks back in Oklahoma, interacted with them every day, liked and respected some and not others, just like white folks. But in Boynton, Oklahoma, in this year of Our Lord 1920, any colored person, no matter how liked and respected, no matter how well off, would be eyed with suspicion and resentment by her white neighbors if she dressed and spoke with Mrs. Gilbert's elegance.

"Do you work here, ma'am?" Blanche spoke to Mrs. Gilbert's back as she rifled through the clothes in the tall pine armoire. Mrs. Gilbert gave her a narrow look and it occurred to Blanche that she had just insulted her rescuer. She corrected herself hastily. "Is this your house, ma'am?"

"No, this little *pied-à-terre* belongs to my employer. She only uses it when she's working in northern Arizona. She's coming out tomorrow from California, so I came here early to open the cabin and set things in order."

Mrs. Gilbert was a lady's maid. Blanche's world fell back into its accustomed configuration. Mrs. Gilbert shot her an ironic glance over her shoulder, as though she had read Blanche's mind. "I'm her personal assistant."

As Blanche drew a breath to ask about the identity of the intriguing businesswoman from California, Mrs. Gilbert held out a voluminous cotton shift. "Strip off that dress, honey. I'll find you some underthings and you can slip into this for the time being."

———

Blanche was sitting at the table, swallowed up by her roomy shift, drinking hot tea and finally beginning to feel warm for the first time in hours, when Mrs. Gilbert returned to the kitchen after hanging Blanche's wet clothes to dry over a wooden chair before the fire.

"What is your plan, now, honey?"

"I don't know. I thought I was going to California. I thought I was going to get married, but he abandoned me in Prescott. I've lost everything I own. I haven't had time to decide what I'm going to do now."

"Where are you from, baby? Where are your people? I can take you back into Prescott so you can send a wire to your parents."

Blanche hesitated. "I can't go home, ma'am. I ran away. I couldn't face my mama and daddy after what I done."

She half expected to be instantly condemned, but Mrs. Gilbert put a sympathetic hand on her arm. "If you were my girl, I'd want you back no matter what you've done."

"I doubt if my parents really want to know what has befallen me. I don't think I can ever go home. I know I can't look them in the face. They have seven other daughters that they can be proud of. They won't miss me." Blanche knew perfectly well that her parents would take her back in a heartbeat. But no matter how her original plans had gone awry, she was free from restraints and expectations and intended to stay that way. She hoped that playing off of Mrs. Gilbert's sympathy would gain her some time to reassess her situation. Her face crumpled and she took a long, dramatic moment to gain control of herself.

Mrs. Gilbert looked skeptical, but she said, "You know your own people, I suppose. If you don't want to go home, what are you going to do with yourself?"

Blanche shook her head. "I don't know, now. I need a job, I guess. Graham—he's the man I ran away with—said he had connections in Hollywood. That I was different from anyone he knew. He wanted to marry me, he said, and get me in the moving pictures, but that ain't going to happen now."

Mrs. Gilbert studied Blanche critically for what seemed like a long time. "The moving pictures, huh?"

Blanche's smile was more than a little bitter. "I was all het up to be a movie star. To marry a rich man.

> ~ *"I would have believed him if he had told me he could make me Queen of England."* ~

"Well, now, don't give up on yourself so quick. Now that you've decided to reevaluate your goals, is there some occupation that appeals to you?"

"At this point I expect I'll take what I can get. I grew up on a farm and my mother made sure I can cook and clean with the best of them. I wouldn't mind working my way out to California eventually, though. I hear it's nice out there. I can't go back to Oklahoma, that's for sure."

"Do you know your way around a kitchen?"

An ironic snort escaped Blanche. "I do indeed. If there's anything my ma made sure of, it's that all her girls know how to cook for one or for an army."

"If you're willing to spend a couple of weeks peeling potatoes, I may have a temporary job for you. Can you stay here in Arizona for a little while?"

Blanche felt a pang of worry. "I don't know. I don't want to run into the man with the carriage again."

"Don't you worry, young lady. Even if that…man did find you, we'll make sure he can't hurt you." Mrs. Gilbert hesitated, considering how much she wanted to say to this odd, damp girl who had shown up on her doorstep. Blanche sat quietly and allowed herself to be judged. If she didn't cut the mustard, there wasn't much she could do about it.

Mrs. Gilbert came to a conclusion and sat back in her chair. "I manage affairs for my employer. She's coming out to Prescott for a short-term job with a company that employs a lot of people, all of whom will need to be fed three meals a day. The cook is looking for help in the kitchen. Well, I say 'kitchen,' but it's really more like a mess tent. Our location is pretty much out in the middle of nowhere. But you're welcome to stay here with me and my employer until the job is finished. I'm not making any promises, but if you're a hard worker and do well, we might invite you to travel with us back to Los Angeles."

Blanche knew she should ask more questions. Who was this "employer" that Mrs. Gilbert was going to such lengths not to name? And what was this mysterious job that was bringing the lady from Los Angeles to the wilds of high desert Arizona? At home, Blanche had hated cotton harvest time, when her mother and aunts had put all the females in the family to work, either cooking for or serving bushels of food to the gangs of itinerant workers. But her situation was desperate and the offer of unglamorous but honest work on the very day she was abandoned in the wilderness was too perfectly timed to refuse. Besides, how could she pass up the possibility of reaching her destination safely while under the protection of someone who did not mean to pimp her out at the nearest mining camp?

"Miz Gilbert," she said, "I've already peeled enough potatoes to feed the entire state of Arizona. I reckon I'm an expert at it. I'd be obliged for the opportunity. Anything to make some money, as long as it's honest."

Mrs. Gilbert's gave a satisfied nod. "Good. I think you won't be peeling potatoes long. Miss Bolding is soft on lost puppies and mistreated little girls."

"Miss Bolding?" Blanche said. Blanche only knew of one person named Bolding—Alma Bolding, star of the silver screen. But Alma Bolding lived in Hollywood in a lavish mansion, not in a cabin in the woods in Arizona.

"Yes, darling, Alma Bolding, the moving picture actress..." Mrs. Gilbert hesitated at the expression of gobsmacked awe on Blanche's face. "...and tomorrow we are going to go out to the location of her next picture to ready the tent where she will put on her costumes and makeup and rest between takes. I will talk to the head cook and ask if he will hire you to assist him in the kitchen. Now, Miss Bolding arrives on the train tomorrow afternoon, and while you are working, I will go to meet her in Prescott and bring her to the set. I will introduce you after you finish work. Miss Bolding is, let us say, larger than life, but don't make a fool of yourself when you meet her. She enjoys meeting her fans, but she hasn't much patience with children."

Blanche was so astounded that her prospective benefactor was actually screen star Alma Bolding that she forgot to be insulted that Mrs. Gilbert had just caller her a child. "I love Miss Bolding," she breathed, struggling to retain her composure. "When she played the doomed Russian empress in *Palace of Intrigue* with Mary Pickford as her daughter, I nearly cried my eyes out!"

Her young companion's starstruck manner amused Mrs. Gilbert. "I'm sure Miss Bolding will be glad to hear that. But now we have business to attend to."

"But why is Miss Bolding shooting a picture in Arizona? I thought she made her pictures in California."

"She does, most of them. This is a Western that she's starring in with her friend Tom Mix, and he likes to shoot out here for the authentic scenery. He used to have a ranch in Prescott, you know, and he still comes out here a lot."

Blanche had thought she couldn't be more over the moon when she found out she was going to meet Alma Bolding, but Tom Mix was just the berries. The great hero of the Westerns was one of the highest-earning movie actors in the world and, on top of everything, he was from Oklahoma.

~*The Slaughterhouse Gulch Gang*~

Mrs. Gilbert showed Blanche to a closet-like bedroom on the second floor with a high, soft bed that felt like a cloud. Blanche felt like she had just closed her eyes minutes before when Mrs. Gilbert woke her early the next day and loaded her down with bags and baskets of supplies to take to the movie set, which was at a place delightfully called Slaughterhouse Gulch, north of Prescott. Blanche's curiosity about how they were going to get there was satisfied when Mrs. Gilbert led her to a small garage located behind the house, where a sturdy Ford Model T sedan was parked. The ever-efficient Mrs. Gilbert packed her supplies neatly in the back and deposited Blanche in the passenger seat after giving the engine a decisive crank. It wasn't far down the narrow mountain road from the cabin to an open field in a gulch with a narrow, fast-running creek cutting through it. Several tents were already set up, and one bare wooden trailer had been hauled in that Blanche would have taken for a gypsy caravan if it had been in the least colorful.

Mrs. Gilbert took her around the set and introduced her to the crew before showing her the small tent on a wooden platform that was to be Miss Bolding's dressing room. The tent was as well-appointed as a hotel room, Blanche thought, with a white bedstead covered with a red quilt, a costume trunk, an armoire and a dressing table, a washstand with fluffy towels, a couple of chairs, and a small oil heater to stave off the mountain chill.

"When Mr. Mills is finished with you for the day, you can come back here and help me with Miss Bolding, all right?"

All right? Blanche would peel a stack of potatoes as high as a mountain if she could wait on Miss Alma Bolding afterwards. "Yes, ma'am," she said.

"Then come with me." Mrs. Gilbert led her to the largest tent, a long, open-sided canvas affair that had been fitted out with a camp stove, prep tables, and banks of long dining tables and benches, where the cast and crew would take their meals.

She met the cook, a very fat man with a bad attitude by the name of Mr. Mills. Blanche figured that his girth and his ill nature indicated that he loved food more than he loved people. He and one put-upon helper were busy unloading staples from the back of a truck—flour, sugar, cans of lard, bushels of potatoes, beans, flats of eggs, bags of various durable vegetables like squashes and carrots. Mr. Mills was not pleased to be interrupted, but he didn't argue with Mrs. Gilbert when she presented Blanche as a willing hand in the kitchen. He barked at the girl to start arranging the plates and utensils in the tall pie cabinet sitting at the back of the tent. Mrs. Gilbert made shooing motions at her, and Blanche set to work, still atingle with anticipation at the thought of meeting real live motion picture stars.

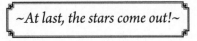

~At last, the stars come out!~

Mr. Mills yelled at Blanche a lot that first day. But he yelled at everyone, and there didn't seem to be much venom behind his words, so Blanche didn't take it personally. Besides, she had been castigated by experts and could tell if a castigator meant business or not. There were a lot of people to feed, but the work itself wasn't as hard as feeding a gang of farmworkers. There were a number of Indians in the cast, which made Blanche feel comfortable, even if they weren't her kind of Indians. They were a jolly bunch who called themselves Yavapais, and when they found out that she was from Oklahoma and pretty much Native herself, they didn't bother to lower their voices in her presence when they cracked jokes about some of the white guys in the crew.

The Californians were a lot of fun, too. Most of them were cowboys, just like her father and brothers and uncles, and they teased the girl gently in a protective way that she found entirely familiar. She had had long practice dealing with just these sorts of men, joking and pretending that she didn't understand a *thing* they were talking about, but wouldn't they like some more stew and here's some bread hot out of the oven? By the time the midday meal was over, she had been adopted by fifty guys and a couple of women. Even the ill-natured Mills realized that his young helper knew what she was doing and therefore mitigated his tirades. In fact, he had grown downright fond of her, though he wasn't going to go out of his way to let her know that.

Blanche didn't exactly enjoy the work, but the motion picture people were interesting and had lots of exciting stories to tell her. She was disappointed that no one very famous had shown up for a meal, though. When she asked Mr. Mills about it, he told her that Tom Mix would undoubtedly eat with the crew later, but he had had experience with Miss Bolding on another set and she usually took her meals in her tent.

This did not surprise Blanche.

Alma Bolding was one of the most acclaimed actresses of the silver screen. She did not need to speak to make her audience laugh, cry, or break their hearts. Her great dark eyes spoke volumes.

Mrs. Gilbert came to the mess tent shortly after the dinner dishes had been cleared away and before the supper preparations had gotten well underway.

"Blanche, honey, Miss Bolding wants to meet you before the story meeting."

"She's here?"

"I told you she was coming in this afternoon. She's been having her costumes fitted." Mrs. Gilbert's voice took on an edge of impatience. "Come on, now, Mr. Mills can't spare you for long."

Alma Bolding was sitting in a camp chair the first time that Blanche saw her. She was dressed in a long, prairie-style western dress and had on a broad-brimmed straw hat to protect her milk-white skin from the Arizona high country sun. She slowly turned her head to look at them as they neared.

Blanche felt weak in the knees. If Alma were any more beautiful, no one would ever get any work done in her presence. Especially the men, who would be running into walls and falling off of cliffs. Alma smiled when she recognized Mrs. Gilbert. Her gaze shifted to Blanche and the smile took on an ironic twist.

"Well, now, Delphinia. I see you've brought me a present."

Alma talked fast, like she had just stepped out of the Bronx and was about to snap her gum, whether she was chewing any or not.

Mrs. Gilbert stepped to the side and pushed Blanche forward. "This is Blanche, Miss Bolding. I found her wandering around in the rain up by the cabin, wet as a fish. Seems she hitched a ride with a man who had ungentlemanly designs on her, so she leaped out of his automobile and ran off into the woods."

Alma's smile widened into an intoxicating grin. "Now, that's the spirit!"

"I've gotten her on here in the kitchen, helping Mr. Mills."

A young man strode over and said, "The director wants to see you, Miss Bolding."

Alma reached out and Blanche took her hand. It was white and soft and Blanche could feel every bone. "I have a feeling that there's a very interesting story here, Blanche, but since Elmo has just called me to discuss the shooting schedule, I'm afraid I'll have to hear about it later."

"Yes, ma'am," Blanche managed, overcome with awe. Buck up before you disgrace yourself, she thought, unable to take her eyes off of Miss Bolding as she walked away. She was vaguely aware of Mrs. Gilbert's hand on her shoulder.

"When Mr. Mills finishes with you for the day," Mrs. Gilbert said, when she finally had Blanche's attention, "come to Miss Bolding's tent and we'll all drive back to the cabin together."

"Miss Bolding is going to let me stay?"

"I haven't asked her yet, but I expect she will, especially if you make yourself useful."

The rest of the day was endless, and not just because of Mr. Mills's bottomless pit of chores for her. She could hardly concentrate on her chopping, serving, and dishwashing for dreaming about her meeting with Alma Bolding. And she was actually going to sleep in the same house as the star!

> ~*Was there no end to the adventures awaiting Blanche once she took a daring leap and flew the nest to freedom?*~

Time marches on, no matter how slowly, and the hour finally arrived when the kitchen was properly packed and secured and Blanche was released from duty. She sprinted across the clearing to Miss Bolding's tent.

"There you are," Mrs. Gilbert said. "Fold that pile of blankets, would you? Miss Bolding will be here…"

She had barely spoken her name before Alma threw open the

tent flap and flung herself onto a stool in front of the dressing table. She was hardly recognizable, and not just because of the thick layer of makeup she was wearing. Her beautiful face was contorted with anger. "What a flaming ass that Elmo is. Remind me to never do another film with him. I swear, if it weren't for Tom and Olive, I'd be out of here faster than you could spit. Delphinia, get this crap off my face, will you? All I want to do tonight is take a bath and get spifflicated." She caught sight of Blanche's reflection in the mirror. "Who are you?"

Blanche froze, a half-folded blanket over her arm.

"This is Blanche. You met her earlier," Mrs. Gilbert said, calm as you please, as she slathered enough cold cream over Alma's face to render her featureless. Blanche could hardly keep her mouth from gaping wide enough to catch a frog.

Alma managed a grunt from under her layer of paint stripper.

"Honey, there is a change of clothes for Miss Bolding in that bag on the floor there. Lay them out on the cot for me, please," Mrs. Gilbert instructed as she wiped away long runnels on Miss Bolding's face with a series of tissues.

Once the makeup was removed, Alma looked more like a real person, still beautiful, but sagging with fatigue. A bit sallow, Blanche observed. Tired, in more ways than one.

Alma stood and stretched her arms out to her side like a three-year-old while Mrs. Gilbert relieved her of her prairie dress, the petticoats, the long black stockings, leaving her standing bare-legged in nothing but camiknickers. She was thin, almost bony.

Alma didn't acknowledge Blanche's presence again. She threw herself on the cot and covered her eyes with a forearm while Blanche busied herself as quietly as she could, fearing that Miss Bolding's abrupt personality change did not bode well for her employment prospects.

She whispered her doubts to Mrs. Gilbert, who reassured her with a smile. "Don't worry about it, Blanche. We'll talk to her tomorrow."

*~Blanche learns that
her idol has feet of clay.~*

Once Mrs. Gilbert had directed the location roustabouts to load Miss Bolding's trunks into the automobile, she roused her famous employer from her nap and deposited her into the back seat along with the rest of the baggage. She gestured for Blanche to join her in the front seat, and the three of them drove back to the cabin in silence.

Mrs. Gilbert hauled Alma Bolding to the upstairs bathroom for a long soak in the tub, leaving Blanche to unload the auto as best she could.

Blanche made several trips to carry in the dozens of boxes and bags. She had not been told where to deposit them, so she made as neat a pile as she could manage on a credenza beside the front door. The final item, a steamer trunk, was almost as big as Blanche herself and certainly weighed as much. But Blanche was nothing if not determined, and somehow finagled the trunk off the back of the auto and dragged it across the driveway, plowing a long, deep rut through the gravel in the process. In order to avoid scratching up the wood floors, she walked the trunk, corner by corner, across the porch and into the cabin. She abandoned it just inside the door and sat down in an armchair, exhausted, to await further instruction and contemplate the vagaries of the day.

When she had gotten up that morning, she had been certain that she had landed on her feet and all her troubles were over. Now that the sun was going down, she wondered what she had gotten herself into. Did the seemingly kind and gentle Mrs. Gilbert expect her to be a general dogsbody, lifting, cooking, cleaning, and fetching in exchange for room and board? Was her idol Alma Bolding really the lively woman who earlier had taken her hand in gentle friendship, or the capricious, self-absorbed creature of this evening? And how badly did Blanche want to hang around and find out?

Badly enough, it seemed. Blanche decided to give her new situation a few days. Maybe even a few weeks. But she also began to formulate alternate plans, in case things didn't work out as well as she hoped.

> ~*An hour later, Mrs. Gilbert finds Blanche*
> *still sitting quietly in the armchair,*
> *surrounded by luggage.*~

"My goodness, honey, did you manage to get that trunk in here all by yourself? I figured it would take both of us."

Blanche's mouth tightened in annoyance. "Yes, ma'am. You said…"

Mrs. Gilbert laughed. "I did say, didn't I? Well, Miss Bolding is bathed and in her dressing gown and will be down in a few minutes—famished, if I know her. So if you'd be so kind as to see if there's anything in the pantry that we can make do with, I'll take some of these suitcases and boxes upstairs. We can unpack the trunk later."

Blanche stood up, not pleased to be in charge of supper after a long day of kitchen patrol, but resigned to doing her duty. She had only taken a step toward the kitchen when Alma Bolding swept down the staircase, dressed to the nines, in full movie star mode. She had on a black, white, and gray evening frock, cut in the latest drop-waist style and covered with peasant designs. The full skirt was short enough to bare six inches of white stocking-covered shin. Her sheer tulle sleeves ballooned out from the shoulder and were secured at her wrists by pearl-encrusted cuffs. Her dark hair was almost completely covered by a close-fitting white silk scarf, its tails hanging halfway down her back. Her elaborate Egyptian-styled earrings were a stunning contrast to the plain headdress. She carried a black cashmere wrap tossed over one arm.

There was a spring in her step and a sparkle in her kohled eyes. That bath worked miracles, Blanche thought.

Mrs. Gilbert looked stunned. "Alma, what are you doing? I thought you were getting ready for bed."

"Elmo is going to pick me up at eight, Delphinia. We're going into Prescott for dinner and a drink."

Mrs. Gilbert's expression changed from one of surprise to one of disapproval. "You have an early call in the morning, Alma."

Mrs. Gilbert's sharp tone didn't daunt Alma in the least. "Don't be an old mother hen, Delphinia. Elmo has to work tomorrow, too. I'll be back in plenty of time to get a good night's sleep and be fresh as a daisy in the morning."

Mrs. Gilbert didn't have time to argue. The distinctive crunch of tires on gravel was followed by the loud "ah-oo-gah" of an automobile horn. Alma threw her cape over her shoulders and sailed out the door with a wave and a cheerful "Ta-ta, girls!"

Well, at least she knows I'm alive, Blanche thought.

Mrs. Gilbert said nothing. She stood with her arms crossed for the longest minute, looking like she had just taken a bite out of a lemon.

Blanche couldn't contain her curiosity. "But I thought she hated Mr. Reynolds…"

Mrs. Gilbert made a disparaging noise. "Miss Bolding's moods run hot and cold. She probably had a disagreement with him about the script and now she thinks she can charm him over to her way of thinking."

"Can she?"

Mrs. Gilbert shrugged. "Probably. Alma Bolding didn't get where she is without knowing how to convince people to do whatever she wants—and think it's their own idea, to boot."

"That's a talent I'd like to have."

Blanche hadn't realized that she had voiced her thought aloud until Mrs. Gilbert gave her a narrow look.

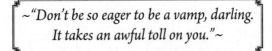

~*"Don't be so eager to be a vamp, darling.*
It takes an awful toll on you."~

"I'm sorry," Blanche said, more meekly than she felt. "Shall I fix up some supper for the two of us?"

"You go on ahead and eat, honey. I've lost my appetite. I'm going to start on this trunk."

Blanche didn't offer to help. She did as she was told and found some cold roasted chicken and a piece of bread to make her supper out of, then cleaned up the kitchen and went upstairs to her tiny bedroom, leaving Mrs. Gilbert sitting in an armchair next to the emptied steamer trunk, knitting.

Exhausted, Blanche fell asleep in her little bed almost immediately, soothed by the piney aroma on the breeze coming in through her open window.

She was wakened out of a sound sleep by loud laughter coming from outside. She had no idea what time it was. Very late, surely, or very early. She rose up on her knees in the bed to look out the window. She had a clear view of the driveway, and though it was as dark as it can only be deep in the woods, the lamplight emanating from the open back door illuminated the scene well enough for Blanche to see Miss Bolding staggering out of an auto, so drunk she could hardly stand. Elmo Reynolds, the director of Tom Mix's movie, was behind the wheel, and judging from the bawdy but barely understandable song he was bellowing, he was as inebriated as his passenger. Mrs. Gilbert came down the steps in time to catch Alma before she ended up splayed all over the gravel. She threw Elmo Reynolds a poisonous look as she guided Miss Bolding into the house. She didn't ask him to stay and sober up before he drove away. He would have to take his chances on the mountain road back to the camp.

> ~*Once again, Alma makes a miraculous recovery following her night of debauchery.*~

Blanche had seen people coming off of a roaring drunk before, so when she arose just after dawn the next morning she dressed quietly and tiptoed down the stairs, expecting that Alma would not wake until much later and suffer from a raging hangover when she did. She planned to ask Mrs. Gilbert what would happen when Alma didn't show up for work on the movie location. Would Alma lose her job before she even started it? Of course, Mr. Reynolds probably wasn't feeling so well himself this morning.

The luggage had been cleared out of the living room. A pillow and blanket were tossed over the sofa. Mrs. Gilbert had stayed downstairs all night.

Blanche could hear activity in the kitchen. She made a detour to fold the blanket, then made her way into the kitchen, determined to order Mrs. Gilbert to bed. Blanche would offer to walk the mile or so to the location this morning and deliver the bad news about Alma to Mr. Mix and Mr. Reynolds.

She stopped short in the kitchen door. Alma Bolding was sitting at the table, already dressed in her prairie frock, piling jam on a piece of toast. Mrs. Gilbert was at the stove, stirring a pot containing something that smelled delicious.

Alma grinned at her, showing no effects whatsoever of her earlier inebriation. Her dark eyes sparkled with a brightness that was just short of unnatural. "There's my lost puppy," she exclaimed. "You darling thing. Mills thinks you're just the best little worker since the shoemaker's elf. Sit down here and let Delphinia feed you before we have to get over to the location." She was talking fast again, happy and good-natured, seemingly over yesterday's pique. Blanche shot Mrs. Gilbert a stunned look.

"Sit down, Blanche," Mrs. Gilbert said. She had not recovered her own good mood. "We have to leave pretty soon."

Blanche lowered herself into a chair across the table from Alma, who was wolfing down her jam-laden toast like she hadn't eaten in a week. "How do you feel this morning, Miss Bolding?"

"Fit as a fiddle," Alma said around her mouthful of toast. "Those pills Dr. Harmon gives me are the best remedy I've ever had for a pumpkin head after a night on the town."

Blanche shot another incredulous glance at Mrs. Gilbert, but Mrs. Gilbert did not turn away from the stove. "Them pills must be a miracle cure, ma'am." As soon as she said it, she caught her breath. She hadn't meant to refer to Miss Bolding's unfortunate state of the night before.

But Alma was far too jolly to take offense. "I did throw off the traces last night, didn't I? But I got what I wanted, so it was worth it. Now, kiddo, tell me about yourself. You sound like the hills of Tennessee or Kentucky to me. How'd you end up wandering through the woods in Arizona after fending off a masher?"

Blanche forgot about the miracle pills, forgot about Mrs. Gilbert's stiff, disapproving posture. She related her entire life story in detail—the slow death by boredom on her parents' farm, the exciting, charming stranger, the rash elopement that was no elopement at all, the escape from the disgusting fat man. She was thrilled that the glorious Alma Bolding was listening to it all with such compassionate interest. Even Mrs. Gilbert had turned around to take in the whole sordid story.

When Blanche finished, Alma clapped her hands to her cheeks, horrified. "Oh, my goodness, darling, what a sorry tale! I don't blame you, mind. Any bright girl worth the name would be up for a stab at fame and fortune. I blame that scum-sucking son of a bitch, that immoral violator of the Mann Act who led you on and treated you like a commodity to be sold. What is the scurvy louse's name? I'll hire somebody to find him and beat the snot out of him."

Blanche could not believe how happy it made her to hear that. But she said, "I appreciate the thought, Miss Bolding, but I don't want to ever have anything to do with Graham Peyton again."

The name seemed to hang in the air after she uttered it. Alma sat back in her chair. She had gone white. "Graham Peyton."

"Yes, ma'am. You know him?"

"Oh, honey, you lucky thing. You have escaped a fate worse than death!"

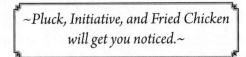

*~Pluck, Initiative, and Fried Chicken
will get you noticed.~*

Since Alma had already spilled the beans about Mills's opinion of her work, on her fourth day of mess duty Blanche felt comfortable enough to ask Mr. Mills to let her take the lunch cart out to the cast and crew on location. The look of harried disapproval he gave her made her think that she had made a mistake in asking so soon, but he growled, "Go on, then."

She didn't hang around long enough to let him reconsider. She threw several towels over the wheeled handcart to keep it warm and fly-free and hurried to today's shooting location about a quarter mile up Slaughterhouse Gulch. Alma Bolding was sitting by herself just behind the cameraman as he shot a scene set in a barroom that carpenters had built right in the gulch. It was a tall, three-sided room with gauze draped over the top to diffuse the bright sunlight. It had a floor, a bar, tables, bottles, and glasses. Blanche marveled at the illusion. It was the first time she had actually seen a scene being shot. The director, Elmo Reynolds, was prowling the perimeter, gesticulating at costar Frank Campeau and two extras who were sitting at a table pretending to confer about something very serious.

Alma turned in her chair when she heard the rattle of Blanche and the cart bumping across the ground toward her. "Ah, there she is! Bring that over here, honey. I'm famished." She threw the towel off the cart and groaned. "Not more rubber chicken."

"Try it, Miss Bolding. I heard you complaining about Mr. Mills's chicken last night. I fried this batch up myself, just for you."

Alma grinned before taking an experimental bite out of a thigh. Her dark eyes widened. "My goodness. What a difference." She examined the thigh like it was a science experiment. "What did you do to make it so juicy?"

"Well, in the first place, it's a thigh and not a breast, and thighs are juicier. Second, Mr. Mills is a real good cook. He can do magic things with chicken I never seen before. But he don't know how to fry it. I swear he boils it first before he fries it."

Alma laughed. "Well, damn, honey, the man is from New Jersey. What does he know about southern fried anything?"

"I didn't exactly tell him he was doing it wrong, but I asked him to let me do the frying this morning. He got all bothered when I didn't boil the chicken first, but I told him that this is the way my mama and grandmas and their mamas back to Eve fried it and I reckon they know more about how to fry a chicken than any fancy chef in Paris, France. He let me go ahead, but I think he just wanted me to have to eat my words. I'll tell you, the cowboys and the crew couldn't get enough of my chicken, and Mr. Mills is the one who had to eat his words. I had to save this for you, Miss Bolding, since the rest of it got ate up."

Alma, who had never learned to boil water, enjoyed Blanche's tale immensely. "I hope Mills doesn't give you any trouble for showing him up."

Blanche shrugged. "I think he was proud of me, but he'd never say it."

"You're a sassy little thing, aren't you?"

Blanche's first impulse was to apologize for stepping out of her place, but she reconsidered. Alma Bolding seemed to like sass. "Well, Miss Bolding, if a chicken is going to sacrifice her life for your dinner, you should at least make it worth her while."

To Blanche's relief, Alma smiled. "You're my kind of gal, puppy."

"Is it all right if I watch for a few minutes?"

"I don't see why not, if Mills can spare you. Just keep out of the way or Elmo will toss you out on your ass."

Blanche stood behind Alma's chair and watched the action as the actress ate. At regular intervals, the director Elmo Reynolds would yell at the actors through a megaphone. He was only ten yards from the action, but the hand-cranked camera was surprisingly noisy, and even though this was a silent movie, the actors were actually speaking dialogue to one another. Blanche couldn't help but laugh when one of the extras threw in a line that was hilariously filthy and had nothing to do with the script. Alma nearly choked on her chicken, and Elmo called a stop.

"What the hell do you think you're doing?" he shrieked.

The extra did not look abashed. "What do you care, Mr. Reynolds? The audience won't be able to hear me, anyway."

"People can read your lips, you idiot. Now just say the lines you were given. And don't let Mix hear you talk like that in front of women. Let's break, anyway. The food cart is here. Fifteen minutes for lunch or we'll lose the light."

Blanche was still euphoric when she wheeled the cartful of licked-clean plates back to the mess tent. She was relieved to see that Mills's minions had already cleaned up after the crew's mid-day meal, so the only dishes she would have to wash were the ones in the cart. But Mills had other plans for her. He waved her over. "Blanche, get your hat. I need to drive into Prescott for supplies before I can start on supper, and I want you to go with me."

Blanche was surprised. Mills usually took his assistant cook with him on these supply runs, and that was fine with Blanche. She had no particular desire to go back into Prescott, but she knew better than to say that to Mills. After all, she told herself, what are the odds that Otto Schilling would be anywhere near the greengrocer's?

> ~ *"You will be mine.*
> *You are mine.*
> *Mine!"* ~

Mr. Mills loaded up the back of his flatbed Model T with empty crates and drove south from Slaughterhouse Gulch to Prescott. To Blanche's relief, he did not go all the way into downtown, but skirted Montezuma Street and turned south on Granite.

He pulled up to a small greengrocer's with a sizable display of late summer and early fall vegetables ranged across the boardwalk in front of the store. Mr. Mills left Blanche outside ogling the produce while he went inside to fetch the proprietor, who, according to the sign on the window, sported the unlikely name of Wu Fan. Most of the vegetables that were piled up in boxes and across tables were things that Blanche would expect to see at this time of year—crisp little apples, carrots, onions, leeks, squashes, peppers, and potatoes. But Blanche was impressed with the healthy displays of some produce that was hard, if not impossible, to find in Oklahoma. The hard little green grapes that grew wild in the woods behind her parents' farm bore little resemblance to these fat, purple fruits oozing juice down the sides of a crate. She had never before seen tiny pine nuts or pistachios. The huge pile of sticky dates looked delicious, and she was so sorely tempted to take a sample that she clasped her hands behind her back like a five-year-old who had been warned not to touch. She was wondering at the small box of hairy little nut-like things labeled "lychee" when a quick movement at her feet caused her to jump back. What had she seen? Was it a rat?

She shuddered and bent over to peek under the sidewalk table, ready to leap back into the truck if she had to. But the bright button eyes staring at her from under the lychees belonged to no rat.

"Hey, dog," she greeted, delighted. "Come on out here and say hello."

The small, unkempt creature of no particular breed stayed where it was, but it did favor her with an enthusiastic tail wag.

She didn't have time to coax it. Mr. Mills reappeared, accompanied by the eponymous Mr. Wu, who was carrying a crate of potatoes almost as big as he was.

"Come on, Blanche," Mills said. "There are a dozen bags and boxes inside. Help us load up."

She tried to ignore the dog as she made several trips back and forth from the grocery to the truck, but it was hard. It was still under the table, but its whiskery nose would poke out and twitch enticingly every time she passed. She couldn't decide what weird liaison had produced such a creature. He was very small, but she didn't think he was a puppy. More like a lap dog, like her great-aunt's Pomeranian, but not nearly so elegant. She had seen a French bulldog once. It was more like that, except much hairier.

She would have spoken to it again, but Mr. Wu caught sight of it and burst out with a cascade of Chinese curses and would have kicked the little intruder if it hadn't beat a hasty retreat.

Blanche loaded a last bag of onions, feeling disappointed that the dog had gone. She stepped out from behind the truck onto the boardwalk and practically bumped her nose on Otto Schilling's waistcoat.

He had her arm in a vice-like grip before she quite knew what was happening.

"Well, I'll be damned! Look who we have here."

Blanche didn't pause to consider the irony of the situation, or plan, or do anything resembling thought. She opened her mouth and screamed like a banshee, all the while kicking her captor in the shins for everything she was worth.

Mills and Wu spilled out of the store, but they were beaten to the rescue by a furry whirlwind of fury that sank its needle teeth into Schilling's ankle and resisted all efforts to dislodge it. Schilling bellowed in pain and Blanche took advantage of the distraction to slip his grip and run into Mr. Mills's arms. Mr. Wu ran into the fray brandishing a nasty-looking metal rod and flailed about with it, unsure whether to aim for the shrieking fat man or the ratty little canine attached to his ankle.

Blanche pressed herself against Mr. Mills's shirt and cried, "Don't hurt it!" But Wu managed to land a kick and the dog yelped and ran off.

Schilling limped back up onto the sidewalk, red-faced and heaving. "I ought to sue you for damages, Wu."

Wu was not intimidated. "I never see that mutt in my life. If not for me, it chew your leg off."

Schilling didn't express his thanks. He had other matters on his mind. He pointed at Blanche.

"That girl belongs to me."

"I beg your pardon?" Mills's question could barely be heard over Blanche's wails of protest.

"I paid good money for that girl. I bought her debt. She owes me. Now, hand her over."

Mills was incensed. "I think not, Mr. Whoever-you-are. This young woman works for Miss Alma Bolding, and if you don't leave forthwith, I will send for the police."

"Hah! The police will be on my side."

"Miss Bolding and Mr. Tom Mix and the entire crew of his latest motion picture will most assuredly not be on your side, you blackguard. Now, leave before the cavalry arrives."

A crowd was gathering, and Schilling could tell that it was time for a strategic retreat. "All right, all right, I'm leaving." He leveled a finger at Blanche. "But this is not over, little girl."

Schilling stalked off and when he disappeared around the corner, Mills pushed Blanche out to arm's length so he could get a good look at her. "Did he hurt you?"

"No, I'm all right." She was panting with alarm, so ghostly white that Mills feared she would faint. "But please, let's get out of here before he comes back."

Mills snapped his fingers to get the grocer's attention. "Add this to my account, if you will, Mr. Wu. I think we'd better make our exit." He gestured for Blanche to get into the truck.

"Can we take the dog?" she asked, then fell to her knees and began scrambling about under the produce tables without waiting for an answer.

Mills started to object, but Mr. Wu said, "That mutt hang around here all the time. If I catch him, I kill him."

Blanche backed out from beneath the grapes, holding the squirming pooch by the scruff of the neck. She clambered into the truck and Mills gave the starter a crank before he got in beside her and shifted into gear. "I think that when we get back to Slaughterhouse Gulch you are going to owe me a story, little girl."

> *~What hideously delightful
> creature is this?~*

When Mills pulled up before the mess tent, Blanche did not hang around. She leaped out of the truck and ran straight to Alma Bolding's tent with the dog in her arms. Alma was in the middle of a costume change and Mrs. Gilbert was on the floor, pinning up the skirt, when Blanche burst in.

"He found me! What shall I do?"

The two women gazed at her as though she had suddenly grown two heads, so Blanche decided more explanation was in order. "I went into Prescott with Mr. Mills and ran right into the man who bought me from Graham, Otto Schilling. He said he owns me! Mr. Mills threatened to call the police but the bad man said the police would be on his side. I have to get out of here."

Mrs. Gilbert and Alma were both standing at her side now, each with an arm over her shoulder. "Don't you worry about a thing, puppy," Alma said. "Nobody owns you, and I've got an army of lawyers who will bring the bastard up on charges."

"But he'll kidnap me."

"Honey, we've got a dozen cowboys and crew who will say otherwise if he tries anything. I'll ask Tom to arrange some guards out at the cabin…" She hesitated, finally noticing what Blanche was holding. "What the frick is this?"

Blanche's panic, which had abated after Alma's assurances, sprang back to life. "He's just a stray, but he saved me from Mr. Schilling. He bit him and I was able to get away. Please let me keep him. I know all about dogs. I'll take care of him. You won't even know he's around."

Mrs. Gilbert looked skeptical, but Alma was already chucking the dog under the chin, much to his apparent pleasure. "Look at this, Delphinia," she said. "What the roving hell kind of a beast do you think it is?"

"A mongrel, for sure. Perhaps part one of those Mexican things, a Chihuahua?" Mrs. Gilbert ventured.

"Looks like he's part rat and part drain hair." Alma was rubbing the creature's ears as it frantically licked her hand.

"He loves you, Miss Bolding," Blanche said. "Please let me keep him."

"Well, of course, puppy." Alma backed off a step and rubbed her saliva-damp hand on the skirt of her costume. "Hey, Delphinia, now we have two lost puppies."

Mrs. Gilbert grabbed Alma's wet hand and began wiping it with a towel. "Blanche, take some rags and soap and wash that thing off in the creek. It stinks. I'm going to go talk to Mr. Mills in a few minutes. And don't think about Schilling anymore. If he shows up again, we'll take care of him." She shot Blanche a stern glance. "But no more trips into Prescott for you."

Blanche clutched the little dog to her breast, limp with relief. "Oh, thank you, thank you both."

After she left the tent with the dog in one hand and a bucketful of bath supplies in the other, Alma and Mrs. Gilbert gave one another a look that indicated they were of one mind.

1926
Santa Monica, California

When you're rich, you think you can get away with anything. And as far as Ted Oliver had been able to see, you could.

Still squatting down beside the accidental grave on the beach, Ted Oliver listened with interest as Officer Poole related his unflattering biography of the late Graham Peyton. Oliver had found that Poole usually tried to do the right thing, which is why he had cultivated a relationship with him. Not many cops cared about the right thing these days. Poole had been with the Santa Monica Police Department since its inception in 1904, shortly after the town was incorporated. In fact, he had been born here, which was probably why he gave a damn about the community.

Santa Monica had been a prosperous enclave for as long as it had been in existence, but it had been a quiet little beach retreat until recently. Now the megawealthy were moving in. The stars of the silver screen, the moguls, oil magnates, and businessmen. The motion picture industry was taking over Southern California, and a filthy industry it was. In the early days, the movie business was wide open, creative and entrepreneurial, but in the past few years, the studio system had been on the rise, geared to making profits and even more profits. The flickers may have been selling dreams, but the reality of the motion picture world was becoming more like a nightmare. Too much money and no morals.

The studios, the press, the law, the business community were all in cahoots. The big studios kept their stable of actors in line with threats of scandal, real or invented. And if they could manage it, they made sure there was scandalous behavior to hold over an actor's head. It wasn't hard. Human nature is weak and it doesn't take much to tempt people. Especially people with big ambitions and bigger egos. Payoffs were rife, drugs were everywhere. In fact, some of the studios had their own purveyors of vice on the payroll. Prohibition was the law, but alcohol was easy to come by. Need a classy young lady to provide entertainment to a dignitary? There were plenty of pretend starlets who'd do whatever necessary for a part.

Plenty of women—and pretty young men, too—who had been lured to Hollywood with promises of fame ended up being traded around like merchandise, locked up in a whorehouse servicing oilmen and producers, virtual prisoners. No money, no prospects, too ashamed or scared to contact their families or the law to ask for help. Not that help would be forthcoming. The police were mostly on the take.

Oliver had never considered himself a pillar of virtue. He knew the way things worked here, and he wasn't above taking the occasional small consideration as an inducement to look the other way. But Oliver did have his standards. Gambling and gin were one thing, but murder and pimping out naive young girls was something else altogether.

After what Poole had told him about Graham Peyton, Oliver

wondered if he really wanted to find out how the bastard had ended up buried under rocks at the foot of a cliff.

He sighed and stood up. "Hal, when you get back to the station, can you find out if anything unusual was going on in the valley around the time that Peyton disappeared? I know he was never reported missing, but my client last saw him alive in 1921."

"Jeez, Ted. Think you can narrow that date down for me a little?"

"In the fall. September, is what I was told. But if you can just go through the incident reports from that fall and see if anything stands out, I'd appreciate it."

"The usual arrangement?"

Oliver removed a ten-dollar bill from his wallet and handed it to the policeman. "The usual arrangement. Oh, and let me know if the coroner turns up anything interesting when he looks over the bones."

Poole pocketed the gratuity. "What are you going to do now?"

"My client's agent gave me the names of some of Peyton's known associates, along with the addresses of Peyton's office and of the place he was living when he disappeared. I figure I'll drive over to Los Angeles and have a talk with his former landlady, see if she remembers anything helpful."

~Oliver begins to piece together the last days of Peyton's life.~

Peyton's last known address was in Los Angeles, in the Westlake District, a section of town that Oliver knew pretty well. The district was popular with actors, full of expensive bungalow courts. Peyton may have been a criminal, but he was a prosperous one. His rented bungalow was located on Alvarado Street. Oliver had called the property manager and was gratified to hear that she lived in the same complex, right across the courtyard from Peyton's former abode. Yes, she remembered

Graham Peyton, and yes, she'd be willing to talk to him about her long-gone tenant.

As soon as he pulled up in front of the bungalow court Oliver realized with a jolt that this was the same place where three years earlier the director William Desmond Taylor had been shot to death by persons unknown. The well-kept two-story Spanish style duplexes may have been high-class, but Oliver wouldn't live in a place with such bad hoodoo on a bet. He parked his Ford on Alvarado and made his way up the sidewalk to the manager's bungalow at the end of the complex, next to the garages. He rang the bell and was greeted by a pleasantly attractive middle-aged woman with a flat middle western accent who called herself Debbie Hall.

After he introduced himself as a private agent working with the police, she invited him into her neat parlor and offered him a cup of coffee. He politely refused. "How long have you been manager here, Mrs. Hall?"

She sat down opposite him in a wingback chair, happy enough to get down to business. "I've been taking care of this complex for a dozen years. My only child is grown and my husband is a lawyer for Sennet Studios. Managing the people who keep the grounds nice and maintaining the units keeps me busy."

"You know most of the tenants and owners?"

"Oh, yes, certainly. Sometimes I feel like my job is more like being a head doctor or a nursemaid than a property manager."

"And you remember Graham Peyton?"

"Of course. He lived in 404½, at least when he was in town. He was often gone for weeks on some business trip or another. He always paid his rent six months in advance. He was a nice man, very charming. But I was glad when he was away on business, because when he was here he was trouble. He was always bringing floozies home with him. There were a lot a screaming fights over there. I tried to stay out of it. A number of actors live in this complex and there's always something loud and obnoxious going on." She hesitated, and Oliver figured she was considering whether to tell him about Desmond's murder. Apparently not. "Besides, it was none of my business," she said, "unless somebody complained. Then I'd have go over there and threaten to call the cops. That usually took care of it."

"Do you remember any floozy in particular? Any names?"

"Like I said, I mind my own business. They all looked alike to me. Young. Too much makeup, not enough clothes."

"Was there anyone who visited Peyton on a regular basis? Besides the floozies, of course."

Mrs. Hall took a moment to consider. "Not that I remember."

"How long was it before you knew he was gone for good? That he wasn't coming back?"

"Well, last I saw him was a couple of months before his rent was due. I didn't think anything of it when I didn't see him again after that, not until his next rent payment was overdue. It wasn't unusual for him to just go away with no warning."

"When was that?"

"Like I said, four, five years ago. It was in the fall, I think, last time I saw him. After he skipped his rent, I went around there a few times before I got the picture. I gave him longer to show up than I would most of my tenants. He had always been Johnny-on-the-spot with his rent. Always paid in cash."

"Did you know how he made his living, Mrs. Hall?"

He was angling for dirt, but Mrs. Hall didn't pick up on it. "I always make sure my tenants have a source of income before I rent to them. He had a nice letter of recommendation from a bank. He told me he worked for the studios, usually Warner or Sennet. He said he was a supplier. He was always dressed nice."

"What did he supply?"

Mrs. Hall shrugged.

Oliver leaned back into the couch. "Did you report his disappearance?"

"No. People skip out on me all the time. The cops would be tired of seeing my face if I reported it every time a tenant left me in the lurch."

"How'd Peyton leave his place? Did you notice anything odd when you cleaned it out?"

The question amused the landlady. "You mean like a closet full of gats or a body under the bed? Nothing odd that I remember."

"What did you do with his stuff?"

"What do you think? I sold most of it."

"Did you find any cash?"

"Yes, he had a small cashbox with about a hundred bucks in it. I confiscated it. He owed me for the two months I let him slide, plus the cleaning deposit."

"How about a ledger? Red leather, about yea-by-yea big, containing a lists of names and numbers?"

"Not that I remember. No books at all, as I recall."

"Do you have anything of his left? A box, a suitcase?"

"I don't know. I might. It would be more in the line of a nice dish or a pillow. Something I could use. Why are the police suddenly interested in Graham Peyton after all this time?"

Well, it took you a while to wonder about that, Oliver thought. "Some people walking on the beach up in Santa Monica found a body at the foot of the bluffs. It has been there for a while. The police believe it's Peyton."

"Is that so?" Mrs. Hall did not seem shocked by her erstwhile tenant's purported demise. "Well, I'm sorry to hear that. So you're trying to find out what happened to him?"

"I'd like to, yes."

The landlady hesitated, then said, "There was one odd thing that happened after the last time I saw Mr. Peyton. I didn't know at the time that he was gone for good. A woman came looking for him. Not his usual female visitor, not by a long shot. There were two men with her. One seemed like her driver, or her bodyguard. He was a big guy in a uniform, anyway. The other man was older, dressed like an accountant. She told me she was Peyton's mother. She paid me a nifty little bit to let her into his bungalow. She said she wanted to leave him a note to let him know she was in town and he should get in touch with her. I kept an eye on her auto—it was a limo, really—from my kitchen window while she was in there. She and the accountant stayed inside the bungalow for quite a while, maybe an hour. Finally she left and I never saw her again. I meant to mention it to Graham when he got back from his trip, but he never did and I forgot about her until now."

Oliver sat up straight. "She said she was his mother? She was an older woman?"

"That's right."

"What did she look like?"

"You wouldn't look twice at her. Old-fashioned. She looked sort of like Queen Victoria. Short, white-haired, dressed in black. Little bit of an accent. I don't know what kind."

"The bungalow that he lived in, I guess you rented it out after Peyton disappeared."

"Of course. There have been three different tenants in that unit in the past five years. There won't be a trace of Graham Peyton left after all this time."

"Say, do you remember what kind of automobile Peyton drove?"

"That, I do remember. He liked a fancy ride, like he was a titan of industry, or wanted people to think so. Had a big old seven-seater Pierce-Arrow touring car."

———

Oliver returned to his walk-up on Santa Monica Boulevard and took a chair at the enamel kitchen table in order to review his notes.

Peyton's bungalow had been cleaned out years ago, and whatever possessions he had left behind had been scattered to the winds. If the landlady had helped herself to fifty thousand dollars, why wasn't she wearing mink and living in a mansion in the Hollywood Hills? Besides, Oliver figured that Peyton hadn't been stupid enough to keep that kind of money in a drawer under his socks.

And who was this old woman who claimed to be Peyton's mother? Oliver had assumed that Peyton had no family. This was an unexpected twist, one that could be worth pursuing.

Since Peyton had told Mrs. Hall that he worked for the Warner brothers, Oliver telephoned his secretary friend at Warner Studios to see what she could find out. Peyton had spread the word that he was a big cheese producer on Broadway, so Oliver rang up Poole and offered him a persuasive inducement to contact the New York City PD and find out if Peyton had had any dealings with the law there.

Oliver spent the rest of the afternoon telephoning banks in the Los Angeles area and asking if Peyton had ever had an account with any of them. He had come up empty. He made a note to see if Poole could help him there, as well.

Speak of the devil, they say, and up he pops. Oliver's telephone rang, and when he answered, Poole said, "Hey, Ted, I've been checking the crime reports from 1920 and '21, and I came across this. It's a report of an abandoned automobile up in Palisades Park, dated October 15, 1921. A Pierce-Arrow touring car. It was parked way at the end of the park, and there's no telling how long it sat there before one of the park employees had it towed. There wasn't any license plate or any papers in the car, and it doesn't look like anybody went to a lot of trouble to trace the owner."

"A Pierce-Arrow. His landlady said he drove a Pierce-Arrow. An expensive auto like that doesn't get abandoned for no reason. Could it be that Peyton got bumped off and his killer tossed him over the cliff, then cleared everything out of the car so it couldn't be traced?"

"It says here that nobody ever came to claim the car, so after a few months the city auctioned it off."

"Does it say who bought it?"

Poole laughed. "Yeah. The L.A. city attorney. Doesn't say how much he paid for it, but I'm guessing he got it for a song."

"Thanks, Hal. Heard anything from New York yet?"

"Naw, not yet. They don't feel the need to roust themselves for the likes of us yokels on the West Coast."

"By the way, do you have any information on Peyton's family? Anybody to notify about the death?"

"No family that I know of. We've checked for next of kin and haven't found any. We'll probably put a notice in the local papers."

"The landlady said that his mother came by looking for him shortly after he disappeared."

"His mother? Well, everybody has a mother, I guess. I'll let the chief know and we'll try to track her down. This woman may have been spinning the landlady a tale. That happens, you know. Maybe Peyton owed her money, or seduced her daughter."

"I'm inclined to believe the latter. I doubt Peyton actually had a mother. Keep me posted, and if I turn anything up I'll let you know." Oliver replaced the earpiece on the hook, removed from his file the photo of Graham Peyton that Mr. Ruhl had supplied him and slipped it into his inside jacket pocket. It was time to apply some shoe leather to the streets of Hollywood, where Peyton's office had been located.

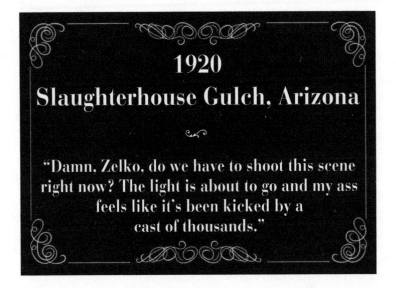

1920
Slaughterhouse Gulch, Arizona

"Damn, Zelko, do we have to shoot this scene right now? The light is about to go and my ass feels like it's been kicked by a cast of thousands."

"Miss Bolding, if you'd pull your knees in when you ride you wouldn't bounce around in the saddle so much."

If Alma hadn't been so tired, she would have been irritated by the unsolicited advice. Especially since it was coming from an idiot stray little girl who had just brought her lunch. As it was, she was amused and a bit grateful to be distracted from her aching derriere. She lifted an eyebrow at the impertinent creature standing near the horse's head, holding the reins. "So now you're an expert on riding as well as chicken frying, are you? Well, I'll have you know, missy, that this horse is the devil incarnate and absolutely refuses to do what he's told. In fact, I'm going to insist that Tom dock his wages."

"There's nothing wrong with this horse, Miss Bolding. He just knows that you don't know what you're doing. You've got to show him that you're the boss."

Alma's eyebrows shot toward her hairline and she loosed a shriek of laughter. "If this horse doesn't know enough to show me the proper deference, then he hasn't been reading *Photoplay* lately. I'm a big star! I'll tell you what, sassy young lady, if you think you can do better, then I invite you to demonstrate." Alma made an impatient gesture at Zelko, the cameraman, who rushed over to help the groaning actress out of the saddle.

Alma half expected Blanche to backtrack quickly and make an excuse, but the girl gave her an eager grin and vaulted up onto the horse's back after a mere nod at the stirrups. The horse sidled, ears perked forward and eyes wide, recognizing that a serious change in his circumstances had occurred.

"Why, I think you have been on a horse before," Alma observed.

"I grew up on a horse farm, Miss," Blanche said, before she pulled the horse's head around and took off down the gulch at a gallop.

Alma clapped her hands in delight.

"Is that your little kitchen maid?"

Alma hadn't realized that her leading man, Tom Mix, had come up behind her. "Delphinia found her wandering around the woods by my cabin just a few days ago and took her in like a stray puppy. She ran away from home with a criminal lowlife and when she realized her mistake she did a skidoo. Delphinia got her a job peeling potatoes for the crew, but it seems our little puppy possesses hidden talents."

"Be danged!" Tom pushed his hat back with his thumb. "That gal can ride, can't she?"

Blanche was acutely aware of their eyes on her as she showed the horse who was boss. Perhaps if she could convince her bene-factors of her mettle, one or the other of them might find a task for her on the set, something that didn't involve potatoes. She turned the horse back toward the watching crowd and when she reached a relative straightaway, she urged him into a gallop before removing one foot from the stirrup, then the other, raising herself up to crouch on the saddle, knees bent, one hand holding the reins and one straight out for balance, her hair streaming in the wind. She had only tried this trick once before, on a dare from one of her brothers, but she had pulled it off then and saw no reason she wouldn't be able to pull it off now. Besides, if she fell and broke her neck, at least that would be the end of her troubles.

The actors watched her race down the gully. Alma pouted. "I'm feeling disgruntled, Tom. That contrary beast wouldn't do anything for me, no matter how nicely I asked."

Tom barely heard her. "Look at that, Alma!"

Alma cut Tom a narrow glance. Perhaps this was an opportunity to help both the girl and herself. "Listen, Tom, I'm getting another one of my brilliant ideas. What say we offer her the job of stunt double for me? We're both slim, brunette, and about the same height. She's enough like me that she could fool the camera from a distance. The fifteen years I've got on her shouldn't make a difference."

"Fifteen years?" Tom repeated with a twinkle.

"Fifteen goddam years, Tom, and don't give me any lip."

Blanche was back in the saddle when she reined in in front of the two stars in a cloud of dust. Alma waved a hand in front of her face and coughed dramatically, but Tom grabbed the stirrup. "What's your name, honey, and where did you learn to ride like that?"

"I'm Blanche, Mr. Mix. My daddy and my grandpapa both raise mules and saddle horses. I been around horses all my life. There's not much I don't know about them." Her desire to impress the star prevented her from mentioning that she had absorbed all her horsecraft through sheer proximity and had never been interested in learning more than she needed in order to do her assigned chores or get to where she was going.

"Where are you from, Blanche?"

"I grew up in the east part of Oklahoma, sir. Same as you." Every Oklahoman living, whether he had seen a motion picture or not, was familiar with their homegrown hero, cowboy star Tom Mix.

"I thought you sounded like home," Mix said, delighted. "I'll tell you what, Blanche. Miss Bolding here has had an idea I think you might like. How would you like to be Miss Bolding's double for the riding scenes in this here picture? We'd sign a proper contract for the duration of shooting. I'd pay you five dollars for every day you appear in front of the camera and an extra five dollars for every stunt."

Blanche blinked down at him. "A double? What's a double, Mr. Mix?"

"That means that whenever Miss Bolding's character is supposed to be riding on horseback, it'll be you on the horse instead of her."

Blanche's forehead wrinkled. "But Miss Bolding is way..."

Alma didn't let her finish. "Don't you say it, missy. You'll be dressed like me, and you and the horse will be far enough away from the camera that no one will be able to tell you aren't me."

Blanche felt her cheeks grow warm with excitement. "I'd love to be in the pictures, and I'll be glad to do whatever you want me to do. But if people will be coming to the picture to see Miss Bolding ride and it's just me pretending to be her, isn't that cheating?"

Tom and Alma both laughed. "Well, aren't you precious?" Alma said. "Come down from yon noble steed, you sweet innocent, and let me tell you how the movie business works."

———

The next two weeks were the most exciting of Blanche's life. Tom was impressed with the skills she already possessed. But he had a lot to teach her about falling, jumping, and fighting, and had some unfamiliar riding tricks to show her from the back of his famous blaze-faced gelding, Tony the Wonder Horse.

With Alma and Mrs. Gilbert beside her, she signed a contract with Tom Mix's production company to perform in *Handsome Stranger* in any capacity she was needed. She was not only filmed riding sedately in the distance, she also hung on for dear life to a wagon bench, next to Tom while he drove hell-bent for leather down a dirt road while a dozen Yavapai Indians dressed like Comanches chased them on horseback. The pursuer in the elaborate war bonnet drew alongside the racing wagon and plucked Blanche off the seat and galloped off as she tried to struggle convincingly while attempting not to wiggle out of his grasp and get trampled.

She also had a bit part in the picture as a Mexican saloon girl during the bar fight scene, hanging around in the background in her off-the-shoulder blouse and full skirt, looking alarmed as Tom and Frank Campeau whaled on each other and busted up the furniture.

> ~*Blanche had never been so bruised and sore in her life. Or so happy.*~

In the space of a month her life had gone from dull to exciting to disastrous. And now, by sheer luck or the grace of God, she had ended up with friends, a dog, and in the movies after all, having the time of her life and actually getting paid for it. On the days she was not needed as an extra or for a stunt, her little pooch followed her around while she did whatever needed doing. Mrs. Gilbert told her that since she was now part of the movie crew she didn't have to make beds at the cabin or ladle soup on the set, but Blanche wanted to keep busy as well as earn the extra twenty-five cents a day.

After one particularly grueling day of shooting, the director,

Elmo Reynolds, told Tom and Alma he didn't need them on location until noon the next day. Tom decided to take his wife, Olive, back to the hotel in Prescott for supper and an early bedtime. Alma made arrangements to go to dinner with Elmo, Zelko, and Frank Campeau. She invited Blanche to join them, but Mrs. Gilbert looked so thunderous that Blanche demurred and the two women went back to the cabin together. Blanche was sorry to pass up an evening hobnobbing with the rich and famous, but in truth she was afraid of going back to Prescott. Besides, she was tired and dirty and happy enough to take a bath and go to bed. She left Mrs. Gilbert sitting in the great room with mending in her lap.

Blanche was woken by headlights and noise like a party going on in the front drive. Judging from the fading stars, it was close to dawn. She opened her door and tiptoed to the loft balcony. Alma was being poured into the cabin by two men whom Blanche recognized as members of the film crew. Mrs. Gilbert, still dressed in the same outfit she was wearing when Blanche left her in her armchair the night before, relieved the men of their burden with a murmured thanks.

Mrs. Gilbert steered Alma up the stairs. She was struggling to support the much taller woman, and when she reached the landing, Blanche made a move to assist. Mrs. Gilbert caught her eye as she stepped forward and gave her a quiet shake of the head. Blanche bit her lip and slipped back into her room. She didn't go back to bed, though. She dressed quickly and went into the kitchen to brew coffee. She thought about starting breakfast but decided to wait until she knew better what was going on. Mrs. Gilbert was upstairs for a long time. When she finally reappeared, the sun was well up and Blanche was sitting at the kitchen table with her hands folded in her lap. Mrs. Gilbert sat down, looking a bit bedraggled.

Blanche stood up and poured her a cup of coffee. "We're supposed to be on set at noon," she noted.

"She'll make it." Mrs. Gilbert didn't elaborate. She rubbed her forehead and took a grateful sip of her coffee.

Blanche very much wanted to ask more questions, but Mrs. Gilbert's attitude deterred her. Instead, she asked, "Can I make you up some eggs?"

Mrs. Gilbert accepted and hungrily ate the scrambled eggs Blanche offered her. The worried look on Blanche's face loosened Mrs. Gilbert's tongue. "I'm going to let her sleep for a few hours. She's not going to feel very good when she wakes up, but a soak in a good hot bath, a couple of Doctor Harmon's pills, and a glass of prairie oysters usually sets her right. Or right enough, anyway. I'm going to try and sleep a bit myself. Would you be a dear and be sure I'm awake by 10:00?"

She stood and was making her way out of the kitchen when she turned and looked at Blanche over her shoulder. "If you hear Alma moving around upstairs, come and wake me right away."

"Yes, ma'am. But if she wakes up, I can go up there and take care of whatever she needs."

"No, darling. Promise me that you won't go upstairs even if she calls you. You come and wake me."

Blanche considered saying that she was not a delicate rose who had never seen a hangover but thought better of it. There was a lot more going on with Alma Bolding than just a couple of nights of indiscreet boozing followed by a handful of happy pills. Besides, the woman deserved to preserve whatever dignity she could salvage.

> ~Sometimes Luck steps in
> when Youth knows not what to do.~

Shooting was scheduled to be finished on the five-reeler by early October. Blanche was too nervous to ask what would happen next, but Mrs. Gilbert approached her after the director called "cut" on the final scene. "Blanche, Alma and I have been talking, and if you're still interested, we'd like for you to come back to California with us."

Blanche's heart skipped a beat. "Mrs. Gilbert, I would like that more than anything. What would I be doing for Miss Bolding? Not that it matters," she added hastily, "because I'll do whatever you need."

"We have in mind that you'll do more or less what you have been doing here on location. I can always use an extra hand with household management. Miss Bolding might have a task or two for you on her upcoming project, which is scheduled to be shot in Malibu in November. She suggested that she could help you get started with a career. We'll proceed on a probationary basis... that means we'll give you a try and see if you measure up," she added, when she saw Blanche's confused expression.

"I'll do my very best. I'm so grateful for everything you've done for me, Mrs. Gilbert, and to Miss Bolding, and Mr. Mix, too. I won't let you down."

"I'm curious, honey. What did you plan to do if we hadn't offered you this opportunity?"

"I didn't quite know what I was going to do with myself. I have a little money now but not enough to do much with. I'd more than likely go into some town around here and find work, at least until I made enough money to move on. I have an aunt in Tempe who would probably help me, but the minute I contact her, she'll let my parents know where I am and they'll come after me."

"Would that be so bad?"

"I miss my family, but I'm never, never going home." Blanche's face set in stubborn lines. "I can't let them know where I am until I make something of myself. I set out to go to California and I'll get there one way or another. It's the land of opportunity, isn't it?"

"Blanche, there are a thousand pretty young girls a day going to Hollywood, hoping for a chance to get into the flickers. Believe me, you won't like the 'opportunities' that most of them eventually have to take advantage of. You stick with Miss Bolding, honey. She likes to help people and you get to be her new project,

I think. She may be a…well, you've gotten a glimpse of what she's like. She's wealthy and she's famous, but I caution you not to follow her example too closely. Yet she has a good heart, and she won't cheat you or use you or sell you to the highest bidder."

Blanche had nothing to say. Mrs. Gilbert's warning gave her pause. But the niggling fear passed quickly. Whatever the future held, it couldn't be worse than what she had already been through. Besides, she had never had so much fun in her life as she had over the past few weeks.

Mrs. Gilbert seemed to read her mind, and smiled. "Miss Bolding likes you, honey. Don't disappoint her."

"Are we going to motor to Hollywood?"

"Oh, Lord, no. You cannot imagine how tedious that drive between here and Los Angeles is. We'll be taking the train. I've already purchased tickets for the three of us on the California Limited for tomorrow night. We're going to let Alma sleep today while you and I close up the cabin. The caretaker, Mr. Warren, will be here tomorrow evening to pick up the keys and to motor us to Ash Fork to catch the 11:32 to Los Angeles. I've reserved two sleeping compartments, one for you and me, and one for Alma, with an adjoining drawing room."

"Can I bring Jack Dempsey with me?"

"Jack Dempsey?"

"My dog. I decided to call him that since he's such a fighter."

That tickled Mrs. Gilbert. "Jack Dempsey. Well, of course. He's ugly as sin but he cleaned up all right. He'll have to stay in the compartment, though."

"I've never had a bedroom on a train. I've only had to sleep sitting up when we'd travel to see my aunt here in Arizona or my grandparents in Arkansas." She hesitated before asking, "Will they make you stay in a separate car, Mrs. Gilbert?"

"No, not on this leg of the trip. Colored folks are allowed to sit wherever they can afford to sit on most Western trains. However, I usually stay in the cabin. I prefer not to deal with the looks I get when I visit the dining car or the club car. Sometimes Alma insists that I accompany her, which is not too bad. Everyone looks at her and ignores me. But this time she'll have you to keep her company and I can spend the trip catching up on my reading, maybe do a little mending or embroidery."

It did not occur to Blanche to think that this was a disgraceful state of affairs. Instead she was happy and impressed that her friend had the option to come and go as she pleased. "I can help you with your sewing. I like embroidery, too."

Mrs. Gilbert smiled at Blanche's enthusiasm. "Is that so? Is there anything you can't do, little girl? Well, if you get tired of being Alma's pet, you can sit with me and Jack Dempsey in the sleeping compartment for a while and sew up some hems."

"How long will the trip take?"

"We'll leave Ash Fork late at night and get into Los Angeles in the middle of the afternoon the next day."

"Will we get to see the Grand Canyon?"

"Not on this trip, honey. Maybe the next time Alma comes out to Arizona to do a picture with Mr. Mix, you and I will make a point of taking the train up there to see it. Now, in the big closet behind the pantry is where I stashed the steamer trunks. Go fetch those for me and let's haul them upstairs and begin packing up Alma's things."

> ~*Blanche's feet hardly touched the floor*
> *as she flew up the stairs with a leather suitcase*
> *in one hand and a makeup case in the other.*~

She had volunteered to pack Alma's delicates while Mrs. Gilbert took charge of hanging Alma's couture outfits in one of the trunks in just the right way. She froze mid-step in the doorway of Alma's loft bedroom. She knew that Mrs. Gilbert was already there, but she hadn't realized that Alma was there, too, lounging on her big bed with Jack Dempsey in her lap, barefoot and dressed in a peignoir, reading the *Prescott Courier* aloud.

"There's a lot of stuff in here about that bomb that went off on Wall Street last month and killed all the people. They're speculating now that Anarchists did it, maybe in revenge for the arrest of those Sacco and Vanzetti persons." Alma's tone was more curious than outraged.

Mrs. Gilbert shook her head. "I don't understand how blowing up a bunch of innocent folks just walking by on the street is going to make anybody have sympathy for your cause." She held up a long evening coat on a hanger and eyed it critically, checking for lint, loose hems, or missing buttons before packing.

Blanche said nothing as she opened the suitcase on top of the dresser and began lifting out Alma's lacy unmentionables, but she couldn't help but think of her Socialist uncle. He was always getting himself into situations because of his union organizing, but she couldn't imagine him purposely killing people, no matter how just he considered his cause.

"Also says here that since the Nineteenth Amendment went into effect, women over twenty-one need to get registered soon if they want to vote in the presidential election next month."

Mrs. Gilbert said something but her head was in the armoire, so her voice was muffled.

Blanche could not stay silent about this. "Oh, Miss Bolding, how exciting. Are you going to register when you get back to California?"

Alma made a sarcastic noise. "Honey, I couldn't care less about politics."

Blanche was shocked. "You don't care that women can vote now?"

"Vote for who, baby? From what I know of politicians, they're all crooks anyway. Us women, we have to take care of ourselves. No man is going to do it for you."

"Maybe women ought to run for office, then."

Alma laughed. "Good luck with that, honey. But I'll tell you what. If you decide to run for Congress someday, I'll vote for you."

Blanche didn't know what to say, so she kept her mouth shut. She had reached the bottom of the drawer when she found a bag of little pink packets full of white powder. The bag was pushed to the back, next to a small wooden box containing a hypodermic needle. Blanche glanced back over her shoulder. Alma was still reading, unaware of Blanche's discovery. But Mrs. Gilbert had turned around and was gazing at her.

"I'll finish that up, Blanche," she said. "You go downstairs and clear out the icebox."

———

Blanche was still in the kitchen an hour later when Mrs. Gilbert came in and put the kettle on for tea. Blanche was dying to ask her about the white powder but bit her lip, afraid to jeopardize her new position in Alma's household.

Mrs. Gilbert sat down and folded her hands on the tabletop before she spoke, her tone matter-of-fact. "I don't know how much you know about Alma. The rags have printed a lot of tripe about her, but it's true that Alma hasn't had much luck with men. She's been married five times and five times her husband turned out to be a jerk, in one way or another."

What this had to do with the powder, Blanche didn't know. But she went along. "If she doesn't like men, then why does she keep getting married?"

Mrs. Gilbert smiled. "I didn't say she doesn't like men. The problem is that she likes them too much. She swears the next one will just be a little fling and then she ends up falling for him and lets him talk her into getting married. Alma acts tough, but a little piece of her dies off every time she gets her heart broken. I think that's why she tries to numb herself with the hooch and the hop."

"But won't that stuff kill her?"

"It might. Not right away, I hope."

"I wish we could help her."

"So do I, darling."

"Are you married, Mrs. Gilbert?"

"Not anymore." She looked down at her hands.

"Did your husband die?"

"He did. But that was a while after I left him."

"What happened?"

"Honey, I'd just as soon not talk about it. It wasn't a pleasant part of my life."

"I'm sorry. I don't mean to be nosy," Blanche said, though she really, really did.

"It's all right. I'd rather you ask me directly than make up stories in your head."

———

The day they were to leave for California, Blanche and Mrs. Gilbert closed up the cabin while Alma slept. Blanche didn't feel like dinner, though she did her best to help Mrs. Gilbert get a tray ready to take up to Alma. Blanche hadn't felt like eating for several days, and this morning she had felt particularly unwell. Nauseated, in fact. The bilious feeling that rose when she had looked at the plate of fried eggs on Mrs. Gilbert's tray caused a sudden panic. What was the date? She looked at the calendar hanging on the kitchen wall. October 12. It had been two weeks—almost three weeks—since her monthly friend was supposed to come for a visit.

> ~"Oh, no, oh, no,
> oh, Sweet Lord, no."~

Terror clutched at her like a hand at her throat. Maybe she was wrong. She put her hand on her perfectly flat belly. Surely she was wrong.

Why had this possibility not occurred to her? Well, it had occurred to her when she first ran away with Graham, but that was when she fully expected to be a married woman before the month was out. Once Graham had abandoned her, the idea that she might have a baby flew right out of her head along with her expectation of marriage. What a complete fool she was.

What now? She couldn't think of what now. She couldn't tell Mrs. Gilbert. What if they dropped her job offer like a hot potato? It was one thing to be on her own in Arizona as a single girl who could work. It was another thing altogether to be on her own as a pregnant, unmarried, fifteen-year-old girl with no money, no friends, and no prospects for either.

No, she had to keep her mouth shut. Soon enough her secret would be no secret, but right now she had an opportunity to get to California and time to figure something out. Besides, maybe she was wrong. Maybe there was something wrong with her.

"Please, Lord, just let me be sick."

> ~Standing on the Precipice…
> What lurks below?
> Is it disaster, or the fulfillment of all her dreams?
> Blanche decides to jump.~

It was almost noon when a man whom Blanche had never seen drove up to the cabin and loaded all the trunks, boxes, and cases into the back of a truck. Mrs. Gilbert introduced her to Bert Warren, the caretaker, who told her to "just call me Bert."

Blanche asked Bert if he would be living in the cabin in Miss Bolding's absence, but he laughed. "No, Miss, I'm just the caretaker. Miss Bolding only uses this cabin when she's here in Arizona making a picture with Mr. Mix. Sometimes she loans it to friends of hers, but most of the time nobody lives here."

Blanche was shocked. Alma's "cabin" was twice the size of the house she had grown up in. It seemed an incredible waste of a perfectly good habitation for it to stand empty for most of the year.

Mrs. Gilbert handed Bert the key to the cabin, and the women piled into the truck for the long drive over barely graded mountain trails to Ash Fork, the nearest stop for the California Limited, the luxury rail liner that ran from Chicago to Los Angeles. The trip was hair-raising, at least for Blanche. Mrs. Gilbert concentrated on her knitting and Alma seemed to enjoy the death-defying ride up and down the winding, cliff-hugging road. By the time they finally reached Ash Fork four hours later, even Alma had had enough. Bert pulled up in front of the Escalante Hotel, another Harvey establishment that served as the train station as well as a hotel and restaurant for travelers. Their train to Los Angeles did not depart until an hour before midnight, so they had plenty of time to rest. Blanche was starving, and was eager to try out the Harvey House restaurant, but Mrs. Gilbert nixed the idea. In the first place, Alma was too famous. Her fans would never leave her alone to eat her dinner in peace. More to the point, Mrs. Gilbert didn't feel like going through the humiliation of being turned away at the door.

So Alma paraded through the lobby in all her glory, with her entourage (Mrs. Gilbert, Blanche, and Jack Dempsey) trailing along behind her, and requested the temporary use of a suite so they could have a quiet dinner and rest before the 11:00 p.m. train to Los Angeles. The hotel staff fell all over themselves to accommodate her, and for several hours the three women and the dog luxuriated in comfort while feasting on steak.

———

The trip to California was a wonder. Blanche was used to train trips spent trying to doze on a hard bench, scrunched up next to one sibling or another, and arriving at her destination hungry, exhausted, and bent over like a question mark. It was amazing how much more pleasant a long journey is when you have a private cabin and an actual bed in which to sleep away the miles. Blanche was surprised to see that it was full daylight when Alma roused her the next morning. The actress was dressed in a long-sleeved turquoise frock with a white scarf around her neck, bright-eyed and ready for action.

"Come on, lazybones, keep me company in the dining car. I'm famished!"

Blanche blinked the sleep out of her eyes and sat up. "My goodness, I haven't slept so well in I don't know how long."

"Train travel will do that for you. Lull you to sleep and whet your appetite".

"What time is it, Miss?"

Alma gave the girl's leg a slap. "Who knows? It is past the dawn, puppy, and we're headed west. We're headed home!"

Blanche's canine bedmate, Jack Dempsey, was bouncing around the berth like a hairy maniac, happy to be alive and in the company of gentlefolk who didn't want to kick him to China. Blanche climbed down from the top bunk and caught Jack Dempsey in her arms as he launched himself at her.

The bottom berth was empty and had been converted back to a seat. "Is Mrs. Gilbert waiting for us in the dining car?"

Alma's beaming grin slipped just a little. "No, Delphinia didn't want to come to the dining car. She's in the sitting room of my cabin, helping herself to a tray that I had brought in for her. We'll drop Jack off to keep her company. Now, slap on some duds, baby. I don't like to eat alone."

In the dining car, Blanche felt less like a breakfast companion than a lady-in-waiting to the queen. It was rare that Alma was able to eat two bites together before someone interrupted her to gush over her beauty or talent or both. Blanche thought that was too bad, because breakfast was a delicious mélange of dishes that she had never eaten before, kippers and fruit cups in syrup and omelets with artichoke hearts. But Alma wasn't bothered at all. She was nourished and energized more by the adulation than by any food.

What would it be like to be loved like that? What would it be like if everyone you met fell all over themselves to praise you, to try and guess what you want before you even know yourself and give it to you? To do anything you ask?

Blanche determined that she would do whatever she could to find out.

1926
Hollywood, California

Hot on the trail, Oliver catches
a faint scent.

Mr. Ruhl had told Ted Oliver that Graham Peyton had kept a one-room office above a clothing store in Hollywood, right on Hollywood Boulevard. Ruhl did not immediately remember the exact address, but he thought that it was somewhere close to the intersection of Las Palmas and Hollywood Boulevard. Armed with a snapshot of a smiling Peyton, Oliver planned to hit every establishment within a mile of Hollywood and Las Palmas, slowly working his way up the north side of Hollywood Boulevard, then back down the south side. The very first place he tried was the restaurant in the middle of the block, an upscale place called "Philippe" (not Phil's, or Philip's or even Philippe's, which is how Oliver knew without setting foot in the place that it was upscale), located directly across the street from Peyton's former office. Philippe had been doing business on this block for some years, and the likelihood was that a man like Peyton, with expensive tastes and the income to indulge them, would have been a frequent customer. Oliver had timed his visit so that he would arrive at about 2:00 in the afternoon, between luncheon and the dinner hour. He asked for the maître d', since a place called Philippe surely had one, and was not disappointed. A tall man with oiled, center-parted hair and the posture of a Prussian general stalked out of the empty dining room and looked down at him as they stood in the marbled entrance. "I am Maurice," he intoned. "How may I assist you?"

Maurice's almost-sneer suggested that the detective was a bit too déclassé for the joint. Oliver suppressed a chuckle at the waiter's bearing. He introduced himself and explained about the skeleton at the bottom of the palisades.

"I'm trying to trace the movements of a man who I expect used to be a regular diner here. This would have been five years ago. Do you have any waiters or staff who have been working here that long?"

"Yes, sir. In fact, I have been the headwaiter here since the restaurant opened. If the man was a regular diner, it is quite likely that I served him. Do you suspect that this man has something to do with the remains?"

"The police are pretty sure the skeleton is all that's left of one Graham Peyton, who had an office just across the street, here. I am investigating the final days of Mr. Peyton's life, and I'm hoping that you can help me out."

The man's eyes widened for a fraction of a second and Oliver felt a stab of hope. He removed the snapshot from his pocket and handed it to the waiter. "Do you recognize the name? Is this him?"

Maurice took the photo and gazed at it for a long moment before handing it back. "Yes, I remember Mr. Peyton very well. He's dead, you say? Well, that is a shame. He was an excellent tipper. I have often wondered what became of him. I rather expected that he had moved back to New York. He was indeed a regular customer here, when he was in town, that is. When do the police believe he died?"

"It was probably in the fall of 1921."

"I don't remember the exact date, but I do remember the last time I saw Mr. Peyton, and that may be about the same time. He was a talent agent, I believe. He was usually with a beautiful woman. Not often the same girl twice, mind you. He was with a young lady the last time he was here. There was an altercation. That's why it sticks in my mind."

"An altercation? What kind of an altercation? With the young lady?"

"No, not with his luncheon companion. He had a regular table, that one over there, by the French doors. He had come in with a blond lass that day. I waited on them, and from what I was able to observe, they were having a pleasant luncheon. I do believe he was on the verge of offering to represent her when another young woman came into the restaurant under false pretenses and made a scene. It was quite the imbroglio. I had to threaten to have her bodily removed, but she left without further ado and Mr. Peyton and his companion finished their meal."

"And that was the last time you saw Peyton?"

"Yes. I can't swear that he didn't come in again sometime when I wasn't on duty, but I never saw him again."

"What can you tell me about the women?"

"The person who created the disturbance was dark-haired. Quite beautiful. Nicely dressed. I've not seen her since."

"Would you recognize her if you saw her again?"

"No, probably not. She was very young, a girl, really. She has more than likely changed out of all recognition after this much time."

"How about the other girl?"

"Oh, yes, I'd recognize her. She still dines here on occasion, with one gentleman or another. We don't cater to single women."

Oliver took a card from his breast pocket and handed it to the waiter. "Next time she comes in, would you give her this and ask her to telephone me?"

"I'll give her the card, but I can't guarantee anything."

"Naturally. Please let her know that anything she can tell me will be kept in the strictest confidence, and may help us find out what happened to Graham Peyton." He placed a dollar bill on the table. "For your time."

1920
California, at Last

Such Stuff That Dreams are Made On...

The California Limited pulled into La Grande Station in the middle of the afternoon. Blanche had spent most of the day with her nose pressed against the window in the drawing room of Miss Bolding's compartment. They had started their morning by traveling through desert so barren that Blanche wondered what God had been thinking when he created it. Some time after they crossed the wide, marshy Colorado River into California, the country began to rise and fall, finally to undulate as they passed through strange, bare, rounded hills that resembled nothing so much as human bodies lying on their sides. Blanche had not formed a favorable opinion of the California landscape, not until they crested the last undulation and the entire San Fernando

Valley spread out under them. She could see a glint of silver in the distance. Could it be? Blanche had no idea how far they were from the Pacific, but she was eager for her first glimpse of an ocean. She had never seen a body of water bigger than the Arkansas River.

The train headed downward and the vista narrowed as they approached Los Angeles, slowing and wending through small town after small town, one running into another, all filled with colorful stucco houses sporting red tiled roofs.

When the train slowed so much that Blanche figured she could probably keep up with it at a walk, Mrs. Gilbert stood up from her seat and started pulling cases off of the rack above their heads.

Blanche caught her breath. "Are we there?"

Alma, sitting across from her with Jack Dempsey in her lap, was enjoying Blanche's excitement. "Almost home, honey. Almost home."

The train slid into a sprawling red brick railroad station with a huge dome that made it look like a cross between a cathedral and a castle. There was a knock on the compartment door and the conductor poked a head in. "Miss Bolding, if you and your party would like to disembark before the other passengers, please come with me and we will unload your luggage."

They were met on the platform by the most amazing person Blanche had ever seen. Was he a man, or was she a woman? He stood somewhere between six and six-and-a-half feet tall and had shoulders out to here and arms like tree trunks. But she had a fine-boned face and blond ringlets that fell to her broad shoulders, Vaseline shining on her eyelids and bright red lipstick that perfectly matched the color of the hibiscus flower print on the scarf around her neck. The black bag trousers she/he was wearing could have been worn by either gender, though young men tended to favor them. The person was standing on the platform as the conductor unfolded the steps from the train car and held out a hand to help Alma dismount.

"Oh, Fee," Alma said, "it's so good to be home. I am perishing for a Collins." She waved vaguely at Blanche, who was descending behind her with the dog in her arms. "Oh, and this is Blanche and her pal Jack Dempsey. We picked them up in Arizona. They'll be staying with us for a while."

The Fee person gave Blanche a smile of surprising sweetness. "Hello, Blanche. It's always a treat when Miss Bolding brings home a new friend." The voice was low and smoky.

Blanche couldn't have been more surprised if they had been greeted at the station by a talking antimacassar, but she couldn't have been more delighted, either. The human species was infinitely more varied than she had ever imagined. This boded very well for her new life in California.

The garden outside the entrance to the station was full of plants as exotic as flora from another planet. Huge fan palms and wicked sword-like monstrosities that Alma called *agaves*. Eye-piercingly bright flowers spilled from pots and hanging baskets. More automobiles were parked on the street in front of the station than Blanche had ever seen gathered in one place, interspersed with the odd horse-drawn carriage advertising tours to places of interest in Southern California. The air was soft, warm, and smelled of vegetation, auto exhaust, engine oil, human beings, fried food, and something salty.

Fee escorted the little party of women to a limousine parked at the curb directly in front of the station. Blanche was aware that they were the center of attention, the crowds of travelers and passersby pointing at them and whispering, but she couldn't decide whether the greater object of their curiosity was Alma Bolding or their giant, unfathomable chauffeur.

Alma Bolding's house was located above Hollywood Boulevard in the brand new subdivision of Whitley Heights, which looked something like a Mediterranean village perched on the tiers of a wedding cake. Fee drove them up the winding access road to the very top tier of the hill and parked directly in front of the main entrance to Alma's Spanish-style mansion. There was no sidewalk, just a stairway that led directly from the street up the hill to the door. The view from the front of the house was a dizzying vista of hills and roofs and treetops. Blanche could look down into the patios and gardens of the houses below. Standing behind her, Mrs. Gilbert said, "That staircase down the hill leads right to Highland Avenue and into the Hollywood Hills." Her arm extended over Blanche's shoulder as she pointed into the distance. "That's Lee Mountain over to the left and those buildings way over there are downtown Los Angeles."

"And we're in Hollywood, now?"

"Yes, honey, we're in Hollywood."

The interior of Alma's mansion was as impressive as the outside. Every room in the house looked out over a terraced interior courtyard with a bubbling fountain, palms, and citrus trees. Mrs. Gilbert's two-room apartment, next to the kitchen, was on the first floor. The whole house was like something out of the *Arabian Nights*, Blanche thought, or the Alhambra, with arched doors and windows, and colorful tiled floors.

Mrs. Gilbert showed Blanche into her lovely bedroom with a canopied bed and French doors leading out to the balcony. The small room was as far from Alma's luxurious suite as it could be and still be located on the same floor. Blanche could hardly believe her luck. She knew she should just keep quiet and enjoy her good fortune while it lasted, but she said, "Mrs. Gilbert, why is Miss Bolding going to so much trouble for me? Does she want something and I'm too stupid to see it? I thought that Graham had my interests at heart, but I couldn't have been more wrong. What does she expect to gain by helping me? It's not like I can do anything for her in return."

Mrs. Gilbert didn't reply at first. She didn't even look at Blanche. She stared into space for so long that Blanche feared she had insulted or angered her by questioning Alma's intentions. "Mrs. G., I didn't mean to—"

Mrs. Gilbert spoke over her. "I never told you how I came to work for Miss Bolding, did I? I married young. He was a charmer, but he was cruel to me. He was a good provider, and my mother told me that no woman could expect better and I had to do my duty. I was cleaning houses in Los Angeles at the time, and Miss Bolding was one of my ladies. That was before she was as famous as she is now. Anyway, I came to work with a black eye one day, and Miss Bolding nagged at me until I told her what happened. I don't know why I did. Most rich white folks don't spare a lot of thought on their servants. But she was so insistent. I figured I'd put her off with some story, but when I opened my mouth, it all came spilling out.

"She blew her top, but not at me. She took me in, gave me a permanent job, and paid for my divorce. She also paid for me to take courses in home management and economics and made me her housekeeper. She was married to her second husband at the time."

As she listened to Mrs. Gilbert's story, Blanche couldn't help but think that even if she had married Graham it wouldn't have turned out well for her. "What happened to your husband, Mrs. Gilbert? Did you ever see him again?"

"Oh, as I said, he died." Mrs. Gilbert's tone was matter-of-fact. "He was found dead not long after I left him. The police never did find out what happened. Not that they tried very hard."

Blanche's eyes widened. "He was murdered?"

"It was no more than he deserved." Mrs. Gilbert shot her a sidelong glance and returned to the matter at hand. "Miss Bolding loves to help people, Blanche, and you are her latest project. Alma looks like she's in clover and everybody just does whatever she wants, but she's had a hard life and money and fame don't erase that. Her immoderate ways are not good for her health. She's in debt and scared of getting too old to make a living in the movies. One of her ex-husbands drained her bank account and another one liked to use her for a punching bag, too. I hope you'll stay, honey, and let her help you, because it'll help her, too, to have somebody else to think of. And don't worry about earning your keep. There will be plenty you can do to help out around here…"

She was interrupted by Alma's voice ringing out from the other end of the hall. "Delphinia, let's throw a party!"

Mrs. Gilbert laughed. "…starting now."

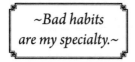

~*Bad habits
are my specialty.*~

Alma Bolding's parties often went on for days. Everyone in Hollywood wanted to be invited. It was a great social coup to even be in possession of one of her gilt-edged invitations. The parties always had a theme, perhaps a scavenger hunt, or a pool party where guests were instructed to come in their bathing suits. And they did. Bathing suits and bow ties with fedoras, or boas and feathered hats. Alma made a grand entrance, sometimes two or three, if the party went on for more than twenty-four hours. She loved to dance, and would drift in and out, usually with a pink lady or gin rickey in hand, always half in the bag and ready to partake in the usual shenanigans with all the bright young things.

Alma had the filthiest mouth Blanche had ever heard on a woman, and maybe just the filthiest mouth she had ever heard, period. It didn't take Blanche long to realize that Alma's drunken binges in Arizona were no fluke. Alma liked to drink. She also took pills to go to sleep at night and pills to wake up in the morning. Alma was only in her mid-thirties, but without the magical skills of her makeup artist and hairdresser, she looked a decade older. She was far too loud, far too frivolous, and something of a slut. There was an endless parade of young snugglepups who came to dinner and often spent the night, none of whom really cared much about Alma, Blanche thought, beyond what she could buy for them.

But Mrs. Gilbert was right about her good heart. Alma was sadly self-aware. Mrs. Gilbert, and as far as Blanche could see, the rest of Alma's staff were all quite protective of her. At first Blanche figured it was because they didn't want to lose their meal ticket, but the more Blanche got to know the maids and the gardeners and the handymen and the chauffeurs, the more she came to realize that they genuinely loved her. Alma had saved many of them in one way or another, just as she had saved Blanche.

Alma decided that Blanche had a future in the motion picture business, so she took the girl shopping for a new wardrobe in Los Angeles, hired a tutor for her, an acting coach, and an elocution coach. She told Blanche she was not going to have an ignoramus living in her house. "Besides, honey, beauty fades but brains never go out of style." Blanche only protested about the elocution lessons. What was the point of suffering to get rid of her Oklahoma twang when the movie audiences couldn't hear her anyway?

"It's not always going to be like that, little biscuit. Someday in the not-too-distant future somebody is going to figure out how to record voices as well as pictures, and then you'd better not sound like you just fell off the turnip truck. But that's not the main reason I want you to learn to talk like a lady. Now, if you want to last in this business, you'd better learn to take care of your own business. Learn to be an actress and not just a star. And if you're going to be an actress, nothing will teach you the craft like starting out with stage work. Now, my friend Damian Kirk is going to be directing his own adaptation of *A Midsummer Night's Dream* at the Morosco Theatre this winter, and I hear he has a small part that would be perfect for you, one of the fairy attendants to Titania. The part has one line and I'm betting that you can get the hay picked out of your teeth enough to deliver it by then."

Blanche was vaguely insulted at Alma's continual denigration of her Ozark Mountain roots, but tamped down her irritation enough to appreciate the opportunity she was being given.

Between shopping for carrots, dusting, and serving canapés to the glitterati at Alma's many parties, Blanche studied literature, economics, and elocution, swam in Alma's blue-tiled pool, exercised, and practiced her one line over and over until late at night, rounding her vowels and making sure the one-syllable words only contained one syllable. "Come now, sisters, let us *dance*," instead of "let us *day-unce*."

One morning out of the blue Alma said, "Let's go down to the hen coop and get you a bob." She didn't give Blanche time to think about it or ask her opinion. Blanche held on for dear life as Alma roared into town in the Bugatti and hustled her into a beauty parlor so exclusive that it didn't even have a name. Alma's hairdresser sat Blanche down in front of the mirror and ran her fingers through the waves of sable that cascaded down Blanche's back. "You have gorgeous hair, sweetie. Why, we could do almost anything with it, and what we want to do is make you look as timely as tomorrow's news. You are a modern girl, sweetie, so let's get modern!"

"I don't know about this, Miss Maloney. I like my hair. My mother always said it was one of my best features."

"Believe me, sweetie, you'll love what I'm going to do to it."

Miss Maloney threw what looked like a sheet over Blanche's shoulders and clipped away like a madwoman while Blanche gritted her teeth and held her breath. But when the snipping stopped, she barely recognized the girl in the mirror with the short, fluffy bob, just like Mabel Normand. She was a new woman, and she loved it.

Miss Maloney looked triumphant. "You are just the cat's meow, honey! And look at this. There must be five pounds of hair on the floor! Don't let that beautiful stuff go to waste. I'll pay you two dollars for it."

Alma wasn't having it. "You'll pay her five dollars, you pill. That hair will make a hell of a wig for a rich balding socialite."

On the day of the audition, Alma gave Blanche a thorough once-over. Hair, clothes, makeup. "You'll do, honey. Will you ever do. That face is going to open doors for you."

Blanche didn't know what to think about that comment.

Beauty is fleeting, that's what her mother had always said. Still... her looks had gotten her out of at least as many messes as they had gotten her into. In fact, it would be downright sacrilegious not to use the gifts God had given her while she still had the use of them. Wouldn't it?

"But I'll tell you what," Alma was saying, "you don't look like a Blanche Tucker anymore. No, indeed. If I had to guess, I'd say you were born in Algiers. No, maybe southern France. Nice, or Monaco. Yes, I like that. You need a French name. Blanche is French for 'white,' which is good, but I don't like the sound. It's flat. Not mellifluous enough. Maybe something Italian, but Spanish is lovely, too. Be mysterious. Keep 'em guessing, that's what I say."

"Oh, Miss Bolding, I love the idea." Blanche especially loved the idea of becoming an entirely new person.

"Now, for a stage name, we want something that says, 'I am a high-class beauty so don't mess with me.' I'll have to think about that." Alma whirled around. "Delphinia, call my publicist! I'm going to make a star!"

But she didn't get the chance, not on that day. At the audition, Damian Kirk took one look at Blanche, standing on the stage with her hat in her hand, and said he had no use for a chubby little girl trying to act like a fairy.

Alma was incensed. "Chubby! Why this girl looks like a string with feet. She looks like a piece of spaghetti that swallowed a peanut. She looks like a..." Alma's voice trailed off. "Where did that peanut come from, honey?"

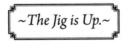

~ *The Jig is Up.* ~

Blanche burst into wet, sloppy sobs. Alma leapt up from her seat in the first row of the theatre and took the steps up to the stage two at a time. She steered the weeping girl off into the wings, sat her down on a stool and handed her a handkerchief.

"Dry your eyes, little puppy. Your nose will swell all up and your face'll get so puffy you'll look like a marshmallow with a hat on. Tell me, honey, and don't worry, Aunt Alma will take care of everything."

By the time Blanche finished her tale, Alma's face resembled a thundercloud. "That piece of shit. I figured you were free of him for good. I have half a mind to send Fee to pay him a little visit. At the very least I'm going to call my lawyer and sue the son of a bitch for child support."

"Oh, no, Miss Bolding, I don't want anything from him. I sure don't want him anywhere around my baby."

"I can understand that, honey. I'd just as soon never see any of my exes again, either. But he shouldn't be allowed to get away scot-free. He needs to pay for what he did."

"Oh, don't worry, Miss Bolding. I intend to make him pay. But right now I suppose I have to think about what I'm going to do."

"Don't worry about anything, honey. I know a great doctor who can take care of you and nobody will be the wiser. He's taken care of me a couple of times. I'll pay for everything and you'll be back on your feet in two weeks."

"Do you mean…? Oh, no, Miss, I couldn't do that."

Alma was taken aback by Blanche's reaction. It hadn't occurred to her that there might be another option besides abortion. This was Hollywood, and an abortion or two was the price of doing business for an actress in Hollywood.

"You mean you want to have the baby?"

"I have to, don't I?"

"No. Do you want to be saddled with a kid at your age, before you even get started in the world? Or would you rather end up married at fifteen to the first schmuck who'll have you, and then spend your days cranking out brats while your husband drinks away the rent money?"

Blanche was startled. A vision of her mother rose—a farm wife with a doting husband and a happy brood of ten living children. She didn't know which scenario horrified her more.

"Miss Bolding, I wouldn't blame you a bit if you threw me right out on the street. You've been so good to me, way more than I could ever have imagined and way more than I deserve. I know you've invested a lot of time and money trying to turn me into a mysterious European princess, but I can't do it now. I'll figure out a way to pay you back. I'll find a job and work till I can't any more, then when the baby comes I'll give it up for adoption."

Alma's eyebrows had practically disappeared under her hat brim. "What a concept! Well, honey, I'm not going to throw you out. Where'd you get such an idea? You're right, I've spent too damn much time and money to give up on you now. Didn't you ever read Shaw's play about Pygmalion? You're my creation and I love you, you pinhead. I was just surprised, that's all. I never knew anybody who didn't either get rid of the little intruder or find somebody to marry so she could keep the tot. If you were older, you could pretend to find the kid in an orphanage after you have him and adopt him yourself, but baby, you're just a baby yourself. You can stay on with me and keep studying, and when the kid is born, we'll find a good place for it. Then we can pick up with your career where we left off." She took a small silver flask out of her pocketbook and slugged down a stiff drink before emitting a huge sigh. "Well, I guess you won't be jumping into any crevasses for me for a while."

More tears started to Blanche's eyes. She had never known anyone like Alma Bolding—crude, rude, and immoral, but kinder and more generous than anyone had a right to be, and she never asked anything in return for her generosity. Blanche found herself reconsidering her entire worldview. It seemed that it was possible to be bad and good at the same time. There was something incredibly comforting in that thought.

> *~Thus followed long, languid days*
> *of paradise, and of reinvention, as*
> *Blanche learns to be someone else.~*

Time slipped past with one day hardly differing from another. Winter was no winter at all, just quiet, muzzy, soft days, each beginning with heavy gray clouds that burned away into misty sunshine. Between lessons, Alma encouraged Blanche to swim in the blue-tiled pool at the back of the property, tend the flower beds, and tried amidst much laughter to teach her to drive the sporty little Bugatti that she kept for tooling around Los Angeles. Christmas came and Mrs. Gilbert hung greenery and red bows over the antique fireplace and brought in pots full of beautiful scarlet flowers from Mexico that she called "poinsettias." The shops on Hollywood Boulevard and Sunset were decorated as well, doing their best to bring the holiday spirit to a distinctly un-Christmassy place. At least the orange and lemon trees put on their own decorations for the season. Blanche did not allow herself to dwell on how much she had loved her giant family's Christmases and how much she missed them. Instead she remained firmly in the moment, only occasionally wondering if they were still looking for her. She knew they were. She knew that her mother would be looking for her until the end of her days.

A few days before the New Year, Alma called Blanche onto the patio. She was sitting in a wicker chair, smoking a cigarette. Standing beside her was the small Asian man whom Blanche had seen only from a distance, working on the landscaping.

Alma gestured at the man with her cigarette holder. "Darling, this is Mr. Hashiyara. I've asked him if he would consider teaching you an exercise program that I think will serve you well in your future film career."

Blanche blinked at the man, who was scrutinizing her as though she were a piece of furniture he might consider buying. Blanche had only known one Asian person in her entire life—her aunt's Chinese housekeeper, Lu, last name unknown, a dumpling of a woman who ran every practical aspect of her aunt's household in Enid, Oklahoma. She doubted if she had spoken two words to Lu in her entire life. She parted her lips to say, "I already know how to garden," but Mr. Hashiyara spoke first.

"Come here, child."

Startled, Blanche looked at Alma, who nodded her encouragement. She took a couple of steps forward. Mr. Hashiyara didn't touch her, simply looked her up and down with his hands folded quietly over his stomach. Finally he said, "Miss Bolding says you have much athletic ability." His English was formal and stilted, but only lightly accented.

Another glance at Alma. Was that amusement that Blanche saw in her eyes? "Miss Bolding is kind."

"You ride horses, yes?"

"Yes. I grew up on a horse farm. I've ridden since I was a little thing."

"You like school? Do you like your teachers?"

Blanche's forehead wrinkled. "I liked my teachers. I like to learn new things, to do new things. I like the tutors Miss Bolding hired for me. But I didn't like going to school."

"Why not?"

"It was boring. What's this all about, Miss Bolding?"

"Darling, Mr. Hashiyara is the possessor of a great and hidden knowledge that has nothing to do with trimming hedges. He has taught me many ways to move my body, knowledge that I have used to keep from breaking something important, like my leg, while leaping over ice floes and falling off of mountains during filming. And I am as athletic as a sofa pillow, so just imagine what he could do for you…" Her gaze switched from Blanche to the gardener. "If he agrees to take you on, that is."

Hashiyara took a deep breath and let it out in a sigh. "Would you like to learn?"

Blanche was still in the dark about what Alma intended to have this strange man teach her, but she felt that tingle of fear mixed with excitement that she had become so familiar with since she ran away from home. "I would like to learn," she said.

Hashiyara stepped back, clearing her path. "Then run."

It was all so bizarre that she didn't think twice. She took off down the garden path and ran flat out around the meandering back garden, around the fountain, up the steep berm and down. The terrace was hardly big enough for her to break a sweat, and when she skidded to a stop on the patio, her breathing had not quickened.

Hashiyara turned to Alma. "I will be here tomorrow afternoon. We will try for one week." Without another word to Blanche, he picked up the hoe he had leaned against the pillar and left.

"Miss Bolding…"

"Mr. Hashiyara is a master practitioner of judo, mysterious physical and mental arts from the Orient, darling. By the time he's finished with you, you'll be able to roll out of a speeding motorcar over a cliff and into a raging flood and not get hurt."

"But what about the baby?" Blanche didn't like to remind Alma of her condition, for fear the offer of judo lessons would be rescinded, but better lose them now before she found out whether she loved them or not.

"Oh, he knows. He won't have you do anything that will harm you or your little bundle. In fact, this may make things easier for you when the time comes." She stood up. "It's time for my rest, now, so run and see if Mrs. Gilbert needs you for anything. Remember that Madame Adele will be here in a couple of hours for your French lessons. Oh, and find something loose and comfortable to wear when Mr. Hashiyara comes tomorrow. Ask Mrs. Gilbert to find you some trousers."

———

Blanche loved her trousers. They were feminine and flowing, and nothing like the hand-me-down overalls and outgrown work pants of her brothers' that she had occasionally worn. Her eyes filled with tears of joy at the freedom she felt when she first put them on. She felt like a powerful female and not just a make-believe male. She loved her martial arts lessons, too, and Mr. Hashiyara for teaching her. He was mindful of her condition but he didn't treat her like tissue paper. The deceptively easy movements he had her do over and over made her muscles quiver and ache, but she persevered. She became strong. Her limbs seemed to lengthen as she added muscle and lost her baby fat. Her cheeks hollowed as her belly grew. When she finally became too big to do the intricate shadow kicks, twirls, and punches, Mr. Hashiyara taught her long, slow, gently flowing moves like a dance, and then had her sit quietly for long periods of time and concentrate on controlling her breathing.

This was exactly what she was doing when she felt her first contraction. She said nothing, but her eyes flew open, as well as her mouth, and Mr. Hashiyara, sitting opposite her on the floor, calmly stood and helped her to her feet.

"Breathe like I taught you. Stand quiet and still. I will tell Mrs. Gilbert. Breathe like I taught you, and all will be well."

———

Giving birth was no more a mystery to Blanche than sex had been, but that didn't mean she wasn't afraid. Her sisters had told her that birthing was horribly painful, but that it was all worth it when you held the baby in your arms for the first time. She only had the pain to look forward to. And she was very young, barely sixteen now, and had heard that the first delivery was especially hard for young mothers.

The doctor and Mrs. Gilbert sat with Blanche in her room as she labored. The French doors to the balcony were flung open to take advantage of the beautiful spring day, and the air was perfumed by pots of flowers hanging off the railing. Between contractions they talked of ordinary things, and Alma buzzed in and out, seemingly more excited than anyone else. Jack Dempsey shared the bed with Blanche until it was time to push, and then he was unceremoniously dumped in the hall.

All in all, the whole experience wasn't any fun, but it wasn't nearly as awful as Blanche feared. And when it was all over, she lay back on her pillows and stared down at the fuzzy-headed little creature in her arms, trying not to care about him.

Mrs. Gilbert, sitting in a chair beside the bed, watched her watching the baby, and said nothing. But Blanche could tell by her expression what was on her mind.

"I can't do it," Blanche said.

Mrs. Gilbert was not surprised. "Are you thinking of keeping him?"

Blanche shook her head. "No, I can't keep him. But I can't give him to strangers. I can't…never see him again."

"You can't have it both ways, honey."

But Blanche had had months to think about this day and formulate a plan. "I think I know a way, Mrs. Gilbert."

**1926
Santa Monica, California**

Oliver receives a call that may lead
him to a Vital Clue.

"So Graham Peyton is dead! I wondered what happened to him."

Ruhl had given Oliver the names of Dix's major brothels in the Los Angeles area. Verbally, of course. No written list existed or was ever going to. There were so many that in order to know where to start, Oliver basically threw a rock and hit one, which happened to be the one closest to his apartment in Santa Monica. The establishment was located in a large house in a tree-lined residential area, on an isolated corner in a nice neighborhood. Oliver wondered if the neighbors had any idea what went on inside. Maybe not. The parking area was located discreetly behind the house. The first floor had been converted into an all-night bakery selling muffins and cakes. It was the most popular bakery in town.

The woman who ran the bawdy house looked more like a schoolmarm than a madam. Tall and bony, with a no-nonsense expression, she ran a tight ship. She had shown Oliver into a gaudy parlor located behind the bakery and served him tea and cakes before getting down to business.

"Mr. Ruhl told me to cooperate, though I don't know what I can tell you." The madam said. She shook her head. "I liked Peyton. He was good-natured and didn't abuse the girls. He was a great supplier of whatever you needed—blow, hooch, mary jane. He liked them young and I could always count on him to bring me fresh, barely used girls. He was Dix's fair-haired boy, too, so if he wanted an occasional tickle, I wouldn't charge him and then he'd put in a good word for me with the boss." A wistful expression briefly crossed her face. "I kind of miss him. I don't know how he died, though, or when. He was just here one day and gone the next."

Oliver tried a little cake with white icing. It was delicious. "What did the girls he recruited think of him?" His question was muffled by a mouthful of pastry.

"Oh, usually they were…reluctant when he'd first bring them in. They'd settle down eventually. I try to keep my girls happy and healthy as possible. It's just good for business. I told him he shouldn't lead them on, tell them he loved them before he recruited them, that he'd get himself in trouble one day. Sued by some girl's relatives for breach of promise or something like that."

"So did he? Get himself in trouble?"

"Not that I know of. He'd always laugh it off. Said he was careful about which girls he chose. Of course, this is not Dix's only pleasure house, so who knows what kind of trouble Peyton got into somewhere else?"

"Can I talk to some of your girls? I'd like to hear what they have to say about him."

"You can ask all you want, none of them are going to know anything. That was five years ago. I don't have any girls working here now who were here that long ago."

"Really? So the whore business has that big a turn-over?"

The woman was pretty sure she had just been insulted. She set her teacup down hard enough to rattle the saucer. "This is a top-of-the-line establishment. If you want a crib joint, you'll have to go elsewhere."

So Oliver did. He visited four separate houses in Santa Monica, Bel Air, and Hollywood that day, and though they were all very different places, with working girls of all possible stripes, he got more or less the same story in all of them. He did manage to find a few girls (not so girlish anymore) who had been "recruited" by Peyton. Many told a common tale—seduced and abandoned, no money, nowhere to go, with little option but to carry on.

Some of the soiled doves seemed content enough with their lifestyle. Some were downright jolly. "I could never make this much money doing anything else," a perky redhead told him. "It beats the hell out of being a shopgirl. Why, I'll be able to buy my own house in a year."

But not all of Dix's employees were so happy. Oliver couldn't help but ask one tired-looking woman, "How do you stand it?"

"Cocaine helps," she said matter-of-factly.

———

Oliver had just arrived home, tired and discouraged, mostly about the sorry state of human nature, and was hanging up his hat when the telephone rang, two short rings and one long. It was for him. He briefly considered not picking up. He had spent a long day trudging around Hollywood and Los Angeles and was desperate for a drink and a bath.

He sighed and picked up the earpiece. "Oliver," he said.

His tone was sharper than he intended, for there was a moment of tentative silence on the other end before a woman said, "Is this the private dick who talked to Maurice at Philippe today?"

Oliver sat down at the table and loosened his tie. "Yes, it is. Ted Oliver, here. Are you the woman who knew Graham Peyton?"

"What's this about?" she said, in lieu of an answer. "Maurice says that Graham is dead?"

"A skeleton with Peyton's wallet on it was discovered buried at the beach a few days ago, after the storm. Been there a long time. I'm trying to reconstruct the last few days of his life. Maurice told me that the last time he saw Peyton he was having a meal with you, Miss…" She didn't take the hint, so Oliver continued. "…and there was an incident involving another woman. Do you remember that?"

"What if I do?"

"As far as I have been able to discover, that's the last time anyone saw Peyton alive. Maurice said you two left together afterwards, so I was hoping maybe you could fill me in a bit on what he did for the rest of that day, or however much longer you know about."

The voice on the other end took on a lighter tone. "I always wondered what happened to the bastard. I didn't kill him, if that's what you're wondering about."

"I never thought you did, Miss…"

"You can call me Miranda."

"…Miranda. I don't want to talk over the telephone. Would you be willing to meet me for a chat? Tell me about the incident at the restaurant and anything else you can help me out with. I'd be happy to pay you for your time."

"Sure. I'd be glad to. For dinner and a hundred bucks."

> ~*"A hundred bucks?*
> *You slay me, Lady!"*~

Miranda chuckled at Oliver's response. "I promise it'll be worth it."

"All I want is information, Miranda, nothing else."

"And all I want is dinner and a hundred bucks. And I promise it'll be worth it."

It was no skin off his nose. K.D. Dix was paying for it. But he said, "It better be. Where are you? Can you meet me tonight in Santa Monica?"

"Yeah, I can do that."

"All right. Seven o'clock at Bay City Italian on the corner of Broadway and Lincoln. How will I know you?"

"I'll be the blonde with the flower in her hair."

Oliver hung the earpiece back on the hook and sat back. A hundred dollars. He'd almost bet the same amount that her information would turn out to be worthless.

**1921
Tempe, Arizona**

Goodbye, sweet Billy Ray.
Have a wonderful life.

Blanche didn't know what had awakened her—the scent of blossoms, the touch of dawn on her eyelids, the rustle and mewl coming from the basket on the table next to her bed. She stood up and leaned over the baby, squinting in the dim light at his perfect face. His eyes were closed still. He was probably dreaming, of what, she couldn't imagine. He had not had time in his fourteen days of life to have had any adventures. Perhaps he was dreaming of heaven, where he had been waiting to be born. Or maybe of the life he lived before starting out on this one. His little mouth pursed and his forehead wrinkled. He looks worried, Blanche thought. Maybe he knew more than he was letting on.

Blanche placed a tender hand on his gently rising and falling belly, and he sighed. *Are you worried, little man? If you are, it's no wonder.*

The morning light was gray and filled with amorphous shapes. The casement window above the bed was open, letting in the sweet, barely detectable aroma of oleander blossoms adrift on the air from somewhere. She sat down on the bed. It was still too murky to see clearly, but she knew all there was to know about the long, narrow bedroom that had once been the back veranda of her Aunt Elizabeth's house in Tempe, Arizona.

The room had been built onto the back of the main house and had its own entrance, giving guests a modicum of privacy. Several tall windows provided a view onto Elizabeth's deep, tree-covered backyard. The flagstone floor was softened by several rugs. The large double bed upon which Blanche sat had been pushed up against the end wall, and a dining table situated against the back wall of the house had been repurposed as a desk.

The world had changed since Blanche was last here, five years earlier—before Graham, before California. Before Mrs. Gilbert, asleep on the cot in the corner, or the baby asleep in his basket. She had been a little girl then, and sick with a lung infection. She was sixteen now, and after all that had happened since she last slept in this room, she supposed she had to think of herself as a woman, whether she felt like one or not.

She had never expected to be here again, at her aunt's house in Arizona. Not now, perhaps ever. If she hadn't been such a fool she wouldn't be here now. But even if she wanted to, there was nothing she could do to take it back, to become the person she had been before.

With Mrs. Gilbert in tow, Blanche had shown up unannounced at her Aunt Elizabeth Kemp's door with the boy in her arms. Elizabeth and her husband, Webster, were rich, at least in Blanche's estimation. They were both lawyers and had their own busy firm, Kemp and Kemp, in downtown Tempe.

Blanche asked Elizabeth to wire Mary Lucas, Blanche's second-oldest sister, who lived with her husband, Kurt, on a farm within walking distance of her parents. Mary was a natural mother, and Blanche could think of no one in the world who would give her little boy a better home. Mary and Kurt loved children and were always collecting odd strays to add to their family. They had enthusiastically agreed to take on one more, and Elizabeth Kemp, Esq., had agreed to take care of the legalities. The day after they received Blanche's wire, Mary and her husband, along with Blanche and Mary's parents, had boarded the train in Muskogee, Oklahoma, and were at this very minute on their way to Tempe, Arizona.

Elizabeth had offered to make arrangements to telephone Oklahoma, and even to pay for the call, so that Blanche could speak to her mother for the first time in nearly a year. Blanche had refused. Her parents finally knew she was alive and well, and that was enough for now.

In the gloom she clutched her two hands together and closed her eyes. There was a verse in the bible…her mother would remember…Sarah or Hannah or someone like that had a baby, and she rejoiced, for now her words gave her power over others. Could that be true? Now that Blanche was a mother, did her words have power? If only she had something that had belonged to him, to Graham. A thing of his that she had stolen. She would press it to her heart.

> ~ *"Curse you," she murmured.*
> *"Curse you. Curse you. I hope you die."* ~

Eventually the baby's thin cry brought her back to the present. She cradled him in the crook of her arm and slid her feet into a pair of crocheted slippers before tiptoeing past Mrs. Gilbert, still asleep on her corner cot in Elizabeth's converted-porch guest bedroom. She carried the boy into the kitchen to warm a bottle in a pan of water on the gas stove. She wished she had a name for him. It didn't seem right to come into the world without your mother giving you a Christian name or your father a last name. But she figured that naming him wasn't her place anymore. She wouldn't be his mother for much longer.

When Blanche opened the screen door into the kitchen, Elizabeth's housekeeper, Felicia, turned to look at her and wiped her hands on her apron tail.

"Sit down, honey," Felicia said. "I'll fix you up some pancakes." Her smile was bright. Perhaps a little strained. "Mrs. Elizabeth got a delivery from Western Union first thing this morning. The adoption papers have come. Your sister and your parents should arrive from Oklahoma very soon."

Blanche said, "Ah." She sat down at the kitchen table with the boy in her lap. "He's going to want a bottle right quick. You want to warm one up for him?"

Felicia set a tall stack of pancakes on the table in front of Blanche and held out her arms. Blanche handed the bundle to her.

"Poor little thing," Felicia murmured, just loud enough for Blanche to hear.

"I'm sorry if you think I'm doing wrong, Felicia," Blanche said as she reached for the syrup. "But I'm not going to change my mind."

~Later That Same Day...~

Blanche, Elizabeth, and Mrs. Gilbert arranged themselves around the dining table in the parlor, Blanche next to Aunt Elizabeth, the adoption papers arrayed before her on the table-top. Elizabeth kept scanning Blanche's face. Blanche had asked to hold the boy again, and she knew that Elizabeth would not relax until the adoption papers were signed and filed at the county courthouse. Blanche looked down at the baby in her lap, sleeping the sleep of the innocent and unaware of the chaos his very existence had caused. Was causing still.

Blanche's mother swore that there was no love like a mother's love for her child. Did Blanche love this little fellow? He had been the source of so much trouble for her. She didn't blame him for it, of course. She gazed at him, trying to see herself, or his father, in his face. He had dark hair, like hers. Otherwise, he looked like every other newborn baby. Cute, delicate. A blank. She felt a curiosity about him. Who is he? Who will he turn out to be? An honest, straightforward man like her father, or a huckster and a liar, like Graham? Are people born one way or the other, or do their parents raise them up to be however they end up being? Her parents were paragons, that's what she had always believed. And look how she had turned out.

No, this was best by far. He should be brought up by people who know how to be parents. He should have that chance.

She looked at Aunt Elizabeth. "Can you show me where to sign?"

"Are you sure this is what you want to do?" There was no judgment in Elizabeth's voice. "Once you sign, there's no going back. This child will belong to your sister and you won't have any say about him."

Blanche shrugged. "I'm sure Mary and Kurt will let me see him whenever I want." She picked up the fountain pen with her free hand, anxious to get this over with. Elizabeth nodded and slid the papers toward her.

"Sign here."

The scratching of pen on paper filled the silence.

Elizabeth's turned over a page. "And here."

When Blanche put down the pen, Elizabeth drew a breath. It was hard to tell what she was thinking. Her dark eyes didn't reveal anything. Well, Blanche thought, maybe a touch of pity. Blanche lifted the baby from her lap and handed him to her aunt.

I don't feel happy, but why am I not sad? Blanche wondered. Why do I feel nothing at all?

Mrs. Gilbert reached across the table and gave Blanche's hand a comforting squeeze. She said to Elizabeth, "Do you know what they mean to call him?"

"They were thinking William Raymond, at least that's what Mary wired, after our Uncle Raymond. Billy Ray Lucas. She liked the way it sounds."

"That's nice," Blanche said, though she didn't think it was nice at all.

Elizabeth leaned forward and clasped her hands on the tabletop. "Mary and Kurt and your folks will be here tomorrow to fetch you and the baby back to Oklahoma, Blanche. Your mama and daddy are heartbroken with missing you. Mary says it just isn't the same at home without you. Your sisters don't know what to do with themselves. They all miss you so much. They are desperate to see you."

"I can't, Aunt Elizabeth. I couldn't stand to face Mama. I don't think I'd even be able to look at Daddy."

Both Elizabeth and Mrs. Gilbert hastened to assure her that her parents wouldn't judge her. No one would judge her. The whole extended family, her parents, her grandparents, her nine siblings and their spouses and children, all of them so badly wanted her to come home.

Blanche knew a kind lie when she heard one. A wave of exhaustion came over her. All she wanted now was for Mary and Kurt to arrive, take their new son, and leave her alone. Let her go to sleep. Let it be over.

The Lucases would arrive late in the afternoon on Monday to sign the adoption papers and take charge of Billy Ray. Elizabeth would file the papers at the Maricopa County courthouse in Phoenix on Tuesday, and then Blanche's parents and the three Lucases would take the train back to Oklahoma on Wednesday afternoon.

Blanche knew that if she were still here when they arrived, Mary and their parents would keep trying to talk Blanche into coming home with them until the moment they mounted the steps to the train going back to Oklahoma. Maybe even try to force her. They would not hesitate to strong-arm her if they could. But Blanche didn't believe for a minute that anyone really wanted her to come home after what she had done.

> *~Unwilling to bear the grief and disappointment*
> *she expects to see in her mother's eyes,*
> *Blanche slips out at dawn.~*

As tired as she was, Blanche was unable to sleep at all that night. She rose before dawn and packed her little carpetbag before waking Mrs. Gilbert. She dressed the sleeping baby in a gown that she had bought for him in California so that he would look his best for his new parents, and the two women crept into the house, planning to leave the baby in the basinet in the parlor along with a note to Aunt Elizabeth.

Elizabeth was sitting in an armchair beside the front door, dressed in her hat and coat, waiting for them.

Blanche stopped in her tracks and for a long moment the women gazed at one another across the dim parlor. "How did you know?" Blanche said.

"The train to Los Angeles leaves at 5:30."

"Don't try to talk me out of leaving. Mrs. Gilbert and me have discussed it and she agrees with me."

Elizabeth leveled a glance at the small Negro woman who was standing behind Blanche with her hands folded quietly before her. Mrs. Gilbert's answering gaze indicated that she didn't agree with Blanche all that much.

Elizabeth said, "You've made your feelings clear, Blanche. It's your decision. Your mother is going to be unhappy, though, when they finally get here and you're gone."

Blanche laughed. "I know it."

Mrs. Gilbert said, "Are you sure you don't want to bring little Billy Ray along to the station and say goodbye, honey?"

"No, he's sleeping so nice. I'll just leave the basket here on the table. Felicia is just in the next room. If he cries, she will take care of him."

She tried not to glance back at the basket when they left the house.

———

Mrs. Gilbert left Blanche and Elizabeth on the station platform while she took the luggage to the baggage car. Blanche could feel her aunt's eyes on her as they waited. She knew Elizabeth was expecting some show of emotion. Tears, perhaps, at losing her little boy. But Blanche only felt a dull nothingness. A void. A weight in her chest where her heart ought to be.

Elizabeth's lawyerly senses were well attuned to her niece's emotional state. "You still have time to change your mind about seeing your folks," she said. "Stay at least until they get here. You don't have to go back to Oklahoma, but you can at least set your mama and daddy's hearts to ease."

"No. How many ways can I say it? They'll try to make me go back there and I won't go back. Not now. Not ever. I couldn't stand it. You tell them, Aunt Elizabeth. You tell them that I'm fine and that I'm sorry as I can be for what I put them through. Tell them that I love them. You'll know what to say. Tell Mama not to worry about me. Mrs. Gilbert takes good care of me. I have a respectable job lined up and I'll write when I get settled."

Elizabeth nodded, satisfied that she had tried her best. Besides, she really didn't blame Blanche that much. She had lived through her own existential crisis a few years earlier. Things generally worked out for the best. Or at least they worked out. "Where are you going now?"

"Just tell them I'm going to California. I have lots of friends there. I won't tell you exactly where. If you don't know, you can't tell Daddy. He'll come after me, for sure."

"I don't look forward to facing your mother. She'll wonder

why I didn't hogtie you and throw you in the closet until she got here."

"I know. I'm sorry about that. Tell her that I packed up and sneaked out in the middle of the night and you didn't know about it until it was too late. Or that I knocked you on the head and made my escape."

"Don't worry, that's exactly what I plan to do. If she thought I let you go without a fight, your mother would kill me dead. Now, if you have any more trouble, or if you need anything, you be sure and contact me. You've already discovered that the world is a rough place for young girls on their own."

Yes, Blanche had discovered that, all right. She didn't tell her aunt that she had also discovered that the world could be as exciting as it was ugly.

She hugged Elizabeth, mounted the steps, and settled herself into a seat next to Mrs. Gilbert. A young woman not much older than Blanche occupied the seat opposite them. A Westerner for sure, Blanche thought. A Southerner would not sit in the same car as Mrs. Gilbert. The train jerked to life and Blanche pressed her nose to the window as it slowly made the long turn out of Tempe and headed toward California. She would have a half-day head start on her family. She hoped that was enough.

I'm coming, Graham, you rat. The thought repeated itself over and over, picking up rhythm as the train picked up speed. *I'm coming. I'm coming. I'm coming.*

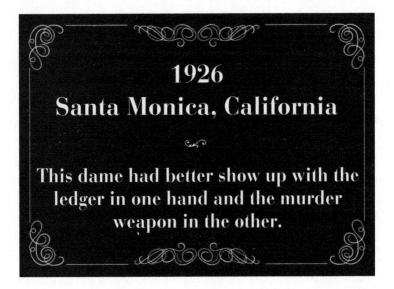

1926
Santa Monica, California

This dame had better show up with the ledger in one hand and the murder weapon in the other.

The woman with the rose in her hair was surprisingly attractive—blond, well-coifed and well-dressed, in a blowsy sort of way. She was rough around the edges, though. Oliver put her demeanor down to her disappointing lifestyle. She dug into Tony's lasagna like she hadn't eaten in a week.

"Graham found me in Indio," she said between shovelfuls. "I was a real appleknocker. I used to hang out at the flickers all day when I could. Graham sat down beside me in the theatre one Saturday while I was watching *The Kid* for maybe the tenth time. He offered to buy me an ice cream soda after the flick. He said he had been on a business trip to New York and was going home to L.A. on the train when he decided to take a break from travel and spotted me in the theater. Told me he was a casting director for the movies and I was just the type of girl he wanted for a new picture that Charlie Chaplin was producing. Charlie was looking for a fresh face to cast opposite him, and he'd introduce me. I ate it up. I met him at the train station that very evening and went with him to Los Angeles. He was a perfect gentleman for a while. He told me he was falling for me."

She pushed her plate away and lit a gasper before continuing. "He got me a room at what I thought was a nice boardinghouse for women, but it turned out to be something else. You know the interesting thing? I didn't even care. I loved the clothes and the parties and the high life. I met all kinds of rich people. Millionaires. And I screwed all kinds of rich people, too." She sighed. "He really did know Charlie Chaplin."

Oliver listened to her tale with a combination of pity and impatience. He had heard it all before, and as sympathetic to sob stories as he was, he really wanted to get down to business. "So what happened at Philippe," he prompted, "when the brunette raised a stink?"

Miranda took a final drag on her cigarette before stubbing it out on her plate. "Oh, that. Well, here's where it gets good. I hadn't been in town very long. That was when I still thought I was going to be in the flicks. Man, Graham was still treating me like a queen. We were in the middle of this elegant feed when this girl with great clothes and a rube accent barged in and raised holy hell. She said that Graham had abandoned her out in the wilderness and left her in the family way to boot. She told him that she was going to make him pay for what he did, and it scared me. He was cool as a cucumber, though. Told Maurice to toss her out, which he did. Then Graham fed me a tale about how in his line of work he met all kinds of cuckoo-birds and this quiff was just looking for some fall guy to support her and her little accident. He swore up and down that the kid wasn't his and he didn't even recognize the slut."

"And you believed him?"

"Sure I did. Willful blindness, they call it. 'Course, it did seem odd that he said he had never seen her before, but he knew where she was from. He called her his 'Tennessee rose' or 'Arkansas rose' or something like that. I remember it like yesterday."

Oliver scribbled the nickname on a napkin. "Where did you go after you left the restaurant?"

Her eyes narrowed. "We went up to my room and had a roll in the hay to celebrate our recent engagement. Then he buttoned up his pants and left and I never saw him again."

Oliver folded his arms. "Well, Miranda, that's an interesting story. So now I know the screamer's name was Tennessee Rose or Arkansas Rose or something like that. That's more than I knew before, but it's hardly worth a hundred smackers."

"Oh, that's not the fun part, sweetie. I had never seen the little bitch before that day, but I remember her face like I have a photograph in my head. I haven't seen her again…not in the flesh, anyway."

"What do you mean?"

"I mean that a couple of years later I saw her up on the screen at Grauman's Egyptian."

Miranda was dragging out whatever her shocking revelation was and enjoying it far too much. Oliver was tempted to grab her by the shoulders and give her a good shake. "You're saying that this Rose person became a movie actress. So don't keep me in suspense."

"Not just a movie actress. I nearly fell out of my seat when I recognized her. I swear to God the brat who threatened to straighten out Graham Peyton grew up to be…

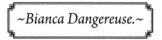

~*Bianca Dangereuse.*~

"You're telling me that the girl who accused Graham Peyton of putting a bun in her oven was Bianca Dangereuse?" Oliver tried and failed to keep the sarcasm out of his voice.

"That's right, sweetie."

"Considering that Bianca Dangereuse is not a real person, I find that less than persuasive."

"Not the character, stupid. I mean the actress who plays Bianca Dangereuse in all them movies. I swear she's the same bird."

"The actress Bianca LaBelle? You think that the knocked-up screamer is Bianca LaBelle? Was this girl French?"

"She sounded to me like she was a yokel from Yokelville, but just because the rags say that Bianca LaBelle is a French princess that don't make it true."

———

Oliver slipped Tony two bits to let him use the telephone with the private line in his office. He would have gone back to his apartment to make the call to Ruhl, but his was a party line, and besides, he thought that if he was going to follow Miranda's sketchy lead, he was going to need some quick help from someone with pull. Ruhl himself answered the telephone, which impressed Oliver. Usually these big muckety-mucks had several layers of lackeys between themselves and the unwashed masses. If Ruhl had given the detective his private number, he must place more importance than Oliver had realized on the search for Peyton's murderer, or the whereabouts of the ledger…or whatever he was really looking for. Oliver had more than a sneaking suspicion that he had not been told the whole story.

Oliver brought his client up to speed on the progress of his investigation. When he related Miranda's tale, Ruhl scoffed. "I would take the word of a two-bit whore with a great deal of skepticism, Mr. Oliver. I seriously doubt if one of the biggest stars in Hollywood had anything to do with Peyton's death. Besides, Bianca LaBelle would have been little more than a child when Peyton disappeared. Still, you say that this woman was fairly certain of the girl's identity?"

"She says she's positive. Of course, people are always saying they've seen John Gilbert at the five and dime or Gloria Swanson walking down the street in Long Beach. It'll probably turn out to be nothing, but we have little enough to go on as it is. Unless you want me to back off, I might be able to turn up a lead if you can get me in to talk to Miss LaBelle for a few minutes."

There was a long silence on the other end of the line as Ruhl considered this. Finally he said, "I have some contacts. I'll get back to you tomorrow. Until then, carry on."

"I intend to, Mr. Ruhl."

1921
Hollywood, California

After leaving her baby to the loving care of
her sister, Blanche returns to Hollywood
to resume her transformation.

Blanche plunged back into her lessons with a vengeance, anything to keep her mind off of the memory of the sleeping baby in the basket on her aunt's table in Arizona. The martial arts sessions with Mr. Hashiyara were particularly therapeutic. Now that she didn't have to worry about pregnancy, she took great pleasure in the strenuous workouts. Especially when he let her break things.

She still helped Mrs. Gilbert around the house. She found that if she wasn't commanded to do it, she enjoyed cooking and really enjoyed the praise Mrs. Gilbert heaped upon her culinary talents. She had hated it when her mother had made her learn kitchen skills, but she had to admit that they had come in very handy.

A couple of times a week, Blanche and Mrs. Gilbert took the

trolley or let Fee chauffeur them into Hollywood to shop for groceries, a nice break for both of them and a chance to spend some
time together. Blanche loved strolling up and down Hollywood
Boulevard, enjoying the sights and people-watching. Sometimes,
she and Mrs. Gilbert caught a movie in one of the grand theaters
in town, and occasionally Fee accompanied them. Blanche had
developed a great fondness for Fee, even if she had not quite
made a decision about the gentle giant's gender affiliation. But
it didn't seem to matter. Fee was clever, competent, funny, and
self-contained. Blanche wondered if Fee was lonely, how he/she
navigated through life, but she was too shy to ask.

The three of them had just come out of the Iris Theater and
were walking down Hollywood Boulevard toward the limousine
when they passed a restaurant called Philippe, and Blanche turned
her head to admire the hat on a woman passing by. If Fee hadn't
been anxious to see Norma Talmadge's new picture at the Iris, if it
hadn't been for whatever business brought the passing woman to
town that evening, if it hadn't been for the woman's good taste in
hats, Blanche would not have turned her head and seen Graham
Peyton through the front window of Phillipe, having dinner with
a young woman, and the course of her life might have turned out
much differently.

But she did see Graham Peyton, and all the hatred and humiliation and anger that she thought she had overcome rose up in
her like a tidal wave.

Mrs. Gilbert and Fee were talking about something and didn't
notice the hesitation in Blanche's step. She was surprised that
they were unaware of the sudden change in her mood, since the
heat of her fury should have scorched the air around them, but
she was grateful. Her friends were none the wiser as she caught
up in two steps and walked with them back to the auto.

Once they had returned to Alma's mansion, she said nothing about her discovery. Graham Peyton was back in town. Mr.
Hashiyara was the only person who had an inkling that something

was up, but he didn't press her about her newfound intensity. She made a point of volunteering to go down the hill into Hollywood at every opportunity—to pick up something for the house or run an errand for Alma or Mrs. Gilbert. She haunted the street around Philippe, not near enough to be conspicuous, but close enough to see the diners come and go. It was several weeks before she caught sight of Graham again. It was about one in the afternoon. He was squiring a different young woman up the steps into the restaurant, a blonde.

Blanche came back the next day, and saw the two of them crossing the street toward the restaurant at about the same time. After they had gone inside, Blanche retraced their path to the building they had come out of and discovered a plaque on the wall next to a stairwell located between two shops: "Peyton Talent Agency. Top of Stairs."

This was the place. This stretch of Hollywood Boulevard. This was where Graham Peyton had his lair.

One fine day in May, Alma decided to ask a couple of friends to supper, and particularly invited Blanche to join the party. This was unusual, since most of the people Alma had over for a quiet meal were either business associates or lovers. It crossed Blanche's mind that Alma intended to set her up with a date, but she banished the thought quickly. Not quickly enough.

Alma's smile was ironic. "Don't worry, honey, I'm not trying to marry you off or pimp you out. These friends of mine are thinking of producing a serial about a daring adventuress, and I told them they should meet you. They're coming for drinks at around five. We'll talk a little business before supper. Be sure to put on some nice rags, puppy."

Blanche didn't know how to feel. Today was the day that she intended to beard the lion in his den. The plan was laid, she had screwed her courage to the sticking point, and she didn't want to postpone the confrontation. Yet…this meeting with movie producers could be her big break.

"Would you like to go downtown with me to pick up the groceries for dinner?" Mrs. Gilbert interrupted her rumination, and she started. Maybe she should take advantage of opportunity when it arose.

"Oh, yes, ma'am, absolutely!"

> ~*After months of Misadventure,*
> *Blanche finally plots her revenge.*~

For her trip to town, Blanche picked out a linen, box-pleated skirt, a cashmere sweater with a fur collar, strappy Louis heels and silk stockings, a cunning little bag, and a hat with a russet pheasant feather adorning one side. She picked out a brooch and a bracelet, and made up her face carefully. When she finished, she hardly recognized the stunning woman in the mirror. Good. If her style and beauty made him rue the day he let her go, then all the better.

Mrs. Gilbert's eyes widened when Blanche came into the kitchen. "You're awfully dressed up for picking out lamb chops."

"Well, Miss Bolding wants me to look nice this evening so I thought I'd practice my makeup lessons, and I guess I just kept going. It feels good to dress up once in a while."

"Well, just try not to get meat juice on your nice jacket."

Fee drove them downtown to the shops, and as soon as they got out of the auto, Blanche said, "Let's split up. We'll be done sooner that way. The butcher is just around the corner. I'll pick out the chops for tonight if you'll get the vegetables."

Blanche was so fidgety that Mrs. Gilbert gave her a sidelong look. "What's going on, honey?"

Blanche had had time to craft an excuse on the trip down the hill. "I thought that if we get done in time I might have time to catch a flick before this evening. I saw that *The Four Horsemen of the Apocalypse* is showing just for this week and I've been dying to see it. I'm already all dressed up, so I don't have to worry about getting ready for Miss Bolding's dinner tonight."

Blanche's delivery was so convincing that Mrs. Gilbert readily bought her lie. Young people were full of energy and restless for adventure, after all. "All right. Pick out nice fat chops and make sure that Guilio understands that they have to be delivered to the house by four o'clock at the latest. I expect it will take me a lot longer than it will you. If you decide to go to the pictures, come on back here first and let Fee know when you'll be home. Don't be late, now, even if you have to leave the picture early."

"I swear," Blanche said. "I'd never disappoint Miss Bolding."

Blanche hit the butcher's shop at a run, made her order, and flew down the street and around the corner just in time to see Graham Peyton and his latest paramour cross the street and go into Philippe, arm in arm. She stood outside Philippe on the sidewalk, shifting impatiently from one foot to the other, unsure of what to do now. Time was of the essence, and she couldn't be sure how long she'd have to wait before Graham went back to his office. Maybe this was better, a public humiliation. She could imagine the confrontation becoming the talk of the town. She decided to take the bull by the horns.

She walked up the steps to the restaurant with as much confidence as she could muster and was met at the entrance by the maître d'. "I'm meeting someone," she said.

His expression was all pity. "I'm sorry, Miss. I'm afraid we cannot accommodate unaccompanied ladies."

Blanche pulled herself up to her full height and lifted her chin in the imperious fashion she had seen Alma use countless times. "I have a luncheon appointment today with Mr. Graham Peyton and his associate. Has he arrived?"

Was that a subtle sneer that the maître d' quickly suppressed? Still, he was all graciousness when he stood aside to usher her in. "Of course, Mademoiselle. Mr. Peyton and his companion have already been seated. Please follow me."

She followed the ramrod straight back down the hall to the dining room, her heels clicking on the marble floor, trying not to stare like a hick at the crystal sconces and peacock feather fans that decorated the walls. He led her across the spacious dining room to a round, linen-covered table near the French doors that looked out onto the fountain in the back garden. Her heart skipped when she spotted Graham.

He was handsome as ever, dressed in a light-colored three-piece suit with a navy blue silk ascot around his neck, his sandy hair fashionably parted in the middle and slicked back from his fore-head. She barely noticed the sylphlike blonde seated at his elbow.

"Mr. Peyton, this young lady says she has an appointment with you?"

Graham looked confused, but only until his gaze shifted from the maître d' to the very attractive brunette standing behind him. "Yes, indeed, Maurice. Thank you."

Graham's companion wasn't pleased to have her luncheon interrupted by a potential rival for his affections. "Graham…" she said. There was a petulant tone to her voice.

"Hang on, honey." Graham didn't take his eyes off of Blanche as he pushed out a chair with his foot. "Have a seat, darling. What can I do for you?"

Blanche did not have a seat. A cold fury crept over her as it dawned on her that he didn't recognize her. "You owe that Schilling guy in Arizona a bunch of money."

The look of hungry delight in Graham's eyes faded. "What?"

"You owe Schilling," she repeated, her voice rising. "He didn't get his money's worth when you sold me to him."

Graham shushed her with a gesture and pulled her down into the empty chair by one arm.

"What the hell are you talking about? Who are you?"

She straightened like a jolt of electricity had gone through her. "What? You were going to get me into the movies. You were going to marry me!"

Graham's luncheon companion gasped. He put a hand on her arm but didn't look at her.

"Oh, yes, my little Oklahoma rose. You're looking mighty slim and tasty. You've got some gams on you. Hey, nice dress. Did I buy that dress for you? I spent a lot of money on you, you know."

"You got your money's worth when you sold me to that disgusting man in Prescott. I don't owe you anything, you son of a bitch."

"Whoa, that's some mouth you've developed, honey. What happened to the sweet little hayseed I rescued from Pigsty Corners?"

But she was just getting started. "You owe me my life back, after you left me in the family way and stranded in Arizona."

He sat back in his chair, visibly relaxed, which infuriated Blanche even further. He had no fear at all of her or her accusations. "You don't say? Well, there's no way I'm the daddy. Where is the little bastard, anyway? Did you keep him? Or did you hunt up a hag with a long stick?"

Blanche stood up so quickly that her chair clattered over backwards. The restaurant fell silent and all eyes turned toward the red-faced beauty in the fur-collared jacket.

"Calm down, honey, you're making a scene. I can't help it if you didn't take advantage of the opportunity I offered you. If you got yourself in trouble, it's your own fault and nothing to do with me." He signaled to the maître d'. "Escort the young lady out, would you, Maurice? Our business is finished."

The maître d' gave her a look that would have withered a sane person, but Blanche was on fire with rage and far from sane. The maître d' crooked a finger and a large man in a tuxedo appeared and lifted the shrieking girl bodily off the floor, hustled her out of the restaurant and dumped her on the street. She tried to rush back in, but he blocked the door with his immovable bulk. "Run along, girl, before I have you arrested for disturbing the peace."

Inside, Graham stood and made a little bow to the room. "Sorry, folks. The young lady mistook me for someone else." When he sat down, he gave his troubled young companion a soothing pat.

"Don't worry about a thing, Miranda. This happens occasionally. I do my best for my clients, but sometimes they're not as talented as they are pretty, and the movie business doesn't work out for them. They're looking for someone to blame, and I'm handy."

"But Graham, what was that about her getting sold and having a baby?"

"I don't know. Like I told her, it sure doesn't have anything to do with me. I can't help it if she's a slut and looking for somebody to support her and her mistake. Now, forget her. I think you have what it takes and I'm going to introduce you to all the most important moviemakers in Hollywood. Your face will grace a thousand screens."

Miranda looked doubtful. "Do you really think that, Graham?"

"You bet." He grasped her hand in both of his. "Besides, darling, I think I may be falling for you, and I'd never do anything to hurt the love of my life."

"Oh, Graham."

He drew closer. "You believe me, don't you?"

Miranda's vision was filled with the sight of her name in lights. "I do, Graham. I really do."

> ~Her nemesis is immune to shame.
> Blanche's vision of doling out a public humiliation
> has turned to ashes.~

Blanche was running along the sidewalk with tears and mascara streaming down her cheeks when Mrs. Gilbert rounded the corner and they nearly collided.

"Where have you been…" Mrs. Gilbert bit off her question in alarm. "Blanche, whatever is wrong?"

Blanche took a deep breath, trying to calm down enough to be able to speak. "I saw him. In Philippe. Graham Peyton, the man who ruined me and sold me like a cow and abandoned me.

I want to kill him." The last sentence came out in a squeak, and Mrs. Gilbert grabbed her arms and shook her.

"Don't say such a thing, Blanche!"

"I hate him."

Mrs. Gilbert quick-marched her down the street to the limousine. Fee saw them coming and leaped out to open the door.

"What?" Fee said, but Mrs. Gilbert shook her head.

Mrs. Gilbert settled Blanche in the back seat and handed her a handkerchief to mop up most of the paint smeared over her cheeks.

"What can I do, Mrs. Gilbert?" Blanche's voice was muffled by the handkerchief as she wiped her nose. "How can I make him pay?"

Mrs. Gilbert put her arm around Blanche's shoulders. "Honey, he deserves to suffer for what he did to you. But your hate will do you more harm than it will him. The best thing you can do is live a happy life. That'll teach him."

Blanche grew still. Her sniffling stopped and she leaned back into the leather seat and straightened her skirt. "He was having luncheon with a girl. He's going to do to that girl the same thing he did to me." Her voice was calmer. She didn't propose going to the police, and neither did Mrs. Gilbert. They both understood how Hollywood worked. "I'd warn her, but if she's as stupid as I was, she won't listen. I'm better, now, Mrs. Gilbert. I'm sorry for making a scene. You can go home, now. If it's all right, Fee can drop me off at the theater. Maybe a flick will help me to forget my troubles. Graham Peyton is old news. I won't try to talk to him again."

Mrs. Gilbert's shoulders relaxed, but she said, "Do you swear?"

Blanche laughed. "My, but you are the cynic, Mrs. G. But you needn't worry. I never want to lay eyes on Graham Peyton again. Besides, I've had enough of being a public spectacle for one day."

"All right then. But be home in time to get ready for dinner. Alma is having Doug and Mary over tonight and wants to introduce you. They've been looking for actors to sign for their new studio."

Doug and Mary! Had this been any other day, Blanche would have been beside herself with joy at the prospect of dinner with Mary Pickford and Doug Fairbanks. As it was, she only thought that now she had less time to carry out her plan.

Once Fee dropped her off in front of the theatre, it took her less than ten minutes to walk back to the restaurant. She didn't attempt to enter again, but waited outside for nearly an hour, until Graham finally came down the front steps with the girl on his arm. Blanche faded back into the shadows until they passed, then followed him and the girl at a discreet distance. She would have been foiled if he had led her to an automobile, but her luck held. Graham and his potential "client" walked across the street to his office. After the couple disappeared inside, Blanche waited on the sidewalk until a light came on in an upstairs window. She checked the sky. The sun had already slipped down behind a building. She had better hustle if she intended to make it back to Hollywood in time to make herself presentable.

"I'm going to get you, Graham," she said aloud, "if it takes me the rest of my life."

> ~Blanche breathes the
> Rarified Air of Fame.~

Mrs. Gilbert was put out. "Where have you been? The Fairbanks' are already here and Alma has been asking for you."

Blanche told her the truth, or at least part of it. "I'm sorry. I tried to find a taxi, but I ended up having to take the trolley back. It took longer than I expected."

"Well, run upstairs and get yourself cleaned up. Alma and her guests are in the living room having a cocktail before dinner. If you hurry, you can join them."

"What shall I wear?"

Mrs. Gilbert gave her a critical once-over. "This is just an informal dinner with friends, so the dress you have on will do."

"Can I borrow a pair of Miss Bolding's Bohemian earrings?"

"No, honey, you're not trying to seduce anyone tonight. Just run a comb through your hair. Wash your face and don't try to put on any more makeup. You don't want to look like a clown. Your own blushing young cheeks are quite colorful enough."

Blanche was irritated at the reference to her youth—as if she hadn't had plenty of grown-woman experiences. But she didn't have time to brood over it. She hurried up the back stairs to her room and threw her hat on the bed. Her wavy hair only needed a little fluffing after being squashed under her hat. She wished that her hair was straight enough that she could wear it close to her head in a fashionable cap, but her thick, dark curls made that impossible. She gazed at her reflection critically. She swiped on the plummy shade of lip blush that Alma had picked out for her and blotted it on a tissue. Mrs. Gilbert was right about her blushing cheeks. The combination of hurry, anger, and excitement had given her an enviable glow.

She skipped down the stairs and would have rushed into the living room had Mrs. Gilbert not waylaid her for a quick inspection before letting her go. "All right, you look downright virginal. Go on in."

As soon as she entered, Alma stood up from her chair in front of the fireplace and waved a kimono-clad arm at her. "There she is! Mary, this is the waif I told you about. My athletic little stuntwoman who Dephinia found wandering in the woods."

Blanche thought she was prepared to meet Alma's guests, but when Douglas Fairbanks stood up, and Mary Pickford turned in her seat on the couch to face her, Blanche stopped in her tracks, suddenly lightheaded. Mary's famous cascade of blond hair was swept into an updo, but she was instantly recognizable as Our Mary.

The stunned look on the girl's face amused Alma no end.

"Close your mouth, honey, and come over here. I promise nobody will eat you."

Mary Pickford and Doug Fairbanks were probably the most famous couple on planet Earth. America's Sweetheart and her swashbuckling hero, two of the founders of United Artists Studios, and two of the most powerful people in Hollywood. But it didn't take long for them to put Blanche at ease. Doug wanted to talk at length about her riding skills. He was impressed to hear of a girl who wasn't afraid to jump off of things and fling herself about. Blanche was charmed by his boyish enthusiasm, and glad that her athleticism interested such a famous person. Ironic, considering the fact that she really didn't like to get dirty and would much rather lie around and eat chocolate than ride a horse or hang from her fingernails over a cliff.

She was more impressed with Mary, though. In the flickers, Mary Pickford usually played a waif of some kind, but in person she made no pretense of being anything other than a sharp-eyed twenty-nine-year-old woman. She spoke to Blanche kindly and wanted to know her story. Blanche told her a somewhat embellished version of the truth.

Over dinner, Blanche mostly sat in silence and listened as the adults talked about their next projects and commiserated about money/studios/directors/writers/fellow actors. Through most of the meal, Blanche could tell that Mary was studying her. The *blanc mange* had been served before Mary spoke directly to her.

"Blanche, Alma tells me that she's advised you to change your name if you're really serious about acting."

"Yes, ma'am. She did suggest that."

"And are you serious about acting?"

"Oh, yes, ma'am. Well, to tell the truth, I don't care so much about being a famous star, but I like it here in California, and Miss Bolding has been so good to me. I've enjoyed what acting I've done. I'd like to do something in the moving picture business, anything that pays enough for me to make my own way."

Mary nodded. "That's smart thinking, dear. Stunt work pays well but it takes a toll on you…"

"I'll second that," Doug interjected.

Mary continued. "So once you're making more than you need to live on, you'd be smart to put as much of your money away, or into safe investments, as you can."

"I'm afraid it will be a long time before I can earn enough money to start saving, Miss Pickford."

"You just remember what I said, dear. There are plenty of people in this racket whose task in life is to con you out of everything you own. You be smarter than they are."

"I'll try, Miss Pickford. If I ever get any extra money, what should I invest it in?"

"I'm not a financial advisor, dear. But if the day comes, you telephone me. I can recommend a couple of trustworthy people to help you." She paused long enough to sample the dessert. "By the way, dear, there's nothing wrong with changing your name. My parents named me Gladys. Gladys Smith." She laughed. "Now, would you pay money to see *Rebecca of Sunnybrook Farm* starring Gladys Smith?"

"I would, darling," Doug said. "I'd pay money to see you mow the lawn. And listen, little Blanche, there's nothing wrong with stunt work. Just make sure you learn to do it right. There's an art to it, you know."

Alma gestured with her wineglass. "Now, Doug, don't start swinging from the chandeliers. I'm making sure she has the right instruction."

Doug laughed. "Blanche, Mary and I have been thinking of producing a series of flicks featuring an intrepid girl who gets into all sorts of trouble, and Alma tells us that you have the talent and plenty of moxie. Lois Weber is writing a script for us, but before we make any casting decisions, would you like to take a bit part in a little picture I'm shooting right now called *The Three Musketeers*? I need a girl who's willing to jump off a balcony."

Blanche felt the color drain out of her face. Was she dreaming? Did he even need to ask? She tried to speak, but her mouth was like cotton, so she nodded so enthusiastically that a couple of hairpins went flying.

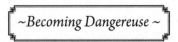

~Becoming Dangereuse ~

Between her lessons, her exercises, and her wildly exciting week on the set of Douglas Fairbanks's movie, Blanche didn't have time to give much thought to plotting her revenge on Graham Peyton. Her one brief scene in the picture required her to climb over the railing of a balcony, slide down a curtain that didn't quite reach the ground, and drop six feet to the cobblestones below. She rehearsed the move only once. There was nothing to it. For her, the fun part of the shoot was being fitted out as a seventeenth-century lady-in-waiting to the Queen of France, having pancake makeup troweled all over her face, and her hair squashed under an elaborate wig with dozens of ringlets. She was sorry that Doug wasn't in the scene with her. No one was, actually. But Doug and Alma did come to the studio to watch.

The dress was gigantic. She felt like she was swathed in fifty pounds of material. Blanche expressed her misgivings to Alma before she mounted the makeshift wooden steps to the back of the false balcony, but Alma simply said, "You can do it."

Blanche stood on the rickety balcony for half an hour before Mr. Niblo, the director, had all the cameras and lights arranged to his satisfaction. She spent the time pondering on how fake the scene looked in real life. The palace she was escaping from had a front and no back. It was all an illusion that the paying public was happy to buy into. She was still lost in her own reverie when Niblo yelled, "All right, girl, let's go."

Blanche grabbed the curtain, threw it over the balcony railing, struggled to lift her skirt-encumbered legs over the rail, and launched herself over. She was infinitely more bottom-heavy than she had been in rehearsal, so rather than slide gracefully down the material, the unaccustomed weight sent her flying to one side like a pendulum. She hung on for dear life as the pendulum swung back in the other direction. She could hear Niblo yelling, but couldn't understand what he was saying. It was too late to worry about it. She decided to make the best of the situation and purposely swung herself back and forth, gaining altitude. Finally, at the top of an arc, she let go and flew over the top of a prop hedge at the side of the pretend courtyard and disappeared from the shot. She landed in a roll, like Mr. Hashiyara had taught her, and stood up. She heard Niblo yell "Cut!" and walked out from behind the hedge as though she had planned the whole thing. Alma and Doug were both laughing hysterically. Niblo looked like he was about to have a stroke, though Blanche couldn't immediately tell if it was because he was overjoyed or ready to commit murder. Apparently, it was a mix of both, for he scolded her until her ears burned, then praised her for her ingenuity.

But all she cared about was the thumbs-up sign that Douglas Fairbanks shot her.

—

There was no call-back the next day, or the next. Alma was between projects, so there was no stunt doubling for Blanche to do. She fell back into her routine of study, exercise, and occasional housework. She read a lot, and played with Jack Dempsey, who was becoming her closest confidant. Even more so than Mrs. Gilbert, for the dog never gave her speculative looks or well-meaning advice about forgiveness.

The old familiar yen for vengeance began to gnaw at her after a week or so. Rather than have to come up with another excuse for a surveillance trip to town, Blanche decided to simply slip away one evening. She often went up to her room to read or study after supper anyway, and no one usually expected to see her again until the next morning.

The sun had set and darkness was falling as she slipped out the back door of Alma's house and made her way down the hill to catch the trolley into downtown. She casually walked down Hollywood Boulevard, past Philippe and past Graham's office on the other side of the street. The light was on in the office window. She strolled up and down the street a few times until she began to feel conspicuous, then walked around the block, circled back, and walked around the block again.

Still a light in the window, still no movement. She rounded the corner once again, but rather than walk all the way around the block, she turned up the alley, and stopped in her tracks. Graham's big, maroon, seven-seater Pierce-Arrow was parked behind his building.

She went up to the auto and stared into it for a long time. The top was down, and the back seat was deep and wide. The interior upholstery was black, and she was wearing a black and purple dress. And it would soon be dark.

> *~Dare she?*
> *She dared.~*

Blanche crawled into the back seat and made herself comfortable. There was no reason to hide until she needed to, and who knew how long she would have to wait until he showed up? Every time anyone crossed the mouth of the alley, she ducked down, but no one turned in her direction. She sat there until night had fallen, alternately berating herself for being a fool, then working herself up into a frenzy of hatred. She heard Graham coming before she saw him. He was feeding his line of bull to some poor idiot. Blanche would recognize that jaunty banter anywhere. It was so dark in the alley that she figured she could have just sat there in the back seat and he would never notice. When she could finally make out two human-sized shapes walking toward her, she hunkered down on the floorboard behind the front seat and held her breath. She heard Graham open the passenger-side door for his companion, then circle around to let himself into the driver's seat.

As he stepped on the starter, turned the key, and shifted into gear, Blanche made a vow to herself that if she ever owned an auto, she would be sure to check the back seat for intruders every time she got in.

He pulled out of the alley and drove off, still loudly talking to his companion over the engine roar. Blanche didn't dare look up or try to judge where they were going, but they drove for a long time. They stayed in the city. She knew that much from their speed and the number of stops and turns he made. Finally the auto slowed and pulled to a stop.

"Here we are," Graham said, his voice loud in the silence. Blanche made herself as small as she could and tried to quiet her racing heart. He got out and opened the door for his passenger, and they walked away. Blanche let her breath out in a whoosh and chanced a glance over the side. The auto was parked on a residential side street. She could see the two figures walking up a sidewalk running between two hulking shapes that she took to be houses. The two disappeared around one of the houses, and Blanche unfolded herself from the floorboard and climbed out.

She had no idea where she was. She ran on tiptoes up the sidewalk where Graham and his tootsie had gone, staying close to the wall of one of the houses. She peeked around the corner in time to see the pair mount the stairs and go into the very house by which she stood. She could see now that this was a bungalow complex around a central courtyard. The Los Angeles area was full of them. When she was on the road with Graham—could it really have been more than a year earlier?—he had told her that he lived in a bungalow. She had visualized a small house, but this complex was hardly small. It consisted of eight expensive

Spanish-style duplexes arranged in a U shape around a central courtyard with a vine-covered gazebo in the center.

Blanche crept down the sidewalk and around the side of the duplex that Graham had gone into. It was located at the end of the complex, where one arm of the U met the bottom. When Graham's ground-floor lights came on, Blanche hoisted herself up on the windowsill and peeked into the living room. Graham was shucking his companion out of her coat. Blanche recognized her as the same blond girl she had seen with him at the restaurant a few weeks earlier. The girl sat down on a long couch while Graham walked over to a sideboard and mixed a couple of drinks. Blanche let go of the sill and dropped to the ground. Seeing him again had stoked the fire of her fury, but the feeling was tempered by a small satisfaction. Now she knew where he lived. She sat on the ground and leaned back against the wall with her eyes closed, savoring the feeling for a few minutes before she had to wrestle with the problem of finding her way home.

By the time Blanche finally made her way back from the Westlake district of Los Angeles to Hollywood and Alma Bolding's house, on foot and by trolley, it was nearly dawn and Graham's address was imprinted on her mind.

> ~If she hadn't been an actress,
> she could have made a living as a cat burglar.~

After her first foray into Los Angeles as a stowaway in Graham's back seat, Blanche studied the trolley route maps and planned out her trip carefully. She dressed in boots and trousers, threw a lightweight black stole over her shoulders, and sneaked out of Alma's house after supper to catch the next car into Los Angeles. She had to change cars twice, but the trip took less than an hour, and she arrived in the Westlake area a little after seven o'clock in the evening. Graham's Pierce-Arrow was not parked in its former spot on the side street so she turned right off the sidewalk and circled the row of covered garages. No sign of the familiar maroon roadster. Still, to be extra careful, she took a peek through the side window of Graham's duplex. No sign of movement. She tried the window and found it unlocked. She slid the sill upwards, hoisted herself through, and dropped lightly onto the kitchen floor. The modern kitchen was equipped with a refrigerator and a gas stove and looked as neat and tidy as if it had never been used. Blanche hunkered down on the floor for a minute, listening, but the house was quiet. Confident that she was alone, she stood up and walked into Graham's impeccable living room. It was the room of a man who entertained frequently. The plush couch and chairs were arranged for conversation. A well-stocked drinks cart held pride of place close to the front door.

She went through the house, every room, upstairs and down. Through the closets and drawers, under the bed. Looking for what, she didn't know. Blanche went back down to the parlor, where her eyes locked onto a secretary's desk sitting in front of a picture window. She pulled down the writing surface and began going through the drawers and cubbies. She found a photo album tucked neatly into the largest drawer and sat down at the desk to look through it. It was full of pictures of women, mostly publicity shots, but she didn't recognize any of the actresses. She thumbed through, half-expecting to see a photograph of herself, even though she hadn't posed for one. It wouldn't have been beyond Peyton to take a snapshot of her as she slept. Under the album she found a green leather-bound ledger containing what looked like lists of random numbers and letters. A code? It meant nothing to her. A large clock sitting on a credenza struck eight, and she closed the ledger and put it back into the drawer. It was late, and she had to get back to Alma's before she was missed, or before the trolleys stopped running. Or Graham came home. She walked through the house, upstairs and down, memorizing the placement of every piece of furniture. She intended to return. After making sure everything was just as she'd found it, she slipped out the kitchen window and slid it closed behind her.

———

After she got her routine down, Blanche managed to get into Los Angeles once or twice a week, sneaking out in the evening and taking the trolleys to Peyton's bungalow. If his Pierce-Arrow was parked on the side street, or in one of the complex's garage buildings, she would hover around the neighborhood for half an hour or so, memorizing the landscape, and then make her way back to Hollywood. If his auto was nowhere to be seen, she would march up the sidewalk as though she belonged and walk around the side of Graham's place. Then it was the work of a moment for her to crawl in through an unlocked window and steal something.

She had no plan. There was no endgame in mind. She only knew that it gave her a tremendous feeling of satisfaction to violate his space. She only took things that she felt he would not miss. A snapshot of a random girl from the photo album. One highball glass from the set on the drinks cart. A pencil. After a few weeks she felt bolder and a bit more whimsical. She took one sock from his dresser drawer. The next week she took one shoe from his closet.

She always approached his house from the back side, toward the street, and never went into the courtyard of the complex lest she be seen and eventually remembered. As it was, she seldom saw anyone on the street at all. A man walking his dog in the evening. A family having an after-dinner stroll. And she was lucky to never meet even those people twice.

She would think about and savor her intrusions for days afterwards. She wished she could have seen Peyton's reaction when his shoe disappeared. She hoped he thought he was losing his mind. It amused her no end that the kitchen window was always unlocked, the only downstairs window in the house that faced the space between two units and was invisible from either the street or the courtyard. How long would it be before it occurred to Graham that he was being burgled? She expected she'd know when he started locking the windows.

~But she wasn't as clever
as she thought she was.~

Mrs. Gilbert had retired to her room after supper and was sitting next to her bed with her knitting in her lap when she heard the distinctive tap tap of dog toenails on the kitchen floor outside her bedroom door. What was Jack Dempsey doing out of Blanche's room at this time of the evening? Usually Blanche took him upstairs with her after supper and he spent the night on her bed. Sometimes the girl left her balcony door open to catch the breezes and Jack took the opportunity to explore. Perhaps he had made his way downstairs in hopes of a treat. Mrs. Gilbert sniffed and laid her knitting aside. She liked the feisty little mutt, but she didn't want him wandering around the house on his own at night.

She pulled on a robe and went into the kitchen to find Jack with his nose pressed to the glass door leading to the kitchen garden. He woofed and looked back over his shoulder long enough to see who had come in, then resumed his staring.

"Jack Dempsey, what are you doing out?" Mrs. Gilbert picked him up, but he whined and wiggled in protest. "What's going on? Do you see something outside?" Mrs. Gilbert put the dog back on the floor and watched him trot back to the glass door. Curious, she joined him.

The kitchen garden was long and narrow, leading to a walkway lined with short fan palms that led around the house and to the front drive.

Someone was out there, moving away from the house on the path. Mrs. Gilbert caught her breath and stepped back. A half-moon illuminated a cloudy sky, giving off enough lambent light to make out shapes but not much detail. Yet Mrs. Gilbert could tell by the way she moved that the figure gliding into the distance was Blanche.

Mrs. Gilbert scooped up the dog, tossed him into her room and shut the door before she slipped out the back to follow Blanche.

Where was this girl going? Her form looked bulky, like she was wearing a hat and coat. The fall nights were cool in coastal California, but if Blanche was just taking a walk around the property a shawl would have done the trick.

Mrs. Gilbert clutched her robe closed with one hand and tried to maintain enough distance between herself and the shadowy figure of the girl to keep her in sight without being noticed. She lost sight of her a few times, but she was easy enough to follow. The concrete staircases between homeowners' properties led inexorably down the hill and out to Highland Avenue. Indeed, Blanche was standing next to the curb when Mrs. Gilbert reached street level. Mrs. Gilbert faded into the cover of a bougainvillea hanging over someone's perimeter wall.

Blanche stood with her hands in her pockets, doing nothing but staring into space. After a few uneventful minutes Mrs. Gilbert was about to give up on the spy mission and make her way back up the hill. She had taken a few steps up the stairs when she heard the trolley bell. The trolley stopped long enough for Blanche to get on before resuming its route.

Mrs. Gilbert was baffled by Blanche's furtive behavior, and curious, but her dominant emotion as the trolley pulled away was disappointment. Mrs. Gilbert liked Blanche. She thought the girl was something special. She was whip smart and a hard worker. But for a teenager who had already proved herself impulsive and willful, sneaking off in the dark couldn't mean anything good.

Mrs. Gilbert sat up for a while in hopes of seeing Blanche return to the house, but eventually gave it up and went to bed. She was relieved when Blanche came downstairs for breakfast at the usual time. She had half expected that the girl had taken off for good.

She said nothing to Blanche about her nighttime adventure and Blanche behaved perfectly normally, offering to fry the bacon, feeding tidbits to Jack Dempsey as they ate. The day progressed as usual and Blanche retired to her room after supper. Mrs. Gilbert kept an eye peeled out the back window all evening. And sure enough, the teenaged night prowler made her shadowy way through the garden that night, and the next, just as the last trace of daylight disappeared.

Alma was making another picture, a costume drama at the Pickford-Fairbanks Studio on Santa Monica Boulevard in Hollywood. The picture was a light romp with lots of romance, so there was no need for a stunt double, but Alma took Blanche with her to the studio several times during the shoot and introduced her to the director and to her costars. Mrs. Gilbert would have thought that between her studies and the excitement of the movie set, Blanche would be too tired to take secret trips to who-knew-where every night. But youth has its advantages.

Mrs. Gilbert considered the straightforward approach of asking Blanche what the hell she thought she was doing, but finally decided to follow Blanche on one of her secret excursions. She'd rather know where Blanche was going and what she was up to before confronting her. After all, Blanche was not her daughter. As long as it didn't concern Alma's household, it was Blanche's problem if she was stupid enough to get herself into something unsavory. Wasn't it?

> ~Blanche had forgotten that
> luck never holds.~

Alma and Mrs. Gilbert left for the studio on their own the next morning, leaving Blanche at home with only Jack Dempsey for company. Blanche was supposed to study lines for an audition that Alma had set up for her the following week. And she really intended to do just that, at least until Alma's Cadillac limousine disappeared down the hill with Fee at the wheel.

She knew her lines pretty well. Graham Peyton had recently returned from a trip and had been at home the last couple of times she paid him a surreptitious nighttime visit. It was a beautiful, soft California fall day, and no one was there to tell her no.

An hour later, Blanche was wandering through Graham Peyton's bungalow. Everything looked different in the daytime. Shabbier, somehow, or maybe just ordinary. She was riffling through kitchen drawers that she had riffled through many times before when she came upon a meat cleaver. She held it up to the light and examined it carefully. Sharp. For several minutes she fantasized about sneaking up behind Graham and burying the cleaver in his back. Or maybe the back of his head. No, his back was better. He'd suffer more.

She went into the living room and made a gin rickey for herself. She was sitting on Graham's sofa with one arm slung along the back, sipping her drink, when she heard someone coming up the wooden steps to the front door. She flew off the couch, glass in hand, and squeezed herself down between the sofa and the back wall just as a key turned in the lock and the door opened.

Graham wasn't alone, but this time his companion was a man rather than an aspiring actress. Blanche's heart was pounding so heard she feared they would hear. Someone sat down on the sofa.

"Can I fix you a drink?" Blanche recognized Graham's voice.

"I'm not staying," the other man said. "This is not a social call, Graham. Do you have the goods?"

Blanche couldn't see them, but she could tell by his tone and the way that Graham deferred to him that the stranger was older. Graham's voice took on a conciliatory tone. Oily, even, Blanche noted. "Now, Ruhl, have I ever let the boss down? Of course I do."

What was this? Blanche forgot her fear, even forgot her hatred, as curiosity overtook her. She oozed forward enough to be able to peep around the side of the sofa, the gin glass still clutched in her hand.

Graham was retrieving a large leather bag from his front closet. He turned toward the sofa and Blanche jerked her head back like a frightened turtle. He must have handed the bag to the man on the sofa, for she heard it snap open.

"It's all there," Graham said.

The man must have been satisfied. "Here's the money for the next shipment. And here's your cut. K.D. has made arrangements for you to meet O'Halloran at the usual place in Chicago on the fifth. Telephone him at this number when you get into town."

Blanche could tell that Graham was standing in front of the man on the sofa. "The fifth? That's pretty quick. I don't know if I can get to Chicago by the fifth."

"Yes, well, K.D. suggests that you go by train this time." Ruhl's comment was tinged with sarcasm. "Your automobile trips take too long and draw too much attention. You're going to pick up the wrong girl one of these days and get yourself shot. Which wouldn't bother me, but K.D. would be unhappy and we don't want that."

"K.D. worries too much. But far be it from me to raise a ruckus. I have a meeting with the Count over at the Sennet studio in a couple hours, but I'll put the dough in the bank and buy a train ticket as soon as I finish with him this afternoon."

"Do it now, Graham. I don't want you to leave fifty thousand dollars lying around your house while you go off to get high."

"Damn it, Ruhl, I'm not going to get high. I'm going to offer him this dope for a better price than K.D. is offering him now."

"We've only ever run that scam in Arizona, Graham. It's too dangerous to try it in K.D.'s own backyard."

"It was the Count's own idea. He's not going to spill the beans to anyone."

Ruhl thought about this. "That could be a very profitable line to pursue. What time are you meeting him?"

"Three o'clock."

"You don't have much time if you're going to get the money deposited and get over to Sennet by three."

"All right. For cryin' out loud! Tell K.D. I'll take care of it. Now get out, Ruhl, and let me go to the can and change my threads so I can hit the road."

Ruhl cautioned Graham to be careful, and Blanche heard the front door open and close. Ruhl had left, but Graham was pacing around the living room, muttering to himself. He called Ruhl a couple of imaginative names before pouring a drink for himself at the cart. Blanche chanced a glance. Graham was still standing at the drinks cart with his back to the sofa. He slugged his drink, picked up what looked like a small suitcase from the side table and put it on the top shelf of the coat closet before he stalked upstairs. Blanche didn't move until she was sure she could hear his footsteps overhead, then she crept out from behind the furniture and placed her empty glass on the cart next to his. (Let him wonder about that!) She fully intended to skitter out through the kitchen window until she heard water running in the bathtub upstairs.

She walked nonchalantly to the coat closet and took the suitcase down from the shelf, sat down in an armchair with it in her lap, and opened it. She had never seen so much money in one place in all her life. She lifted her head and listened to Graham splashing around in the tub. What would happen if she stole the suitcase?

Graham would be in loads of trouble if all the money disappeared. Would his associates kill him? Probably. She didn't know much about the crime world, but she knew that drug dealers and bootleggers were brutal and unforgiving.

No, tempting as it was, it was too much. Still, he owed her. She pulled out a small bundle of fifties and stuffed it down her blouse before replacing the bag and slipping out the window.

She could feel the money next to her skin all throughout the trolley rides back to Hollywood. Passengers would smile at her as they got on and off. *I probably look like the cat who ate the canary,* she thought. It was nice to be smiled at, to be noticed, though, so all the way home she cultivated an enigmatic little smile.

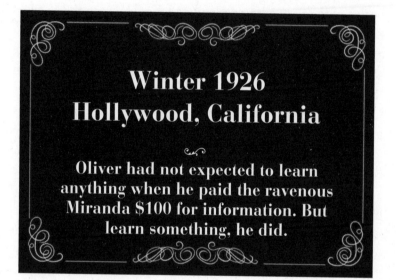

Winter 1926
Hollywood, California

Oliver had not expected to learn anything when he paid the ravenous Miranda $100 for information. But learn something, he did.

And after that luncheon, it had taken some pull from some powerful people for Oliver to gain permission to meet with Bianca LaBelle at her fabulous Beverly Hills estate. Even though he figured it would lead to nothing, Oliver had been happy enough to spend a few unproductive minutes in the company of a glamorous movie star. But Bianca had turned out to be nothing like Oliver expected. No brainless Hollywood ingenue, she. No, there was something about this woman that scared him, and scared him good. He had thought that he was going to ask her a few questions and get on with his life, but she had turned the tables on him, and against his better judgment—almost against his will—he had agreed to keep her informed on the progress of his investigation. Why had he done that? Bianca LaBelle was *Dangereuse* indeed.

After he answered Bianca's summons and let her wrap him around her little finger, Oliver spent the next few days completing his shoe-leather investigation. The building in which Peyton's office was once located had been sold, and the office space had a new tenant who had never heard of Graham Peyton. Half of the businesses on this particular mile-long stretch of Hollywood Boulevard had changed hands in the years since Peyton disappeared, and half of the remainder had different staff. A few people were still there who recognized Peyton's snapshot and remembered waiting on him for one thing or another, but aside from the headwaiter at Philippe, Oliver didn't find anyone who remembered his name or had any idea what had happened to him, or admitted to it.

Oliver revisited the bungalow court on Alameda several times, coming back again and again to knock on doors until someone answered who would talk to him. Only a few of the tenants had lived in the complex long enough to have known who Peyton was, and no one admitted to being well acquainted with him or even to wondering what had become of him. Oliver had just knocked on one particular front door for the fourth time in a week and was about to give it up as a lost cause. He was hoping that he wouldn't have to pump the landlady for the names of the people who had lived here while Peyton was alive, but that was his next move. He was wondering how much the information would cost him when a breathless woman flung open the door, causing him to start.

"Oh, sorry," she panted. "I was upstairs when you knocked. What can I do for you?"

She was just past the first bloom of youth, rosy-cheeked, with a sleek cap of light brown hair. Oliver immediately pegged her as an actress or would-be actress.

He introduced himself and gave her the same spiel about the skeleton and tracing Peyton's last movements that he had been rattling off to all and sundry. He was surprised when she said, "Yeah, I remember Graham. He's dead? Sorry to hear that. I just figured he moved out. We were friendly enough, but didn't really socialize. I had a bunch of leftover roast once and took it to him. He thanked me and was very polite. I liked him, but I could tell that he was a scallywag. Girls over all the time. But then most of the people who live in this complex are scallywags. Mostly motion picture people, you know. Some famous people have lived around here, and I've seen famous people coming to visit their friends. I don't know if Mr. Peyton worked in the business. He never said. I thought he must be a traveling salesman. He was gone a lot, often for long periods of time. "

"Did you recognize any of his visitors?"

"Nobody famous. Not that I noticed. Oh, except once. Right before he left on one of his trips, Alma Bolding herself asked me which bungalow was his! I nearly fainted."

The hair rose up on the back of Oliver's neck. "Alma Bolding. Are you sure?"

The young woman seemed insulted that he'd ask. "Well, of course. I'd hardly mistake some regular person for Alma Bolding."

"Did she go into his place?"

"She did. She didn't even knock, just walked right in."

> *~A little time out for
> Zanzibar Gold~*

The afternoon was well along by the time Oliver got back to Santa Monica. He was driving up Third Street toward his apartment when he noticed that the Criterion Theater was showing a Bianca Dangereuse adventure called *Zanzibar Gold*. He braked so quickly that he nearly bumped his head on the steering wheel. He pulled over to the curb and parked amid a chorus of horns from cars that had been behind him when he stopped in the middle of the street.

He paid his twenty cents for a ticket and settled himself into a seat in the middle of the darkened theatre. It was a weeknight, so the crowd was sparse. He had arrived in time for the opening credits. The story had something to do with Bianca foiling a plot by renegade slave traders to rob a train carrying British gold so they could…do something about buying ivory or slaves or wives. Oliver wasn't quite clear on that point. However, it was exciting.

Oliver's favorite part was after the renegades had hijacked a train full of schoolgirls, when Bianca leaped off a roof and onto the top of one of the cars as the train sped past. She crouched down on the shingles atop the depot until the train was whizzing by under her, then stood up and took a flying leap, hit the top of the caboose behind the cupola, rolled to the end, and caught herself before she was flung off onto the tracks. For a moment she flapped along behind the caboose like a human flag, then pulled herself up and dropped onto the platform at the back, where a British soldier opened the door and she disappeared inside. It was all rather silly, but Oliver had to admit that if Bianca LaBelle really did do her own stunts, she was amazingly athletic. Like all Bianca Dangereuse pictures, she saved the day with a little help from her sidekick Butch Revelle, and the last shot of the movie was a close-up of Bianca's face and her famous quirky, knowing, little smile.

After *Zanzibar Gold* ended and the shorts were showing before the next feature, Oliver sat in the dark and tried to think of what connections there could be between Bianca LaBelle and the grisly fate of Graham Peyton. Even if Peyton had taken advantage of LaBelle when she was a girl, that didn't mean she had anything to do with his death. He took advantage of a lot of girls. Oliver would have simply chalked it up to the fact that Bianca was one of many Peyton-hating women that he would eventually uncover. But what about the Alma Bolding connection? What did she have to do with all of this? The first time he saw Alma, she had implied that she knew Peyton. How? Peyton was a boy when Alma first became famous, so she was probably not one of his seducees. What was she doing at Peyton's bungalow shortly before he disappeared?

Ruhl had told him that the missing ledger contained incriminating information about important people. Could Alma Bolding be one of them? Surely Bianca herself was not one of the names in Ruhl's book. When Peyton disappeared in 1921, Bianca was a nameless teenager and not yet a movie star worth blackmailing. Old enough to be judged for her morals, but he couldn't imagine her as a teenaged money-launderer or politician-briber. Oliver gave an unconscious shrug in the dark. Maybe she was a girl mobster and he was just naive.

When Oliver finally got home, he telephoned the number that Bianca had given him and was surprised that the woman who answered the telephone put him right through. He asked Bianca if he could make another appointment to see her. After all, she had asked him to keep her apprised of his progress, and by the way, he'd like to ask her a few more questions. "I could come by tonight," he offered.

"I'm sorry, Mr. Oliver, but tonight I'm throwing a little shindig. We just finished a picture and I'm having a wrap party for the cast and crew and a few close friends."

Oliver had drawn a breath to ask when would be convenient for her when she said, "You're welcome to come, if you wish. Come around nine. I'll leave your name with the gatekeeper."

He removed the earpiece from his ear and gave it a dubious once-over. Was he really being invited to a Hollywood party? He regained himself quickly. "Will Miss Bolding be there?"

"Yes, certainly."

"Would you object to my talking with your guests? Would that be too intrusive? I promise I won't connect your name in any way to the person I'm investigating."

She answered with a throaty laugh. "I trust you know what you're doing. Intrude away, Mr. Oliver. Intrude away."

After Bianca rang off, Oliver sat back in his chair with the receiver still in his hand and pondered his next move.

> *~Oliver climbs back up the mountain,*
> *takes a terrifying fall.~*

Oliver waited until midnight to head back up the canyon to Bianca's estate. He knew how Hollywood parties went, and wanted to be sure all the guests arrived before he did. He drove to the gate, where a uniformed guard with a clipboard came out of his little booth and gave the battered Ford a skeptical once-over.

Oliver spoke before the guard had a chance to shoo him away. "I'm Ted Oliver. Miss LaBelle invited me."

The guard's skepticism deepened, but he checked the guest list, found Oliver's name, didn't believe his eyes and looked again. "All right," he said with reluctance. "Park that jalopy over to the side."

"Thanks, pal." Oliver strove not to sound put out. Sometimes the schlubs who worked for the high and mighty were snobbier than the high and mighty themselves. He wound around the long drive and parked behind the Cadillacs, Hispano-Suizas, and Rolls-Royces. Two or three liveried chauffeurs were bunched together around a silver limo, smoking. They gave him a collective stink-eye as he walked up to the front door.

Fee, the same unusual creature whom he had met the first time he was here, was stationed at the door with a list of her own. Oliver categorized the person as a "she" this evening, since she was wearing a perky blond wig and a backless gold-sequined evening gown that was split up one side. Fee's muscular bare shoulders and one bare thigh were smooth and hairless, though they did look more suited to bench-pressing than tangoing. Still…"Nice dress," Oliver said, as he handed her his hat.

"Thanks. Go on in, Mr. Oliver. Just follow the noise."

That wasn't hard to do. Most of the action was centered in the white-carpeted living room, which judging by the state of most of the guests who were tromping in and out of the house from the pool area with glasses of wine in their hands, would not be so white tomorrow.

Oliver hesitated when he saw that it was a costume party. Bianca hadn't mentioned that. Most of the partygoers were masked, but Oliver recognized several of the more famous guests. There was Daniel May, who played Bianca Dangereuse's partner in crime, Butch Revelle. In the corner, where the eight-piece jazz band was making the joint jump, Dorothy Dwan, dressed as a pussycat, was cutting a rug. And over there, in full cowboy regalia, Tom Mix and Will Rogers were seated on the long couch with their heads together, engaged in a raucous conversation. Oliver didn't recognize the rest. Either their disguises were too effective or they were behind-the-scenes types like directors and scriptwriters. He wandered through the crowd, hoping the guests took his shabby suit for a Little Tramp outfit. Nobody paid him the slightest mind. A handsome devil in tails was noodling on a grand piano, though the noisy jazz band rendered the effort futile. Even so, a slender young thing dressed as Cleopatra was hanging all over him.

Oliver went through the sunroom, where a lot of canoodling was going on, and out the French doors to the pool area. The trees and cabanas were hung with paper lanterns, giving the scene a dreamlike quality. He spent a lot of time walking around the property, hoping that none of the drunken revelers gathered around the pool ended up at the bottom of the deep end. No one was sober enough to notice.

He had been wandering around for almost an hour, inside and out, checking out the guests, before it dawned on him that he hadn't struck up a conversation with anyone. He went back into the living room and had the bartender fix him a drink.

"She likes to stay in control of herself."

Oliver started when Alma Bolding spoke. He had not heard

her come up behind him. Of course, he could barely hear himself think over the frenetic noise the jazz band was pounding out.

"What?"

Alma was clad in an outlandishly elaborate Queen Elizabeth costume, complete with pearl-encrusted red wig and stark white makeup. She smelled like a perfumed distillery and was unsteady on her feet. "Bianca. You've been looking for her. She ain't staggering around with the rest of us drunks. Bianca likes to stay in control."

"I got that impression when I talked to her the other day," Oliver said.

"I know you want to question her. Don't think you're going to be able to trip her up, young fellow. She's too smart for that. She knows how to protect herself. She knows how to stay out of trouble and knows everybody's dirty little secrets just for insurance."

"How did you come to be such good friends with Miss LaBelle?" The question had nothing to do with his purpose for being there. He knew he shouldn't ask, but he couldn't help himself. A veteran actress could be jealous of beautiful up-and-comers, and it was a rare thing that older actors actually promoted and mentored someone who could replace them in the fickle hearts of the fans. Alma Bolding was well known in the business for being difficult. Bianca LaBelle was a movie star in her own right. She certainly did not have to put up with Alma's eccentricities if she didn't want to.

Alma dodged the question. "It's a long story."

"Most people don't help their stunt doubles become stars."

Alma shot him an ironic look and finished his thought for him. "Especially harridans such as myself, you mean. Why should I care? I don't have to act anymore. I'm loaded."

"And now so is she, thanks to you."

"Oh, not just me, believe me. The girl has what it takes." Alma hesitated, then said, "I wouldn't give a tiny fly's fart for most of the brainless sluts who think they want to get into the movies.

But Bianca…after all that she's been through, after all the things that the usual thugs and shits and bottom-feeders our business has to offer have done to her… Well, I keep trying to educate her, but in spite of it all, the basic decency still hasn't been beaten, screwed, or cheated out of her. Not yet." Alma's smile managed to convey affection and bitterness at once.

"I'm not looking to trip anybody up, Miss Bolding. Actually, it's you I'd like to talk to."

Alma's painted eyebrows shot skyward. "Me? I don't know nothing, sonny, and I wouldn't tell you if I did. Why do you care what happened to that poisonous toad, anyway? Why, I think that if some citizen had walked up to him on Rodeo Drive in the middle of the afternoon and shot him in the head, the district attorney would have given a medal to the guy who pulled the trigger."

That made Oliver laugh. "I agree with you, there."

"Then what's the point?"

Oliver studied the actress, trying to decide the best way to proceed. She was three sheets to the wind, probably no inhibitions at all. Anything she said to him right now would be either the unvarnished truth, a lie, or a damned lie. Either way, tomorrow she probably wouldn't remember talking to him at all. "How about it, Miss Bolding? Would you be willing to find a secluded corner right now and tell me how you knew Graham Peyton?"

She emitted a high-pitched sound that was halfway between a laugh and a shriek. "Up yours three ways from Sunday, young man."

Oliver tried not to smile. Alma was awful, and he couldn't help but like her. He'd try her again when she could see straight. "So where is Bianca?"

Alma gestured toward the hall with her martini glass, slopping gin on the rug. "She's in the kitchen."

> ~*Bianca had never been taught how to charm,*
> *but she did wonders for an amateur.*~

Oliver walked through the house, heading in the direction Alma had indicated. He passed through the library room where Bianca had asked him to keep her informed, down another long hall with walls of blond brick, a couple of closed doors on one side and on the other, floor-to-ceiling windows looking out onto a citrus orchard. Must be nice to be rolling in moola.

Bianca had unusual taste in decor, he thought—spare, bold lines, simple white and chrome furniture accented with splashes of bright color. She liked art. Statuary and small *objets* were scatted about on table tops and shelves, in corners, and even hanging from the ceiling. The walls were mostly bare except for the black, white, and gold light sconces, but every once in a while he would come across a painting, usually something large and in an odd style that was unfamiliar to him. A painting ought to look like something, in his opinion. But then what did he know about art?

He opened one of the wood-and-metal double doors at end of the hall, into a formal dining room dominated by an oval mahogany table with an eye-catching inlaid fan pattern made of ebony. A door in one corner of the large room was unassuming enough that Oliver figured its purpose was to let waiters slip discreetly in and out of the kitchen while serving dinner to the glitterati.

He pushed open the restaurant-style door and found himself in a kitchen that was bigger than his entire apartment. He was too busy gawking at the shiny chrome fixtures to notice that the maid who had served him sandwiches on his first visit was stalking toward him, until she said, "Sir, you can't be in here. Let me escort you back to the party."

"It's all right, Norah. Let him come in. You can go. We'll be fine." Bianca was sitting on a stool at a marble-topped kitchen island. She was wearing a black velvet sheath dress dripping with jet-beaded fringe. The front of the dress was basically nonexistent, cut so low that one false move would leave Bianca with no secrets. A sleek man with dark hair and eyes was sitting next to her. Norah stood aside, looking doubtful.

Bianca put a hand on her companion's shoulder. "Hello, Oliver. I'm glad you could make it. This is my friend Rudy. We were just taking a little break from the merriment. Rudy, this is Ted Oliver. He's handling some business for me."

The dark man stood up, all old world elegance and grace, and said, "Pleased to meet you." He had a thick Italian accent.

Oliver held out a hand while trying not to swallow his tongue. "Likewise, Mr. Valentino." Oliver's face felt like it was on fire. He figured he must look like a fireplug, but neither Valentino nor LaBelle seemed to notice.

"Rudy, would you excuse us for a moment? Mr. Oliver and I have things to discuss."

"Of course, *cara*. I must return to the party before Pola wonders where I've gone. I feel much better now, *grazie*. Your drink you make me is a big help."

Rudolph Valentino, the most beloved romantic star in all the wide world, cast Oliver a narrow look as he left. Bianca gestured toward his vacated stool and bade Oliver have a seat. "Rudy doesn't mean anything by that squint, Mr. Oliver. He's blind as a bat. I'm worried about him, though. He's been having terrible stomach problems for a while."

"You run in rarified company, Miss LaBelle." Oliver hoisted himself onto the seat. "But then you're pretty rarified yourself."

"Yes, well, fame isn't all it's cracked up to be, Mr. Oliver. Not when you have to live in a fortress to keep from being loved to death." Her inscrutable smile appeared and was gone. "Not that I'm complaining. It's nice to have enough money to do what needs to be done. Speaking of doing what needs to be done, I assume you have garnered some information that you think will interest me?"

He filled her in on his investigation, including Miranda's tale of the screaming teenager who confronted Peyton at Philippe. He carefully watched Bianca's face when he told her about the woman who saw Alma at Peyton's bungalow shortly before he disappeared, but her expression gave nothing away.

All she said was, "Have you asked Alma about that?"

"I talked to her for a minute just before I came to find you. She's not in any condition to answer questions right now."

Bianca nodded, unsurprised. "I don't know what she was doing there, but I can guess. You know that Graham supplied drugs to some of the studios. You've heard of the Count?"

"I've heard he hollows out peanut shells and fills them with cocaine, then sells bags of 'peanuts' to actors on the set."

She inclined her jet-and-feather-adorned head in assent. "Alma has had her battles with that demon in the past. Alma was one of the Count's good customers, but she always preferred to make her purchases wholesale rather than retail. Graham was a wholesale supplier. She was probably going straight to the source. You can question her all you want, but drunk or sober, I doubt if she'll remember much about that time." Her small smile reappeared. "You don't look like you're buying my theory, Oliver. Have you begun to form one of your own?"

"I think you know a lot more about the death of Graham Peyton than you're letting on, Miss LaBelle, and I think it may have something to do with Alma Bolding. Why else would you want to pay me money to keep informed about my investigation?"

The statement seemed to startle her. "You think she bumped him off?"

"Maybe. Or she may know who did. I do think you're the kind of girl who would go to a lot of trouble to protect someone you care about. Somebody like Alma, say."

Her expression said that she didn't care for the implication. Bianca pondered the white marble floor for some time. When she lifted her head to look at him, Oliver was startled anew by her gold-flecked green eyes. "You've been straight with me, Oliver, so I'll be straight with you. The truth is that I did come to California because of Graham Peyton—indirectly, that is. I was fifteen, bored, and susceptible to his guff. He persuaded me to run away with him. He didn't have to persuade very hard, I admit."

She paused, looking wistful. "You can't retrieve a deed long done or a time gone. Do you know what it is to long for something so badly that it feels like your heart is being pulled right out of your body? That's the way I felt."

Oliver was oddly disturbed by her story. Suddenly he didn't want her to go on, to make herself so vulnerable. He held up a hand to silence her. "Miss LaBelle…"

But she ignored the gesture. "It took me a long time to realize that what I longed for was not Graham Peyton. It was adventure. And do you know, I still long for adventure? Adventure is my one true love, I think." She straightened and shook off her thoughtful mood. "Fortunately, I met Alma and Tom Mix in Arizona and they rescued me before I could end up working in one of K.D. Dix's brothels. I was lucky to escape. I was aware of Graham's disappearance a few years ago. Like everyone else, I expected that he met a bad end, and I was frankly relieved that he was gone. I've been quite successful since I've been in Hollywood, Mr. Oliver, and I have lived in some anxiety that my past association with that…person would be discovered and end up splashed all over the tabloids. If you were able to find the woman who recognized me from the altercation at the restaurant, it's just a matter of time before one of the tabloids finds her, too."

"And as for Alma, if somebody saw her at Graham's bungalow, I wouldn't be surprised if she was there to give him a piece of her mind. Trying to protect me somehow. She knew that Graham and I had a history and she was determined that he leave me alone. But I'll bet everything I own or ever will own that Alma Bolding never killed anybody. So do not bring up her name to K.D. Dix. I'll pay you any amount of money you want. Dix will jump to conclusions and I don't want Alma hurt."

"Miss LaBelle, I'd never make idle accusations about anyone, especially to a mobster."

"Promise me, Oliver. Dix is evil, and Alma is weak."

"Miss LaBelle…"

She spoke over him. "Oh, for heaven's sake, call me Bianca. All this Miss LaBelle stuff is getting on my nerves. As for why I'm interested in finding out what happened to Graham Peyton, well, that's very personal, Oliver. But I promise that it isn't because I am involved in any of his criminal enterprises, or ever have been, or know anyone who has."

Oliver had no reason to take her word for it, but he was relieved nonetheless. If she really had fallen pregnant by Peyton, like Miranda said, he could understand her desire to keep it quiet. He said, "Well, if it makes you feel any better, I don't think anybody is going to find out for sure what happened to Graham Peyton. I think the simplest answer is the most likely. He got caught skimming money from the wrong people and ended up tossed over a cliff. I think the money is long gone and if there ever was a second ledger, the book got burned up in his landlady's incinerator five years ago. Dix is wasting his money trying to find out what happened to that ledger. If it hasn't turned up after five years, it's not going to turn up now."

"I'm inclined to agree with you, Oliver. I hope your client does, too. K.D. Dix is not somebody you want to cross."

"So everyone keeps telling me." He stood up. "Well, I'd better let you get back to your guests. Oh, and by the way, I caught a showing of *Zanzibar Gold* this afternoon."

One sculpted eyebrow rose. "Indeed? Are you a fan of the Dangereuse flicks? What did you think?"

"It was quite a romp. I was impressed."

She seemed pleased. "I learned how to do stunts and not kill myself from my sensei, Mr. Hirayasu. It takes a lot of work to make all that climbing and fighting and falling down look easy. Besides, I enjoy knowing that I could knock you on your ass if I wanted to."

Oliver grinned. "I especially liked the part where you jumped on top of the caboose."

Bianca laughed. Her Mona Lisa smile broke open like the sun breaking through clouds, into a gleaming, extravagant, tooth-filled grin that transformed not just her face but her whole being. She was transcendent, and Oliver nearly fell off his stool. He almost didn't hear her when she said, "That was an accident. I was supposed to land on my feet and walk across the top of the car. I was lucky I didn't break my neck. It looked swell on film, though."

Oliver tried to make his feet move in a straight line as he walked through the party and out the front door into the night. This was trouble. He was lightheaded and could hardly breathe. He had never been thunderstruck in his life, but this had to be what it was like. Damn it damn it damn it. What was he going to do now?

He had a strong feeling that both Bianca LaBelle and Alma Bolding knew something about Graham Peyton's death. But unless the situation changed, he would never hear the whole story from them. Bianca LaBelle was box office gold, and as long as she was a top moneymaker, the studio bigwigs weren't going to let an inconvenient incident like murder interfere with her. What if Bianca LaBelle really was protecting Alma Bolding? What if, God forbid, Bianca herself was involved in shilling drugs or hooch or whores or murder? Could anyone who looked like that be evil? Would it matter? Who would he tell if she was? Certainly not K.D. Dix.

In the short time he had been here in paradise he had learned that Southern California law enforcement was not the stellar institution one would hope. He had been trying to stay out of the mud, but it was hard. He didn't know how much longer he was going to be able to last. If Bianca was dirty, he was going to have to choose between her and his soul. He had the sinking fear that when the time came, he would make the wrong choice.

———

Bianca LaBelle watched Oliver leave her kitchen, but she was in no hurry to return to the party. She got up from her seat at the counter, retrieved a bottle of milk from the refrigerator, and poured herself a glass. Lies came easy to her these days. Too bad they were necessary. Still, things were going her way. The instant that Oliver had fallen for her, she knew it. She always did.

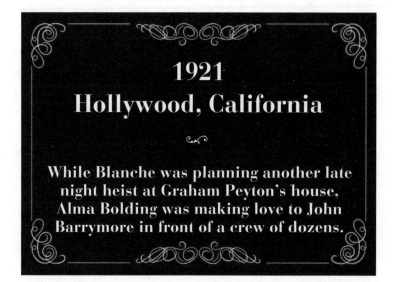

1921
Hollywood, California

While Blanche was planning another late night heist at Graham Peyton's house, Alma Bolding was making love to John Barrymore in front of a crew of dozens.

Mrs. Gilbert sat in her usual unobtrusive spot in a corner of the cavernous studio on Santa Monica Boulevard, well behind the cameras, but close enough that she could see everything. As Alma's scene played out, Mrs. Gilbert thought about Blanche's secretive trips into Los Angeles and made plans to confront the little sneak as soon as she got home. She would have done it this morning if Alma hadn't insisted that she come to the location with her today. Alma liked to hear Mrs. Gilbert's opinion of how things had gone. She especially liked the fact that Mrs. Gilbert's opinion was always complimentary.

After the director called cut, Alma wended her way around the Klieg lights and cables, only knocking over a few things with her antebellum hoopskirt, and gingerly sat down on a hoop-friendly stool next to Mrs. Gilbert's chair.

"I swear that if that knucklehead Barrymore treads on my train one more time I'm going to klop his kop."

Mrs. Gilbert smiled. Alma always opened with a complaint. "You move so gracefully in that monstrosity of a dress. Besides, I thought you two really had some heat between you in that last scene."

Feathers smoothed, Alma allowed herself to relax. "Well, I do think that last shot went well. And thank God that was my last scene for the day. I can't wait to shuck this getup. It'll be a treat to get home."

Mrs. Gilbert checked the pendant watch pinned to her blouse. "Gosh, it's probably already dark. It'll take an hour to get you out of that costume. We won't get home until nine or ten. Do you want to stop at Victorio's and get something to eat?"

"God, no. That asshole treats you like dirt. If I didn't love his pastrami so much I'd never spend another dime there. We'll rummage around and find something at home. I want to run lines with Blanche before we go to bed."

———

Once they finally, finally made their way home, Mrs. Gilbert ensconced Alma in the kitchen and went upstairs to Blanche's room. She knocked, but the only answer she got was from an overexcited Jack Dempsey, who had been in solitary far too long for such a small-bladdered dog. Mrs. Gilbert opened the door and a hairy streak flashed by her ankles. "Blanche?" she said, and stepped into the room, expecting to see that the girl had fallen asleep, but the room was empty. Mrs. Gilbert switched on a bedside lamp. The top of the little desk was strewn with script pages lying over an open book of full-color art prints. She had been studying, like she was supposed to. This was a big place, and it could be that Blanche was somewhere else in the house, reading in the study, or enjoying the cool night air in a lounge chair on the sunroof. It could be, so Mrs. Gilbert would have a look around even though she knew Blanche was off on one of her late-night excursions.

She caught sight of something odd on top of the bureau and stepped over for a closer look. It appeared to be a shrine. No, if it was a shrine it was an odd one. It was a collection of masculine things, arranged in a pattern like a wagon wheel, a circle with spokes. A spoon, a man's black sock, a wing-tipped shoe, a highball glass, a cigar-cutter. A handkerchief. Mrs. Gilbert picked up the pocket square and examined it. The initials GP were embroidered in black thread on one corner. With a heavy sigh, Mrs. Gilbert deflated and sank down onto the bed. "Oh, Blanche," she breathed.

———

Alma was confused by Mrs. Gilbert's report. "What do you mean, she's gone? Where could she go at this time of night, and by herself?"

Mrs. Gilbert said, "I have an idea. She's been sneaking out. I don't know how long this has been going on. I've only known about it for a little while. Last night I followed her in my Ford, just to see where she's been going. She's been taking the trolley into Los Angeles and visiting someone in the Westlake part of town, on Alameda. I suspect I know who, but I won't say until I know for sure."

Alma had been sagging with fatigue since they left the set. Suddenly she was electrified. "That stinker! You think she's got herself a honey?"

"I don't know, Alma. I hope she's not into anything that can hurt her. You know she's an 'act now, pay later,' sort of girl."

"Well, I don't know either, Delphinia, but I'll be damned if I'm going to pay for another adoption or an abortion. Or bail. Why didn't you tell me about this?" She punctuated her question by jabbing the air with her turkey sandwich.

"You've got enough on your mind. I meant to confront her myself this evening, but it looks like I missed my chance."

"You say you know where she's been going?"

"Yes, more or less. I saw where she got off the trolley."

Alma stood up from the round kitchen table. "Get your coat. We're going to get to the bottom of this. You can drive. Go wake up Fee in case we need some muscle."

"Fee's visiting family in Carmel tonight," Mrs. Gilbert said, "so we're on our own."

————

Blanche made a thorough inspection of the bungalow complex to make sure that Graham's auto was not there. She had been taking bolder and bolder risks. He would be gone on another trip after today. She knew she should wait until he was safely gone, shouldn't take the chance that he might be upstairs asleep, but she had been left her on her own all the livelong day. She had tried to be good, and she was good until nearly her bedtime, and Alma and Mrs. Gilbert still weren't home. One more opportunity to make trouble for the man who had treated her like garbage was too tempting to pass up.

By the time she left Alma's house it was already dark, so she had made the trip by cab. The cabbie dropped her off a block or so south of Graham's place on Alameda, and she took a casual stroll up the sidewalk and around the corner onto Fourth Street. No Pierce-Arrow. She slipped between Graham's duplex and his neighbor's, hoisted herself up and tried to slide Graham's kitchen window open. It was locked. Blanche dropped to the ground and uttered an oath. She wasn't as surprised as she might have been. Anyone with fifty thousand dollars in his closet would think to lock his ground-floor windows.

But she hadn't come all this way to give up so easily. The upstairs bedroom window was situated above her usual entrance, and she could see that he had left it open a crack. She had worn her boots and jodhpurs. She could climb a tree, climb a rope, climb a rock face. There was no earthly reason she wouldn't be able to shinny up the side of a house.

———

Mrs. Gilbert parked on Fourth Street a little way down from the corner of Alameda. When she had followed Blanche's daytime jaunt, this was where she had seen the girl disappear between two bungalow units.

In the passenger seat next to her, Alma leaned forward to peer out the front windshield. "I think I've been here before, or somewhere close, anyway. Edna Purviance lives around here. Mostly movie people live in these places all up and down Alameda. Maybe Blanche got herself involved with somebody she met on one of my locations." She opened the car door and set one designer shoe on the sidewalk. "I'm going to… Oh, my God!" She slammed the door shut and slid down in the seat. "Look who just drove up."

A maroon Pierce-Arrow with the top down pulled over and parked a few yards in front of them. A natty man with fair hair got out and walked down the sidewalk between the bungalows.

"Who is it? I don't recognize him," Mrs. Gilbert said.

Alma answered in a stage whisper. "It's Graham Peyton, his own depraved self. I used to see him all the time at that speakeasy I liked to go to, King's, passing out dope like it was candy."

Mrs. Gilbert was too shocked to hide. She leaned forward over the wheel until her nose was practically touching the windshield. "Oh, Blanche! What is she doing, Alma? She's got what looks like an altar in her bedroom with his stuff on it. She swore to me that she'd never try to see him again."

Alma flung the open car door and flung herself out onto the pavement. "Come on, Delphinia. We're going to put a stop to this right now."

Mrs. Gilbert and the actress followed Peyton's route and emerged into a garden-like courtyard. A rectangle of expensive duplexes faced a vine-covered gazebo. Graham Peyton was nowhere to be seen.

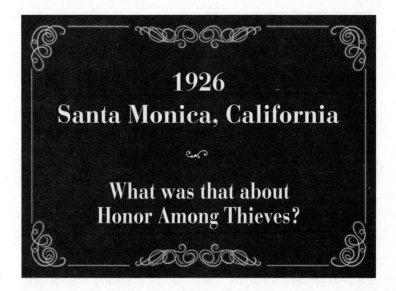

1926
Santa Monica, California

What was that about
Honor Among Thieves?

Very early in the morning, frantic pounding on Oliver's apartment door caused him to scramble out of bed and rush into the front room while pulling a robe on over his union suit. Ruhl was standing on the landing.

"Dix wants to see you."

Oliver scrubbed his stubbly face with both hands, still half awake. "How did you know where I live?"

"Don't be stupid. Let me in. I have to talk to you."

Ruhl pushed past him and plopped down at the kitchen table. He looked gray and sweaty.

Oliver couldn't decide whether to be alarmed at the summons or annoyed at the intrusion. He settled on both. "What's wrong?

What does Dix want with me? I can't tell him any more than I told you, not yet anyway."

"Listen, Oliver, when you talk to Dix, don't say anything about the ledger."

Now Oliver was confused. He lowered himself into a chair opposite Ruhl at the table. "What do you mean? There isn't anything to say. I haven't found out what happened to the ledger."

"I mean, don't bring it up at all. Dix isn't interested in the ledger, only in what happened to Peyton. Have you found any evidence that he was killed? Or that his death was an accident?"

"What's the deal? What's in that ledger that you don't want Dix to see?"

"Look, there were two ledgers. Peyton was skimming. Dix would give him cash to make a purchase and he'd take some off the top and pay the supplier a little less than he told Dix he had. If K.D. finds out…"

"What if he does? What can he do to Peyton now? Kill him deader?" Oliver's eyes narrowed as the truth struck him. "You were in it with him."

Ruhl clutched at Oliver's arm. "You can't mention the ledger to Dix. Peyton was a dope, but he kept meticulous records. He listed every payment he made to…anyone."

Ruhl was really scared, Oliver thought, and Ruhl didn't look like a man who scared easily. "Dix doesn't know about the second ledger. Why did you even ask me to find it? If I was in your situation I'd keep my mouth shut. That ledger has been gone for years and is unlikely to turn up now."

"So has Peyton, and he turned up. I thought he took a powder and took the book with him. But if it's out there and Dix finds it…"

"Calm down, Ruhl. It's no nevermind to me. If Dix doesn't bring it up, neither will I."

Ruhl looked marginally comforted. He pulled a white linen handkerchief out of his breast pocket and mopped his brow. "I'm glad you understand. I'll personally add another grand to your fee as a reward for your cooperation."

"Thanks. I appreciate your generosity." Oliver's words belied the contempt he felt for the old weasel. So much for the idea of honor among thieves. He studied the old man's pale face for a minute, wondering if he, Oliver, should be afraid now that Ruhl had confessed his double dealing. He had been working under the impression that Ruhl was only a mob accountant without either the authority or the *cojones* to order a hit himself. But what if that assumption was a mistake? What if Ruhl was an enforcer? What if he had been responsible for Peyton's demise, thinking he could retrieve the ledger before Dix found it and keep all the doubly ill-gotten profits for himself? If that was so, Ruhl must have shit himself when Peyton disappeared and he realized that the book was out there somewhere.

If that were true, why would Ruhl risk involving an outsider five years after the fact? No, Ruhl didn't kill Peyton. He had to have believed for all this time that Peyton was still alive and still in possession of the ledger. Ruhl only cared about the book. K.D. Dix was the driving force behind the search for Peyton's killer. A giant, crushing force was on the loose, and Ruhl was terrified that he was about to get steamrolled.

Oliver was feeling distinctly unhappy that he had agreed to take on the case, no matter how much money he had been offered. You can't spend your riches if you're dead.

Ruhl stuffed his handkerchief back into his pocket. "Well, get dressed, then. Let's get this over with."

"Now?"

"Yes, now. Don't worry. Dix doesn't expect miracles and won't pull your arms off like you were a fly. Just be straight about your progress. It's early days yet."

Before he went into the bedroom to change, Oliver offered Ruhl a snort to steady his nerves. The old guy looked like he could use it.

Ruhl's limousine took up more than its share of parking spots at the curb in front of Oliver's building. The driver was the same black-suited hulk with the crooked nose that Oliver had seen both times Ruhl met with him at Bay Cities. Oliver slid into the back seat of the auto next to Ruhl, wishing that he had had time to fry some bacon and eggs. He'd regret dying on an empty stomach.

Neither man was in the mood for small talk, so they made the hour-long trip in tense silence, out of Santa Monica, east through downtown Los Angeles, through Chinatown, and up into the hills, all the way to Pasadena. Oliver had only been to Pasadena once in the two years he had lived in Southern California, but the sight of mansion after mansion lining Orange Grove Boulevard, known as "Millionaire Row," had stuck with him, so he was surprised that the limo turned off Orange Grove and drove back into a secluded area north of town, backing up to the San Gabriel Mountains. Oliver understood why when they passed through the gates of a parklike estate. For K.D. Dix, living on Millionaire Row would have been slumming it.

1921
Los Angeles, California

❧

Blanche had learned that calm breathing
really helps when you're in a Situation.
And, Brother, was she in a Situation.

Blanche took her time wandering through the duplex, as usual.
She peeked into all the drawers she had peeked in before, and
rifled through his clothes. She chose a necktie with a subtle thistle
design embroidered all over it and stuffed it into the pocket of
her jodhpurs. She went back downstairs and mixed a drink for
herself, a finger of something amber and about a half-pint of
seltzer. She had never succumbed to the allure of liquor, but if it
caused Graham the slightest distress that his stash was mysteri-
ously disappearing, she'd drink it. She sat down at the secretary's
desk to finish her drink in comfort, casually looking through the
drawers and cubbies. The photo album with headshots of young
women was still there, with the green ledger still lying underneath

it. She shifted the ledger and discovered a small notch at the back of the writing surface that she had never seen before. Curious, she hooked a finger in the notch and lifted it up to find a hidden compartment below. Inside were a snub-nosed revolver lying on top of a red leather ledger. Two ledgers? She leafed through the book, comparing the numbers and letters in the red book to the ones in the green book. They were similar, in a code that meant nothing to her, but not exactly the same.

The differences must mean something to Graham, though, she thought, or he wouldn't keep the red book hidden. She replaced the book and gun and did her best to leave the desk like she found it. It was time to get down to business.

She opened the door of the front closet, took down the small suitcase, and carried it to a side table to open it. Graham had not gone to the bank as he had promised his co-conspirator. The money was still there, with one small indentation where she had lifted her bundle of fifties. She wondered if Graham had noticed yet. She chose another small bundle from a pile on the opposite side from the one she had taken earlier and stuffed it down the front of her blouse. She walked into the closet to return the satchel to the top shelf, and didn't hear the front door open.

———

Alma stalked all around the circle of the courtyard, hunting for a clue as to Blanche's whereabouts, with Mrs. Gilbert close behind her. She was just about to mount a random front porch and pound on the door when a girl in evening wear rounded the corner. Alma accosted her. "Excuse me, honey, do you live here?"

The girl stopped in her tracks, her big blue eyes growing even bigger as she recognized the star. "Oh, my goodness. Yes, Miss Bolding, I live right here with two of my girlfriends. Can I help you with something?"

"Do you know Graham Peyton?"

"Yes, he lives two doors down from me." She extended her arm. "Right there. Can I…"

But Alma had no time for pleasantries. She strode up the steps to Peyton's bungalow with her companion hot on her heels, opened the door, and walked right in.

Graham Peyton hadn't stopped to wonder what a girl was doing in his front closet with K.D. Dix's fifty thousand dollars in her hands. He crossed the room in a trice, grabbed Blanche by the collar and jerked her out so forcefully that the briefcase flew open and bills scattered everywhere. There was no time for her to scream or make any sound at all. He put his hands around her throat and squeezed before she could take a breath. She could feel her windpipe collapsing. Black spots appeared before her eyes and the light faded. Her last thought before unconsciousness enveloped her was that he was going to get away with her murder. She should have taken all his money when she first had the chance.

> ~*And just when you think things are as bad as they can be…*~

Blanche swam back up out of the darkness to see Alma's and Mrs. Gilbert's concerned faces hovering over her. She gasped a ragged breath and clutched her throat. It hurt. She didn't know whether she had been lying on the floor for minutes or days, but she was alive.

"Oh, baby," Alma breathed, "you total dope, he almost killed you!"

Blanche tried to speak, but her voice didn't work and she mouthed her question.

Mrs. Gilbert interpreted. "Where is he? He's here. Alma smashed him over the head with a whiskey decanter while he was throttling you. He's out cold. Can you sit up?"

Blanche nodded and her two rescuers helped her into a sitting position. Graham was sprawled facedown on the rug, his arms splayed out beside him. Blood oozed over the back of his head and onto one of his shoulders. Blanche managed to get to her knees and crawled over to him.

"You have some very big explaining to do, young lady." Alma's Bronx staccato was hot and rapid as machine-gun fire.

Blanche pushed Graham's head over so she could see his face. She was barely aware that Alma was speaking. She made a croaking noise and Alma hesitated.

"What did you say?"

Blanche cleared her throat and tried again. "I think he's dead, Miss Bolding. I think you killed him."

~Blanche takes the reins.~

Alma was hysterical. "I'm ruined! I'm ruined! What a scandal!"

"Hush, now, Alma, before everybody in the complex hears you." Mrs. Gilbert was doing her best to calm the actress down, but drama was both Alma's forte and her fall-back position. Blanche was still sitting on the floor next to Graham's body, watching in silence. Thinking.

"I'll call the police," Mrs. Gilbert said. "It was justifiable. You kept him from killing Blanche. You're a hero."

Alma wasn't buying it. "Don't be silly. What are the police going to do? Do you know what this guy did for a living? And look at all this dough! What was that venomous beast up to?"

"Well, we can't just leave him here and stroll out like nothing happened."

"Why not?"

"Alma, honey, you were seen."

While the women were talking, Blanche staggered to her feet and went into the kitchen to pour herself a drink of water, then returned to the living room and flopped down on the couch. Alma and Mrs. Gilbert were too concerned with their situation to pay her any mind.

She cleared her throat. "Graham was a criminal," she said, and the women looked at her, surprised to hear her speak. Her voice sounded husky. "He was going to use the money to buy drugs for somebody named Dix. But he was in cahoots with another man, a guy called Ruhl, to cheat his boss. They were going to sell the drugs for less than their boss thinks he's paying for them and keep the difference for themselves."

The color drained from Alma's face. "Oh, sweet bejeezus. Dix is the biggest criminal on the West Coast. And this idiot thought he could embezzle from him? I don't want to run afoul of a bunch of mobsters."

"It's pitch black outside," Blanche pointed out.

"And?" Alma said in the tone one uses when confronted with the obvious.

Blanche ignored the sarcasm. "Can either of you drive a Pierce-Arrow roadster?"

Mrs. Gilbert let go of Alma's arm. "I probably can. You have a plan, honey?"

"We have to get rid of the body so nobody will ever find it. Graham was supposed to leave for Chicago tomorrow with the money. It'll be days before anyone even notices he's missing. If we hide the body and the money, his criminal friends will think he did a bunk. By the time they figure out he's gone for good, who will think to make a connection between Graham and Alma?"

Alma was unconvinced, but willing to keep an open mind. "How the hell are the three of us going to get him out of here without being seen?"

Blanche stood up. "Let me think." She paced around the room for a few minutes, eyeing all the possible items that could be of use. She found a set of keys in a bowl beside the front door and pocketed them. "Mrs. Gilbert, help me roll him up in this rug. Alma, you pick up the money and put it back in the case."

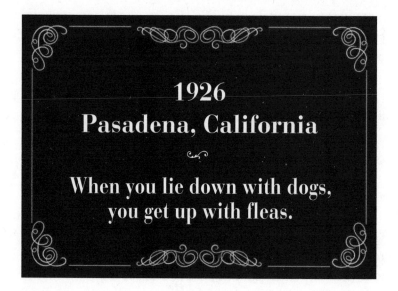

1926
Pasadena, California

When you lie down with dogs,
you get up with fleas.

K.D. Dix's sprawling Nouveau mansion must have covered an acre all by itself. The house was a work of art, all carved wood, stained glass, and subtle colors that blended into the surrounding forest. Oliver and Ruhl were ushered into a two-story foyer by a uniformed butler, who led them on a mile-long hike down a hall to a sunny parlor whose comfortable overstuffed furniture was as old-fashioned as the architecture of the house was modern. "Wait here," the manservant ordered. "Tea will be brought shortly. Please make yourselves comfortable."

Oliver wondered if the man was making a joke. "Comfortable" was the last thing either he or Ruhl felt. Much jittering and pacing ensued as they waited.

Oliver half expected to be left to stew for hours. That was a common technique for softening up a witness. But they were only left on their own for a quarter of an hour before the door opened and a short, dumpy, white-haired woman dressed in black entered, carrying a silver tea service. Ruhl and Oliver stood up until the woman placed the tray on a table, then took a seat on the divan before bidding Oliver to sit also.

"Ruhl, you can go," she said without taking her eyes off of Oliver. Ruhl hastened to obey. Before he left the room he shot a warning look at Oliver.

Oliver was confused. Dix's wife? A secretary? He remembered that the landlady at Peyton's bungalow complex had mentioned that an old woman who resembled Queen Victoria had shown up looking for her son shortly after Peyton disappeared. Was this the same woman? The Queen Victoria description fit the bill. "You're Graham Peyton's mother," he said.

She nodded. "I am."

"I don't understand. Do you work for K.D. Dix?"

The woman looked amused. "I am K.D. Dix, Oliver. For the past few weeks you've been working for me."

Surprise caused Oliver to forget himself. "You're K.D. Dix?"

"Pull your eyes back into your head, boy. When I heard that Graham's body had been found, I gave Ruhl the task of hiring someone not associated with me to look into his death. Ruhl came up with you. I'd like to find out if my purchase has been worth the money."

Oliver could hardly grasp the fact that this murderous whoremonger and dealer in illicit intoxicants resembled his grandmother. "You're K.D. Dix?"

Dix was used to his reaction. It was the same with anyone who met her. She counted on it. She carried on patiently. "Mr. Oliver, when Graham's body was discovered, Ruhl suggested that someone within my organization may have had a connection to his death. Now, I have quite a lot of resources at my disposal. I don't have to rely on someone who is not on my payroll to look into my son's death, but Ruhl suggested an independent investigator would be wise and I went along with it. However, I learned long ago not to put all my eggs in one basket, if you'll forgive the cliché. I have been keeping an eye on you."

"You've had somebody following me?"

She shrugged. It was a small matter to her. "That, and other things, too. You have a good reputation among your former clients."

Oliver's low-grade fear turned into anger. "I don't appreciate being kept on a leash, Miss Dix…"

"Mrs. Dix. No, I imagine not. I am aware of everyone you have spoken to on this matter. Some information that you have uncovered interests me. That Graham kept a secret ledger, for instance."

Oliver swallowed his words. He didn't ask how she had found out.

But she told him anyway. "I spoke to Debbie Hall, Graham's landlady, after you went to see her. She told me that you asked her about a missing ledger. Five years ago, after Graham disappeared, I went to his house myself and removed anything that might lead back to me. He did keep an account of the business he did for me. I recovered that ledger. It did not have a red cover. I'm curious to know why you asked Mrs. Hall about the existence of a missing ledger with a red cover?"

If Oliver told Dix the truth would he be signing Ruhl's death warrant? If he lied, would he be signing his own? He decided to dance around the truth for all he was worth. "Mrs. Dix, I was fishing, trying to come up with any sort of motive for murder. Two sets of books would do it, and most account ledgers are red or black. I haven't found anything. Even if such a thing exists and it can be found after all this time, whatever information is in it is so old it could only be of limited interest for someone like you who surely has many other ways to wield…influence." Oliver was aware that Dix's rather stilted way of speaking was beginning to affecting his own delivery.

A smile creased Mrs. Dix's sweet, round face. "True. Still, if there is a second ledger, I want to know about it. I knew that Graham was skimming, and I long suspected that he had an accomplice. I'd like to know who that was, and if a second ledger exists, it could tell me. I would not have lasted as long as I have if I did not insist on respect. I do not want anyone to think he can take something that belongs to me and not pay a terrible price."

"Even after five years?"

"Especially after five years. But what I really want to find out is how Graham ended up dead at the bottom of the palisades. And if someone put him there, I want to know who. Graham enjoyed courting danger. When he disappeared, Ruhl thought he had run, but I knew that he was probably dead. Yet in spite of my not inconsiderable assets, I was never able to find out what happened to him. Now that his remains have been found, I hope that some fresh clue to his murder was unearthed with his bones. Graham Peyton caused me much heartache, but he was my son, Mr. Oliver, so it matters to me very much."

"If I do manage to find out that he was murdered and who did it, what do you plan to do about it?"

"I plan to make the killer pay, and pay dearly."

"Mrs. Dix," Oliver said, "I have been doing my utmost to discover what happened to Peyton, and will continue to do so if you want. But it may be that his death really was an accident. Or if he was murdered, there may very well be nothing left to lead to his killer. But if I do find that he was killed and also find out who did it, I have to warn you that I will go to the police with the information." The instant the words left his mouth, Oliver regretted them. *What am I doing? I'm no hero. Am I trying to prove I have a shred of honesty left?*

Mrs. Dix smiled in a way that did not make Oliver comfortable. "Be my guest, Mr. Oliver. If you find the bastard who murdered my son, you can tell the President of the United States himself. It won't keep me from having my vengeance."

Oliver's heart fell to his stomach with a thud. "It might take me a long time to get to the bottom of this. It may take years, even, to come up with anything at all."

"I've already waited years. I'm a patient woman. Don't worry, Mr. Oliver. I'll cover your expenses, no matter how long it takes. From this moment until you tell me what I want to know, I am your only client."

Oliver left the house through the front door and leaned up against a column on the veranda to roll a cigarette and think the situation over. He flapped his jacket lapel with one hand while he smoked. He had sweated through his white shirt.

What to do? The old woman looked so harmless, which scared Oliver more than if she had been a six-foot tall thug with a shiny suit and a cauliflower ear. He was relieved that at least the whereabouts of the second ledger was only a side issue to her. He knew he wouldn't rat out Ruhl unless his own life depended on it. Getting involved with K.D. Dix was a bad idea. What would he do if he did find out who killed Peyton? Oliver was not a paragon of virtue, and he didn't have any particular sympathy for this theoretical murderer, but the idea of giving up some poor schmuck to bloody revenge was too much for him. Yet he didn't want to run afoul of Dix and end up buried at the bottom of a handy cliff himself.

Ruhl waiting for him in the limo. Oliver slid into the seat next to him and lit another cigarette off of the previous butt. "So tell me, Ruhl, how did Grandma Dix get into the whore business?"

Ruhl made a shushing noise and nodded at the back of the driver's head. "Keep your voice down. Listen, K.D. is into a lot more than the whore business. And when she shot her pimp in San Francisco back in '81 and took over his operation, she didn't look anything like your grandma, believe me. She's had to be twice as tough as any man to survive, and she learned that lesson well, so don't underestimate her."

"I won't. But you certainly did, Ruhl. She knows that I've been asking about a ledger. I managed to put her off for the moment, so she doesn't know you're connected."

Oliver thought the old man might be sick. "God, I should have known she'd keep an eye on you," Ruhl said. "If you do find it, what will you do?"

Oliver thought about what Dix's reaction would be if she found out he wasn't telling her everything. "You'd better hope it don't turn up, Ruhl. I like living."

> *~Like a moth to the flame...~*

As soon as Ruhl dropped him off at home, Oliver was overcome with a desire to talk to Bianca. It was irrational. He didn't want K.D. Dix to have Bianca in her sights. Besides, if he really wanted to pursue this investigation, Alma Bolding was the woman he should be interrogating. But sense didn't figure into it. He picked up the telephone receiver but reconsidered. How was Dix keeping him under surveillance? Was there a listening device planted somewhere in the apartment? Was the telephone operator on Dix's payroll? Oliver put his jacket back on and slunk to his car, keeping close to walls and shrubbery, then drove to Beverly Hills by the most circuitous route imaginable. When he was reasonably sure that he was not being followed, he drove up the canyon to Bianca's front gate and rolled down his window to talk to the guard.

"Is Miss LaBelle at home? I need to speak to her."

The guard recognized him. "I'm sorry, Mr. Oliver, but you are not expected."

"Would you please let her know that I would like to see her? I have some important information for her."

The man's pleasantly bland expression didn't change, but he sounded weary. When it came to people trying to get in to see the great Bianca LaBelle, he had heard every ploy there was. "I'm sorry, but if you would like to see Miss LaBelle at her home you are welcome to telephone her secretary and make an appointment."

Oliver was disappointed, but he did admire the man's efficiency. He took a different circuitous route back to Santa Monica, parked behind his building, and sneaked upstairs. He fried an egg for his supper and pulled the curtains before he ate. He didn't feel like putting on a show for whoever was tailing him.

He was just rinsing off his one dish when the telephone rang, two shorts and a long. It was for him.

"I understand you want to see me," Bianca said.

"Yes, thanks for calling. I wasn't sure you'd remember me. I have a copy of the script I told you about at your party last week. You were kind enough to say you'd read it."

Bianca got the picture immediately. "Of course I remember you. I thought your story idea was very promising. I'm free right now. Would you like to come to my place for a nightcap?"

"You're very gracious. I'll be there as soon as I can."

Oliver replaced the receiver, feeling slightly ridiculous at the ruse. But if someone was listening, it was better to be safe than sorry. Every third person in Southern California was trying to get a script read, so who would doubt that Oliver was as well?

~*The Big Squeeze*~

This time Bianca met with him in the white living room in front of the massive fireplace. Fee, male-ish again in tails and spats, did not leave the room but stood sentry at the entrance. Bianca was dressed for an occasion of some sort, a vision in a pink chiffon gown with a pearl-covered belt around her hips. A pearl-studded headband sporting a spray of white baby's breath offset her cropped cloud of sable waves.

She offered him a drink. Oliver declined and made himself comfortable on the couch opposite her. "You're looking particularly luscious. Am I delaying a night on the town?"

"I'm going to dinner with friends." She dismissed his compliment with a wave and got down to business. "It's no wonder you were afraid of our being heard over the telephone, Oliver. I understand you met with K.D. Dix today."

He exploded. "Jesus H. Christ! Why do you people need me? Why don't you just spy on each other and leave me out of it?"

Fee took a step forward, but Bianca stopped him with a glance. "Don't bust a blood vessel, Oliver," she said. "A friend of mine saw you get into a limousine with Ruhl. It was an accident that I found out at all. Then you came by here this afternoon and asked to see me. What did you learn from Dix that I need to know?"

"Why didn't you tell me Dix is a woman?"

Bianca favored him with her enigmatic smile. "I thought it would be a nice surprise."

"Did you know that she's Graham Peyton's mother?"

He was perversely pleased to see that he had surprised her for a change. "No! But that makes sense. I always wondered why she's never stopped looking for him."

"Have you ever met her? She is one scary bitch. Mainly because she looks like your old granny but you know she'd happily rip your throat out if you cross her. I told her what I know, which ain't much…yet. I also told her I'd keep trying to find out what happened to Peyton because I was afraid not to. Look, Bianca, what do you know that you're not telling me? I can't protect you if I don't know how you're involved."

"Protect me? You think you could protect me from K.D. Dix? I don't think so. Even if you could, you don't need to. Even Dix would have a hard time getting to me. As for what I'm not telling you about my youthful involvement with Graham Peyton, it has nothing to do with his criminal activities, or my protecting Alma or anyone else. It only has to do with our personal relationship years ago, when I was young and stupid. I don't want my name dragged through the mud."

Oliver was relieved. "I'm glad to hear it. Peyton led many a young girl astray. I've met a few of them and any one of them would have been happy to throw him off a cliff. I don't know your story, Miss LaBelle, but it does seem like you turned out all right. I will take that drink, if you're still offering." He leaned back, feeling relaxed and chatty. "You know, it was Ruhl who hired me in the first place, and it turns out that he's more interested in finding a ledger that Peyton used to cook the books than in finding out why he got killed. Poor old crook is terrified that Dix will find out that he was in cahoots with Peyton to double-cross her. Seems they used their booty to invest in a side business of their own in Arizona."

She straightened. "Is that so? Graham was stealing from his own mother? I'm not surprised he and Ruhl were tied up in something shady together. Is Ruhl still running the same scam, or did he give it up when Graham died?"

"I don't know. I didn't ask and he didn't volunteer to tell me. He probably is, or he wouldn't be as worried as he is."

Bianca stood up and took a turn around the room. Oliver watched as she paced, trying to figure out why she was suddenly interested in Ruhl, but distracted by her long, silk-stocking-clad legs. She stopped abruptly and turned to face him. "Ruhl has been doing Dix's dirty work for years. He probably hired you because you're expendable. He thinks nobody will care when you disappear without a trace. You know that Ruhl is as much a danger to you now as Dix?"

Yes, that had crossed Oliver's mind. He had already been figuring how far he was going to have to run. But to Bianca, he said, "Why would Ruhl be worried about me? Even if I do come across this red ledger, I'm going to give it to him. I'm not going to tell Dix about it. I don't mind being a snoop, but I don't relish being an accessory to murder."

"He'll do anything to keep his secret from Dix, and the best way to keep a secret is to make sure you're the only one who knows it. If I were you, Oliver, I'd forget about the body and the ledger, change my name, and take a permanent trip to China. I told you that I'd pay you to keep me informed, and you've done that. Wait here while I get you some traveling money. Fee, get Mr. Oliver that drink."

"Wait a minute, I can take care of myself," he said, but Bianca had already disappeared down the hall. Oliver didn't know whether to be scared stupid or royally pissed. He took the shot of Scotch that Fee offered him and slugged it down.

Fee's expression was a combination of amusement and sympathy. "I'm afraid Miss LaBelle is something of a force of nature."

"Yeah, well, I don't like dames telling me what to do. Not K.D. Dix and not Alma Bolding and not Bianca Freaking LaBelle." He stood up.

"You might as well take your money before you leave," Fee said. "And don't pack your bags just yet. I have a feeling that you're not going to have to go anywhere."

"What's up, Fee? Do you know what the hell is going on with all these broads? If you do, I'd sure appreciate a heads-up."

The soft-spoken giant shrugged. "How should I know? Miss LaBelle is smarter than me. Even if she burned down an orphanage on Christmas Eve while the whole town watched, you wouldn't be able to pin it on her because she's smarter than you. She's smarter than most of us. All I know is that Miss LaBelle always figures out how to take care of everything."

1921
Los, Angeles, California

Valkyrie

The women rolled Peyton up like a blintz in a Turkish-style area rug that was not quite long enough to conceal his entire body. They had to decide whether to let the top of his head hang out one end or his brown Oxfords hang out the other. They chose the shoes. Mrs. Graham hung a towel over his toes, which looked odd but effectively disguised the fact that the rug they were transporting had feet. There was only one exit in the bungalow, and it led directly into the courtyard. They considered stuffing the body through the kitchen window and letting it fall onto the sidewalk between houses, but the three of them weren't strong enough to lift the dead weight high enough.

In the end, Blanche took a nonchalant midnight stroll through

the courtyard and determined that no one was about. Alma stood
sentry while Blanche and Mrs. Gilbert manhandled their burden
out the front door, around the side of the house to the curb, and
heaved him into the boot of his own car. In case they were seen,
they had concocted a cover story about picking up a carpet that
they had bought from a resident and the only time they could
do it was after midnight. It sounded fishy even to them, so they
were fortunate they didn't have to use it.

The three women crawled into the front seat of the Pierce-
Arrow together to catch their breath and come up with part two
of their body disposal operation.

"Mrs. Gilbert," Blanche said, "I'll drive the Ford and you follow
me in the Pierce-Arrow. Alma, you ride with Mrs. Gilbert. If she
gets stopped for some reason, nobody is going to question her
if you're in the car."

"Where are we going?"

"I know just the place."

The two cars left Los Angeles, drove west to Ocean Park and
up the coast highway to Santa Monica. The moon had risen by
the time Blanche pulled off the highway onto a secluded beach
below the palisades and parked behind a rocky outcrop where
the autos couldn't be seen from the road. She got out of the Ford
and directed Mrs. Gilbert to park the Pierce-Arrow behind her.

The three stood on the sand with their heads together and
whispered, as though their dead passenger might hear their plan if
they spoke up. "I've been here with Jack Dempsey a million times,"
Blanche said. "Autos only drive by on this road in any numbers
on holidays, heading out of town, and I've never known anyone
to stop here. You could sit behind this rock until doomsday and
nobody going by on the road would see you."

"Do you plan to bury him here?" Mrs. Gilbert sounded doubtful.

"I figured we could throw him in the ocean."

That idea met with general approval. After all, where could
secrets be buried deeper than the ocean?

They hauled the body out of the boot of the Pierce-Arrow and lugged it to the water's edge. "Oh, my God, he moved!" Alma dropped his feet and danced around in disgust. "Did he move?"

Blanche and Mrs. Gilbert struggled not to drop their bundle onto the sand. "No, for heaven's sake, Alma, he's dead as Moses," Blanche groaned. "He's just limp and squiggly like noodles. If you aren't going to help, then get out of the way."

The ocean's breath was cold, the water black, vast, and forbidding. Blanche and Mrs. Gilbert waded out into the deep, carrying Peyton as far as they could manage and still stay on their feet, then let the ocean take their burden before they slogged their way back to shore. They stood on the sand, wet and bedraggled, and watched the dark form of the rolled carpet float on the somewhat less dark water for several minutes.

"Surely the rug's pile will get waterlogged and drag him down." Mrs. Gilbert sounded hopeful.

Alma dashed any hope. "Damn, he's coming back! The tide is coming in. Shee-ut, we chose a great time to toss him in the drink."

"If we just leave him here, won't he wash out to sea when the tide goes out?" Blanche was not entirely sure about the workings of the Pacific Ocean.

"No," Mrs. Gilbert said. "That won't be for hours and hours. And until then he'll wash up on the beach, here. We can't take the chance that somebody will find him before the tide takes him out."

Alma turned to Blanche. "But you said nobody ever comes here."

Blanche shrugged. "I've never seen anyone, but what do I know? I'm not here twenty-four hours a day." She put her hands on her hips. "Where are the sharks when you need them?"

"If we had a rowboat," Mrs. Gilbert said, "we could fill his pockets with rocks or something and row him a long way out before we dropped him over the side."

"Well, we don't have a boat," Blanche pointed out.

"Drag him out again," Alma suggested. "Then stab him in the belly a few times and let all the air out of him so he'll sink."

Blanche's lip curled. "Oh, Alma, ick. Besides, I forgot my shiv."

By this time the body had washed back up onto the beach, a sodden carpet roll with feet. Blanche snagged the roll and pulled it out of the surf and onto the sand. The rug slowly unfurled as she tugged. Peyton flopped out on his back in the lapping waves.

"Oh, Lord," Alma moaned. "He's gone all white. His fingers twitched, I know he twitched!"

"Will you relax?" Blanche said. "It's just the tide coming in."

"I'll roll him back up." Mrs. Gilbert leaned over the body, but before she quite realized what was happening, the presumed corpse's hand shot out to grab her ankle and jerk her off her feet into the surf.

~It's Alive!~

Alma shrieked. "Delphinia! Save her Blanche oh my god he's still alive kill him kill him!"

But Blanche had disappeared.

Peyton rose up on his knees like a sodden ghoul, straddled Mrs. Gilbert's supine form and got his hands around her neck.

Mrs. Gilbert pried at the fingers to no avail, desperate for air, while Alma pounded ineffectually on the living corpse's back. But he was unstoppable.

Alma may as well have been an annoying fly for all the impression her pounding fists were making as the undead Peyton pressed Mrs. Gilbert's head deeper under the rising water.

Blanche reappeared out of the night like an avenging angel with a tire iron in her hand, and whacked Peyton across the forearms. He made a feral sound and loosened his grip long enough for Mrs. Gilbert to gasp air, but he didn't let go. Blanche drew back again and hit him in the head with everything she had, and was rewarded with the sound of cracking bone and a howl as he fell over sideways into the surf. Mrs. Gilbert rolled out from under him and Alma pulled her to her feet. The two women clutched one another in horror as Blanche kicked the still figure in the side.

"That's for all them girls that didn't get away." Her voice rang out over the waves as she kicked him again. "And that's for Billy Ray who can't never be mine!"

She stood over him, poised to hit him again with the tire iron if he tried anything, until the tide had come in so far that his arms began to float. He never moved again.

She calmly stepped away and dropped the tire iron onto the beach before turning toward her appalled companions. "Can y'all help me carry him back over there to the bottom of the cliff? We'll have to bury him under the rocks on the far side of the railroad tracks."

Mrs. Gilbert was sobbing, tears streaming down her face. But Alma gathered herself quickly.

"Too bad we didn't think of that before we lugged the carcass all the way over here."

"It's a good thing we didn't or eventually he'd have woke up and dug himself out. Well, he's dead now. It'll be a lot easier to get him across the beach if we drag him." She picked up one corner of the waterlogged carpet. "Damn, this thing weighs a ton. It'll take us forever to drag him across on this. Alma, give me your coat."

"What? I paid a bundle for this coat."

"You can afford to buy another one. Unless you want to carry him."

Grumbling, Alma removed her expensive full-length lambswool coat and Blanche rolled the body onto it, its legs sprawled over the hem. She dragged it across the sand, across the deserted two-lane highway, its head bumping over the tracks, to a rockfall at the base of the bluff. Blanche and Mrs. Gilbert and even Alma spent the rest of the night burying the corpse under rocks. The sun was coming up when the wet, dirty, exhausted trio laid the last rock over the final resting place of Graham Peyton.

Alma stretched and groaned. "I feel like I've been pounded within an inch of my life. I'm going to take a four-hour-long bath and sleep until next June."

Mrs. Gilbert, who really had been pounded within an inch of her life, wasn't so sanguine. "What if they find him?" Her voice was a painful rasp.

Blanche sat back on a rock and tucked a strand of dark hair back behind her ear. "They won't find him. Mrs. Gilbert, do you suppose I'd be able to drive that big Pierce-Arrow?"

It was a relief for Mrs. Gilbert to speak of something normal. "It's easier to drive than my auto. I'm sure you could."

"Alma, drive Mrs. Gilbert home in her car. Call your doctor friend to have a look at her tonight. Try to get some sleep before you have to be on set this afternoon."

Alma gave her a sharp look. Blanche had taken charge. Alma was happy to let her. "What are you going to do?"

"I'm going to drive this auto up to the top of the cliff and abandon it. If they ever do find him, maybe they'll think he fell."

"How will you get home?"

"Don't worry about me, Alma. I'll get home. I can take care of myself."

Alma laughed. "No kidding."

~Our little girl has Teeth and Claws.~

Neither Mrs. Gilbert nor Alma had much to say as they drove back to Hollywood. They had been traveling for half an hour before Alma said, "Delphinia, how do we get ourselves into these things?"

"You have to stop bringing home strays, Alma."

"I thought she was a pussycat, Delphinia. I didn't realize that we got ourselves a lioness. Who's Billy Ray?"

"Her little baby. That's what the sister named him."

"Ah," Alma said, enlightened. "Well, no wonder. Did you see how beautiful she looked while she was mashing the bastard's head in? She was lit up. She was on fire."

Mrs. Gilbert shot her an incredulous glance. "Are you serious? It was horrible. Alma, are you all right?"

"I'm fine, Delphinia. She saved your life. *La belle dame sans merci.*"

———

Blanche did not abandon the car right away. She stopped at a dump and got rid of the Turkish rug, then drove back to Peyton's bungalow and shimmied through the window to clean away all evidence that anyone other than Graham Peyton had been there that evening. She cleaned herself up as well, washing her filthy face and hands, brushing the dirt from her clothes and boots, combing and arranging her dark wavy hair. She took a silk scarf from Peyton's closet and tied it around her neck to hide the bruises. She took the small suitcase with her when she left, along with the remainder of the fifty thousand dollars, a snub-nosed revolver, and lying right on top of the money, one red leather-bound ledger. She drove the Pierce-Arrow back to Santa Monica, up the California Incline, along Palisades Park to the very end, and off the road to a secluded spot behind a stand of palms. She parked the vehicle close to the fence by the cliff edge, removed the license plate, and threw the key over the side.

She walked back through the park and made her way down to the trolley stop, casually swinging the small suitcase like a girl who had just returned from a trip to grandmother's house. No one cast her a glance.

1926
Santa Monica, California

Everybody, sooner or later, sits down
to a banquet of consequences.
—Robert Louis Stevenson

Another early morning knock on his door roused Oliver from a troubled sleep. His first conscious thought was, Oh, lordy, not Ruhl again. His heart took a leap as his last conversation with Bianca LaBelle came back to him. Was Ruhl here to shut him up for good? Oliver briefly considered not answering but dismissed the thought quickly. That would only delay the inevitable. He pulled his loaded .38 from his bedside table and slipped it into the pocket of his robe before he took a deep breath and went into the front room.

He flung open the door and his eyes traveled down from where Ruhl's head should have been to look into the sweet face of K.D. Dix, standing on the landing in all her black-clad glory. A brick-shaped man with a crooked nose was behind her, looking distinctly large and protective.

Oliver's mouth flopped open like a hooked fish. He couldn't think of anything to say, but stood aside as she pushed past him. He was provisionally comforted by the fact that she was looking pleased with herself.

"Where did you find the ledger?" she said.

Oliver blinked at the unexpected question. "I didn't."

Dix made herself as comfortable as she could on his seat-sprung sofa. "Well, your snooping around must have shaken it loose because it showed up in my mail yesterday. It's in code, but not much of a code, so now I know who was using Graham to cheat me. Graham always was an easy mark. Why he did it I don't know. I'd have given him anything he wanted. The package was postmarked Los Angeles, so I'm guessing one of the people you questioned either had it in his possession or mentioned your visit to whoever did. And I'm also guessing that one of those people is responsible for my son's death."

Oliver swallowed. "So what do you want me to do now?"

"Keep digging, for now, Oliver. Find out who killed my boy and don't stop till you do. I'll let you know if I want anything else." She opened the drawstring handbag on her lap and dug around in it, just like a normal woman would do. She withdrew an envelope and handed it to him. It was full of cash.

And that was that. Dix left, along with her jumbo-sized companion, and Oliver stood for a long time with the envelope in his hand, cold as ice. He felt like he was in a vise, unable to escape, squeezed between a black widow and a woman called Dangereuse.

He was still standing there when the telephone rang, two shorts and a long.

———

The man's arm swayed back and forth as though he was waving goodbye to life. It was the last movement he would ever make on this earth. Long strands of Brilliantined hair on the top of his head bobbed slightly in the tiny waves of the incoming tide. He lay facedown in the sand. He had not been on the beach very long. The back of his expensive serge suit was barely damp.

Oliver looked back at the cliff behind the beach, across the road and beyond the railroad tracks. The body lay only yards from where Peyton's skeleton had been found.

"Help me turn him over," Officer Poole said.

Turning over a corpse is harder than it sounds, especially if it's a wet corpse. It took both of them to flip the dead man onto his back. His steel gray eyes were open, his face mottled. A bullet hole creased the center of his forehead. The water had washed away most of the blood.

Poole took stock of Oliver's expression. He looked sick. "You know who he is?"

Oliver nodded. "His name was Ruhl."

> *~And now, who is the villain of our tale*
> *and who is the hero?~*

Will Ted Oliver have to choose between his soul and his life?

And what of Bianca? Will she ever have a relationship with her son? Will her family forgive her and welcome her back into the fold? Can she save Alma Bolding from destroying herself? Can she even save herself?

Will the evil K.D. Dix discover who killed her son?

Join us next time to find the answers to these questions and many others as we continue...

> *~The Adventures of Bianca Dangereuse, Episode 2.~*

Real or Not?

Many of the people, places, and circumstances mentioned in this book actually lived, but neither Bianca LaBelle or her movie alter ego, Bianca Dangereuse, ever existed. Nor did the actress Alma Bolding. I did name Alma after my aunt, Alma Bolding Bourland, a sweet, country woman with simple needs and desires who would NEVER have behaved as outrageously as the fictional Alma. My aunt would have enjoyed being famous, however. Other completely fictional characters include Dephinia Gilbert, Ted Oliver, director Elmo Reynolds, Zelko the cameraman, Del Burke the publicist, actor Daniel May, Bianca's costar Damian Kirk and his movie character Butch Revelle.

There really was a movie called *Stella Maris* made in 1920, starring Mary Pickford and Conrad Tarle, and *The Three Musketeers* in 1921 with Douglas Fairbanks. *The Three Musketeers* was a blockbuster in its day, but there was no scene of a young woman swinging on a curtain from the balcony. Perhaps it was cut. None of Bianca's movies were ever made—*Palace of Intrigue, Handsome Stranger,* or *Zanzibar Gold.* They should have been, though.

Bay Cities Italian Deli has stood on the corner of Broadway and Lincoln in Santa Monica since 1925.

A restaurant called Philippe was established in 1908 in Los Angeles. I needed a fancy restaurant in Hollywood, so I moved Philippe to Santa Monica and classed up the joint. As of 2019, the Original Philippe still exists, now located at 1001 N. Alameda in Los Angeles.

By 1926, an effective type of listening device called a "Detective Dictograph" was readily available. It was an intercom-like gadget with a sensitive microphone that could be hidden anywhere in a room, such as inside a clock or a lamp. It was intended for surveillance work, and during the 1910s and 1920s, law enforcement and detective agencies often used it to gather evidence in quite a number of criminal cases.

About the Author

Donis Casey is the author of ten Alafair Tucker Mysteries: *The Old Buzzard Had It Coming, Hornswoggled, The Drop Edge of Yonder, The Sky Took Him, Crying Blood, The Wrong Hill to Die On, Hell With the Lid Blown Off, All Men Fear Me, The Return of the Raven Mocker,* and *Forty Dead Men*. This award-winning series, featuring the sleuthing mother of ten children, is set in Oklahoma during the booming 1910s. Donis has twice won the Arizona Book Award for her series, and been a finalist for the Willa Award and a nine-time finalist for the Oklahoma Book Award. Her first novel, *The Old Buzzard Had It Coming*, was named an Oklahoma Centennial Book in 2008. Donis is a former teacher, academic librarian, and entrepreneur. She lives in Tempe, Arizona.